P9-DNT-392

THE GIRL NEXT DOOR

BOOKS BY PATRICIA MACDONALD

Stranger in the House

Suspicious Origin

Not Guilty

THE GIRL

NEXT DOOR

A NOVEL

PATRICIA

MACDONALD

ATRIA BOOKS
NEW YORK   LONDON   TORONTO   SYDNEY

ATRIA BOOKS
1230 AVENUE OF THE AMERICAS
NEW YORK, NY 10020

LIBRARY OF CONGRESS CATALOGING-IN-PUBLICATION DATA

MACDONALD, PATRICIA J.
THE GIRL NEXT DOOR / PATRICIA MCDONALD—1ST ATRIA BOOKS HARDCOVER ED.
P. CM.
ISBN 0-7434-2361-5
1. MARRIED WOMEN—CRIMES AGAINST—FICTION. 2. CHILDREN OF MURDER
VICTIMS—FICTION. 3. MOTHERS—DEATH—FICTION. 4. SUBURBAN LIFE—FICTION.
5. YOUNG WOMEN—FICTION. 6. UXORICIDE—FICTION. I. TITLE.
PS3563.A287G57 2004
813'.54—DC22   2004047693

FIRST ATRIA BOOKS HARDCOVER EDITION JULY 2004

10   9   8   7   6   5   4   3   2

ATRIA BOOKS IS A TRADEMARK OF SIMON & SCHUSTER, INC.

MANUFACTURED IN THE UNITED STATES OF AMERICA

FOR INFORMATION REGARDING SPECIAL DISCOUNTS FOR BULK PURCHASES,
PLEASE CONTACT SIMON & SCHUSTER SPECIAL SALES AT 1-800-456-6798
OR BUSINESS@SIMONANDSCHUSTER.COM

To my friends Craig, Michel, and Daniel Gras, and to Josephine Halfpenny, who brought us together. Happy Birthday, Nan!

ACKNOWLEDGMENTS

Special thanks to Rich Terbeck at the New Jersey State Parole Bureau for patiently, thoroughly answering my questions. And my apologies to Rich for any liberties I took with the facts!

Thanks, as ever, to Art Bourgeau, Jane Berkey, Meg Ruley, Annelise Robey, and Maggie Crawford for tough questions and brilliant suggestions.

PROLOGUE

NINA AVERY tried to concentrate on her highlighted script. Even though she loved to act, and was thrilled with the part she had landed in the school play, she could not focus on learning her lines. She was distracted by the April breeze that drifted through her bedroom window, and by the fact that it was Friday and school was over for the week. But most of all, she was distracted by thoughts of Brandon Ross, the boy who lived next door.

His family had moved in last November, and she had met him at Christmastime. Her mother, Marsha, had invited the new neighbors to a holiday party. Brandon's father, Frank, was balding and stocky. His mother, Sheila, was blond, stylish, and thin. The party ended, not surprisingly, in an argument between Nina's parents. Her mother accused her husband, Duncan, of flirting with Sheila. Duncan insisted that Marsha had ruined the party all by herself by drinking too much egg nog and getting sloppy.

But the party wasn't ruined for Nina. She had fallen head over heels for Brandon.

Unfortunately, she hadn't seen much of him in the months that followed. They took the same bus to school, but in the winter everyone ran to the bus stop at the last minute to avoid the cold. Now that spring was here, Nina had been leaving the house early just so she might be able to spend a few more minutes with Brandon before the bus arrived. He was taller than Nina, and a year older. At fifteen, he had broad shoulders and soft brown hair that fell over his forehead. His eyes, when she dared to meet them, were brown with flecks of gold in them.

"No, you listen to me, Marsha. I have patients waiting for me. I left my practice to go over to that school and be humiliated . . ." her father shouted.

Nina sighed and returned to reality. She knew very well that it wasn't only spring fever and Brandon Ross that were distracting her. It was impossible to memorize lines over the sound of the shouting from downstairs. Her parents had just returned from the high school, where they had been summoned to discuss her brother Jimmy and the problems he was having. It didn't sound like it went too well. Their angry voices spiked up the stairwell and mushroomed in the hall.

"Your patients can spare you for an hour," her mother retorted in a sarcastic tone. "You don't hear me complaining because I couldn't work this afternoon."

"Excuse me, I'm a doctor. I'm not just dabbling in a paint box," Duncan replied.

"You see, Duncan?" she cried. "This is your attitude. Nothing is important but you. My painting is a waste of time. The children are a waste of time. This is why Jimmy has problems. Because you have no time for him," Marsha shouted. "Because you're too busy with your . . . *other interests.*"

Jimmy was now sixteen, and had started hanging around

with a garage band called Black Death. In a lot of ways, Nina thought Jimmy was sweeter than her older brother, Patrick, but lately he got into fights, cut school a lot, and came home glassy-eyed from the Black Death rehearsals. The band's lead singer, Calvin Mears, was a known drug user whose single mother did not seem to care what he did. A lot of girls thought Calvin was hot. He was lean and mean, with shoulder-length blond hair and haunted-looking gray eyes. Nina thought he was a little bit scary. She had heard the rumor that he had gotten a ninth-grader pregnant. Her brother Jimmy was the opposite of Calvin. Girls thought he was cute, too, but in a different way from Calvin. He was tall and broad-shouldered, with curly black hair and a face that was scarred up from a million child-hood scrapes. He acted as the band's general grunt and Calvin's personal bodyguard. No amount of punishment had succeeded in keeping him away from his new friend.

Nina couldn't understand why her mother blamed her father for Jimmy's behavior. Her father was a hero in her eyes. Just last year it had been in all the papers when his astute diagnosis and quick treatment had saved the life of their mailman's young son, who had a rare, often fatal blood disease. Nina liked everyone to know that Dr. Avery was her dad.

But Nina's mother was always mad at him. Her father would try to avoid the arguments, but her mother would persist. And then he would snap back with something mean—that she was a nag, or she drank too much, or she had let herself go. Which wasn't fair either, Nina thought. It was true that she didn't look much like the raven-haired beauty in her wedding picture. Her hair was graying now, and she was pudgy. But it didn't help anything when her dad, who was still fit and handsome, brought up her mother's shortcomings. Nina sighed. She loved them both so much. Why couldn't they just get along? But arguing had become a way of life for them. It was sickening. It gave her a stomachache.

Nina heard the front door slam. She went to her open window and looked out. Marsha Avery, wearing sneakers and her old green sweatshirt, her face like a thundercloud, was crossing the front lawn, toting her paint box and her large zippered portfolio. Nina knew where she was headed. At one end of their street was the Madison Creek Nature Preserve. A state-owned woodland, it was her mother's favorite place to paint. The woods ran along the banks of a burbling stream, and its winding trails were overgrown and shady. Nina started to call out to her mother, but then she hesitated. Nina and her brothers all pretended not to hear the arguments between their parents. She didn't want her mother to know that she had been listening.

Nina rested her elbows on the windowsill, her chin in her hands, and breathed in the balmy April air. The New York suburb of Hoffman, New Jersey, never looked more beautiful than it did in the spring, and Madison Street was especially pretty. There were large, comfortable old houses and lots of trees fuzzy with new leaves and buds. If you turned right out of the Averys' driveway, it was a short walk to the quaint downtown shopping area of Hoffman. If you turned left, you were headed for the preserve. It wasn't the ritziest part of town. That was the horsey area of estates called Old Hoffman. But Nina loved her street with its towering elms, lush gardens, and gas streetlamps.

Today, though, instead of cheering her up, the loveliness of her neighborhood made Nina feel more melancholy than ever. Melancholy and lonely. Her thoughts drifted back to Brandon Ross. "He'll never like me," she said aloud. She turned her head and looked into the mirror over her bureau. She had long, wavy black hair and creamy skin with no zits, knock on wood. She had often been told that she was beautiful when she smiled. But why smile? If Brandon thought about her at all, it was probably to think how boring she was.

Nina heard a car engine stopping and she looked out the

window again. A shiny Jeep with the sunroof open was pulling into the wide driveway beside her father's car. The Jeep belonged to Lindsay Farrell, a beautiful girl with straight platinum-blond hair. Her dad was some kind of mogul in New York and they lived in Old Hoffman. Nina thought she had never seen teeth as dazzling as Lindsay's or eyes as blue. Lindsay got out of the car, as did her passenger, Nina's older brother, Patrick. Patrick was a dreamboat with brown curly hair and an athlete's body. He looked like a younger version of his handsome father, and together he and Lindsay looked like some *Vogue* advertisement for the good life.

Patrick came up close to Lindsay and tilted her face up to his with one finger under her chin. Just then the front door slammed again, and Nina saw her dad come out into the driveway, glowering and rattling his keys.

Patrick and Lindsay jumped apart. "Hey, Dad," said Patrick warily.

Nina's father mumbled a greeting and headed for his car.

"Dad, did the mail come?" Patrick asked.

"I don't know. Check the box. I'm heading back to the office." He climbed into his car and began to back out of the driveway.

Nina sighed and turned away from the window. She lay down on her bed, pushing her script to the floor, and looked up at the ceiling. She didn't feel like learning lines. She didn't care about the play. She was overcome with a combination of weariness and the jitters. Nina closed her eyes. "Life sucks," she said.

The phone beside her bed rang. Nina picked it up.

"Nina," said a familiar voice. "It's Brandon, next door."

Like she didn't immediately recognize his voice. Nina scrambled up and sat Indian style on the bed. She was shaking all over, glad he couldn't see her.

"Hi," she said. "How are ya?"

"Okay. I'm fine." He spoke in a rush, as if he wanted to be finished with an unpleasant task. "Nina, I was thinking . . . do you like . . . um . . . Julia Roberts?"

"Of course," she said. "Who doesn't like Julia Roberts?"

"Well, that new movie she's in is downtown. You wanna go see it tonight?"

Nina couldn't believe her ears. It was Friday. He was asking her to go to the movies on a Friday night. She wanted him to say it again. "Tonight?" she asked.

"If you're not doin' anything," he said.

This was how it happened, she thought. In an instant, with one simple question, your life was utterly changed. "I'm not," she said.

"I don't know the time," he said. "I have to call the theater."

"I have a paper," she said eagerly. "I'll look it up." She promised to call him back and hung up feeling numb. She had a date. A real date! With the boy she liked most in the world. This day, which had seemed so bleak, now seemed magical. Of course, she still had to ask her parents, but her mother would say yes. She had to.

The paper, she thought. I've got to get the paper and call him back. Nina clattered down the stairs and spotted the *Hoffman Gazette* on the coffee table. She stopped to read the caption under the photo of a familiar face on the front page and then checked the index. Her hands were still trembling as she turned to the section that had the movie schedule. Just as she found the listings, she heard a war whoop from the kitchen. Putting down the paper, she walked over to the kitchen door.

Patrick was embracing Lindsay, a letter clutched in his hand. A torn envelope lay on the kitchen table. When he spotted Nina, he waved the letter at her.

"I got into Rutgers!" he cried. "I got accepted."

Nina beamed at her brother. "Patrick, that is so cool." So now it was certain. In the fall he would be going to college.

Sometimes, though she hated to admit it, she thought she might miss him.

As if to remind her of how sentimental she was being, Patrick let out a loud belch.

"Patrick, ugh," said Lindsay, grimacing.

Patrick released Lindsay and came over to Nina, lifting her briefly off her feet.

"Does Mom know?" asked Nina.

"Not yet," said Patrick.

"They're going to be really happy," said Nina, hoping, selfishly, that perhaps her parents would be reconciled, however briefly, by this good news.

Patrick set Nina down and stared again at his letter. "I can't believe it," he said.

"I always knew you'd get in," Nina said, although that was not entirely true. Patrick's acceptance at college had never been a given. He wasn't much of a student.

Patrick seemed to have a sudden realization. "I've got to call the brainiac!"

Nina knew who he meant. Gemma Johnstone, the smartest girl in the senior class, was Patrick's tutor. Searching the paper for the movie times, Nina had just noticed the picture of Gemma, accepting the Delman Prize, which was given to the best scholar in the school. Gemma had gotten early admission to Princeton months ago. With Gemma's help, Patrick had worked hard and brought up all his grades.

Lindsay knew who he meant, too. She tossed her shiny blond hair like a glimmering curtain. "She wasn't in school today."

"Where was she?" Nina asked.

Lindsay shrugged. "Still sick, I guess. Yesterday she had to leave early."

Patrick had dialed the number and was leaving a message. "Gemma, it's Patrick. I've got big news. Call me."

Just then the back door opened and Marsha Avery came in, looking glummer than when she had left the house earlier.

"Hello, Mrs. Avery," Lindsay said politely.

"Mom," Patrick cried. "Look." He waved the letter at her. "I got in."

Marsha frowned, and then her face cleared. "Let me see!" she cried. She took the letter and scanned it. Her gloomy expression vanished. "Oh, Patrick, that's wonderful, darling. Just wonderful. I'm so proud of you. I knew you could do it." She beamed, and hugged her son. "Did you tell your father?" Marsha asked.

"He went back to the office," said Patrick.

"You better give him a call," said Marsha.

Patrick took the phone into the living room, with Lindsay following behind him.

Nina wanted to protest that she needed the phone to call Brandon, but she knew this was more important. Marsha began to put her painting equipment back in the closet. She unzipped the green paint-spattered sweatshirt that they all referred to as her camouflage outfit.

"How come you're back so soon?" Nina asked.

Marsha's expression darkened again. "I had to leave. There was a lot of commotion there. Police everywhere. TV reporters. It was a zoo."

"Police?" Nina asked. "What were the police doing there?"

"You know that baby that was kidnapped?" said Marsha. "The Kilgore baby?"

Even Nina, who paid little attention to the news, knew what her mother was referring to. Everybody around there knew. April Kilgore, a cocktail waitress, and her baby had moved in with her new boyfriend, a guy named Travis Duffy, who had a history of child abuse from his first marriage. One night, while April was working the late shift, the baby disappeared. Duffy insisted that the child had been stolen while he was asleep on the couch. The police had been investigating it for a couple of months now. "Yeah. What about it?" Nina said.

"Someone said they found him."

"The baby? He was in the park?"

"Well, found his remains, I should say. Apparently a dog was digging there . . ."

"You mean the kidnappers killed the baby?" Nina asked, confused.

"Oh no," Marsha scoffed. "There never really was a kidnapping. Nobody believed that story for a minute. That boyfriend of hers was lying through his teeth. But they'll get him now. Now that they've found the body. I blame the mother, for leaving the baby alone with him. She knew he had a violent history. What was she thinking?"

Nina didn't really understand and, in truth, didn't find it all that interesting. Not compared to what was on her mind. "Mom," she said. "I have to ask you something . . ."

A tap on the kitchen screen door interrupted her. They both looked up.

"Excuse me. Is Patrick here?" asked the girl at the door.

"Oh hi, Gemma," said Nina shyly. "He's here. Come on in."

Gemma entered the kitchen. "He called me but I didn't get to the phone in time. I tried to call back, but . . ." Her large brown eyes stood out against her pale skin and her brunette hair looked greasy. She was dressed as always in baggy overalls and a shapeless T-shirt. Nina felt protective of the shy, studious girl who was often the butt of jokes.

Patrick came back into the kitchen and hung up the phone. When he spotted Gemma, he rushed over to her and lifted her up just as he had lifted Nina.

"Gemma. Guess what?" he cried. "I got accepted at Rutgers."

Two spots of color appeared in Gemma's cheeks as he set her back down. "Patrick. That's fantastic!"

"Patrick, are you ready to go?" Lindsay asked impatiently.

Patrick stretched, his shirt riding up over his taut, tanned abdomen. "I guess so."

"Wait a minute," said Marsha. "Where are you going?"

Patrick threw an arm around his mother and squeezed her. "We're going to celebrate. Probably hang out at the mall. Have a bite to eat at T.G.I.F.'s."

"Why not take Gemma with you?" said Marsha. "After all, without her help . . ."

"Oh no, really," said Gemma, blushing. "Patrick did the work."

"Besides, she's still under the weather," said Patrick breezily. "Look how pale she is. She's been out of school for two days. But I am going to buy her a present." He turned to Lindsay. "You can help me pick something out."

"That's not necessary," Gemma said.

"Maybe some nice shampoo," said Lindsay.

Gemma reached up and touched her hair self-consciously. Nina glared at Lindsay. She couldn't think of a sufficiently acidic retort.

"Okay, we're out of here," said Patrick. "Come on, Gemma. We'll drop you off."

"If you see Jimmy . . ." said Marsha anxiously.

"I'm not planning on looking under any rocks," said Patrick. Then he relented, noticing his mother's hurt expression. "Why don't you call Calvin's? Maybe that little creep's mother will know where they are."

Marsha shook her head in disgust. "That woman is so worthless. She doesn't care what they do."

"Well, I'll send him home if I see him," said Patrick. "Gemma, are you coming?" Patrick headed out the screen door with Lindsay, Gemma trailing them.

Marsha watched them go thoughtfully. "If that girl gets any thinner she's going to disappear," she said.

"You know, I saw her at the park yesterday when I was

painting," said Marsha. "I wonder why she said she was sick?"

"I don't know," said Nina in exasperation. "But she just got the Delman Prize so I doubt she's playing hookey or flunking out. Mom, I have to ask you something."

Marsha glanced at her watch, and then picked up the remote. "Let's see if the early news is on. They might have something about the Kilgore baby." She switched on the TV in the corner above the sink and changed the channels until she found the local news. "What is it?" she said.

"Can I go to the movies tonight with Brandon . . ."

Her mother tore her gaze from the TV screen. "With Brandon? Is this a date? Fourteen is a little bit young for a date."

"It's just the movies," Nina cried.

"It better be. 'Cause if I find it was anything else," Marsha warned her.

"It's nothing else." Nina rolled her eyes.

"The movies and then straight home. You hear me?"

"I hear you." Nina felt a little deflated by her mother's response. This was her very first real date. She had expected her mother to be excited. To ask her all about it, at least. But her mother's attention was now absorbed in the TV news. She was watching it intently.

"The baby's remains were found wrapped in a black plastic trash bag," the reporter in the blue coat was saying on the screen. "We have reports now that the child had been suffocated, and buried in a shallow grave . . ."

Marsha let out a gasp of horror.

"When asked about speculation that this could be the missing Kilgore baby, a police spokesman had this to say . . ."

It was sad, Nina thought. But it really wasn't her concern. She had a date tonight. A date. With Brandon Ross. She floated up the stairs to her room to call and tell him the screening times and plan her outfit.

BY the time the movie was over, and Nina and Brandon had streamed out of the theater with the other moviegoers, the night sky was black and spangled with stars. Nina wanted to grab the people who walked by her and shake them, and make them realize the improbable thing that was happening right under their noses. Nina Avery was on a date.

At least, she thought it was a date. So far, Brandon hadn't even held her hand. When we're walking home, she thought. That's when he'll do it. It will seem natural to just grab hands and walk along.

But now they were walking up Madison Street, and coming ever closer to their houses, and still he hadn't touched her. He was talking easily to her, telling her about his plans for the summer and his ideas about high school, but he kept his hands resolutely to himself. Maybe he just wants to be friends, she thought in despair. Maybe he just needed somebody to go to the movies with him. She felt her mood sinking as their houses came into view. That was probably it. It wasn't a date at all. Just two friends going to see a movie.

"Nina, is something wrong?" he asked.

She shook her head, and tried not to look tragic. She plastered a smile onto her face. "No, nothing," she said. "That was fun. I'm glad we went."

Brandon looked over toward his house. "I'd invite you over to my house, but I see my dad's car is back and my mom went upstairs with a headache before I left. They might not want any company."

Nina yawned, as if the very idea of spending another moment together was tiresome. "I better go in, too. I'll see you, Brandon."

He gazed at her with a troubled look on his face, and for

one second she thought he might be going to lean toward her and kiss her, but then he backed down off the front step. "Okay, I'll see ya," he said.

She opened the front door, wanting to escape from his sight. It was a disaster, she thought. There was no other way to describe it. In her mind she'd rehearsed how she was going to tell her mother about it. Her mom was always interested in the details of Nina's life. Earlier, when Nina left the house, her mother had been brooding and had hardly said good-bye. Nina knew she was distracted by her worries about Jimmy. And that fight with her dad. But by now she would be more relaxed, her cheeks flushed from the evening wine, that familiar half-smile on her face. She would be ready to listen.

Nina stepped into the front hall and was surprised to find that it was dark. Instantly, she felt alarmed, her fretting over the date forgotten. Nobody around there ever went to bed that early. Besides, her mother wouldn't turn the light out when Nina hadn't come home yet. And there was something else. A funny smell. Somebody had to be here. Both of her parents' cars were in the driveway. "Mom?" she called out. "Dad?"

There was a light on in the living room. From the looks of it, it was only one light—maybe the standing lamp by the bookcase. She followed the dim arc of light and walked into the living room. It took a minute for her eyes to adjust, to register what they were seeing. And then she let out a gasp and a strangled cry.

"Nina," her father said.

He was crouching on the oriental rug in front of the coffee table, looking up at her. His broad even-featured face was pale and sweaty. He was disheveled, still wearing his shirt and tie but no jacket. The front of the shirt was splotched with something dark. On the rug in front of him lay her mother, clutching the newspaper from the coffee table, as if she had pulled it down with her when she fell. Marsha's eyes were open, and there was a look of panic frozen in them. The front of her turtleneck was ripped, and there was a huge dark splotch over her chest. Her jeans and even her white socks were speckled with dark spots. Near her head on the rug was a knife. Nina recognized it. It came from the block in the kitchen. It, too, was stained.

"Mom, oh my God!" Nina started to rush toward her mother.

Slowly, Duncan rose to his feet, waving his hands at her. "Nina," he said. "Don't. Don't come any closer."

"Mom," she cried in a hoarse voice. "Mom. What's wrong with her?"

"Honey, your mom is . . . gone," he said. "I came in and found her like this."

"You mean . . .?"

"She's dead. Yes." He approached Nina gingerly, as if she were a rearing horse.

"No, she's not dead!" Nina cried. "Don't say that." She lunged toward her mother, but he intercepted her and held her back.

"No. There's nothing you can do. Someone's stabbed her."

"No. That's crazy. Let me go!" Nina cried frantically. "Mommy!"

"Honey, stop. She's dead. Believe me. I'm a doctor. I know when someone's dead. Come on. Get away from her. I don't want you to see her like this."

"Mommy," she whimpered.

"Don't go near her," Duncan murmured, holding her. "Come on. We have to go in the kitchen. We have to call the police. Come with me." He steered her away from her mother's body, although Nina could not tear her gaze from the horrible, incredible sight. Supporting one another, they stumbled into the kitchen, which was lit only by the light over the stove. Nina slid on something wet and slippery. She looked down just as

Duncan flipped on the switch for the overhead light. Nina saw that her own sneakered foot was resting in a scarlet puddle. She looked up. Blood splattered the cheerful, fruit-garlanded wallpaper and smeared the checkered tile floor.

"Oh my God," said Duncan.

Nina began to scream.

1

NINA seated herself on a cold metal folding chair in the back of the parole board hearing room. She was one of the first to arrive. The train from New York City to Trenton had left her with an hour to spare. She smoothed down the skirt of the claret-colored knit dress she was wearing. It was a rich shade that matched her garnet earrings and went well with her long black hair and her white skin. When she chose her clothes that morning, she had been conscious of wanting to look vibrant in contrast to the drab group that made up the parole board. She wanted her father's gaze to pick her out as soon as he walked into the room, so he could see the encouragement in her eyes.

The door behind her opened and Nina shifted around in her seat, wondering if it was Patrick arriving. She saw that it was an elderly couple shuffling in, the woman leaning on a cane. Nina turned back around and faced the long table at the front of the room. Maybe Patrick wouldn't show up this year. She hoped he wouldn't. But she feared that he would. It wasn't as if either one of them could ever forget about it.

Her thoughts drifted back to that horrible night fifteen years earlier and the jumble of nightmarish images she could never shake. She remembered hurling herself into Patrick's arms when he arrived home that night, shaken and bewildered, accompanied by the cops who had gone out to search for him. She could still see her eighteen-year-old brother, sobbing against their father's shoulder like a small boy, insisting that it couldn't be true. And then the three of them looking on in equal measures of horror and outrage as the detectives produced Marsha's rifled purse and empty wallet, which they had found on the bedroom floor. After that, the questioning, the endless questioning. Detective Hagen, gray-haired and sharp-eyed, suggesting, over and over, that Duncan had been slow to call for help. Too slow. The expression in Patrick's eyes beginning to change. Anger beginning to dawn there.

The door behind the conference table opened and the twelve members of the board straggled in, shuffling papers and conferring with one another. They were, as always, a stolid-looking bunch, more men than women, more white than black, all solemn, their suits a somber array of blue, black, and gray. Some of their faces were familiar to her. A couple of them were new. Year after year, these proceedings had a sameness to them. Normally, it seemed, they ended in disappointment. A few times, waiting out in the echoing corridor, Nina had seen genuine joy as a prisoner was given a second chance unexpectedly early. She told herself that she was not being unrealistic in hoping that this time she would be the one rejoicing. This year she had reason to hope.

Someone whispered her name, and Nina looked up to see Patrick entering the room, followed by his wife. She smiled, but her heart sank. She'd been hoping he might give their father a break, considering all that had happened recently, but no such luck. He was here, as usual. Without looking around, Patrick seated himself in the middle of the bank of seats on the other side of the aisle from her. He glanced over at her and nodded. Gemma poked her head out from behind Patrick and mouthed, "Hi, Nina." Nina smiled weakly back at Gemma.

So Patrick was here as usual and Jimmy, as usual, was not. To be fair, Jimmy had made great progress in his life from that night when their mother was killed. That night when he returned home high on drugs, trailing an equally doped-up Calvin Mears. Her father had ordered Calvin out of the house, and held Jimmy's forehead when he vomited at the sight of their mother's blood in the living room and all over the kitchen. Nina had often thought, although her father had never admitted as much to her, that the reason he refused to go to the police station that night, the reason that he insisted on having a lawyer before the police asked any more questions, was because he feared Jimmy would be busted for drugs. But Patrick scoffed at that notion. Their father's actions that night gave rise to Patrick's first suspicion, later confirmed in his mind by a jury's verdict, that Duncan was the one who had murdered their mother.

Nina straightened up as the head of the parole board, Arnold Whelan, instructed the bailiff to bring in prisoner #7796043. The bailiff went out the side door and came back into the room after a moment accompanied by a thin, gray-haired, gray-complected man in an orange jumpsuit who had his hands handcuffed in front of him. Nina felt the familiar stab of pain at the sight of her father, restrained that way, as if he were likely to be violent.

Duncan Avery did not look around, but sat down in the chair facing the board.

"Will the clerk please read the prisoner's file?" asked Arnold Whelan.

The clerk cleared his throat. "Duncan Patrick Avery, on August eighteenth, 1988, in the township of Hoffman, County of Bergen, New Jersey, convicted of the crime of murder in the second degree." The clerk then read a history of Duncan's applications and denials for parole. When he was asked if everything in this file was accurate, Duncan said gruffly that it was.

Mr. Whelan then announced that the board would hear testimony from two new witnesses on behalf of the applicant. He called for Stan Mazurek, and a burly young man in a wheelchair wearing a midnight blue law enforcement uniform was pushed up to the front of the room by a young woman with lustreless brown hair. The woman was wearing a V-necked tunic over stretch pants, and on the front of the tunic was a large round laminated pin that had a photo of two smiling little girls in red dresses seated, one behind the other, against a Christmas tree backdrop. The woman put the brake on the chair and gave Mazurek a quick kiss before she sat down in the front row, far from where Duncan Avery was seated.

"Now, Mr. Mazurek, you are, as I understand it," said Whelan, looking at the papers in front of him, "a guard at the Bergen County State Prison, where Mr. Avery currently resides."

Dr. Avery, Nina silently corrected him.

The guard nodded in agreement.

"And you are here today to support the applicant's petition for parole?"

Mazurek shifted uneasily in the wheelchair and put a protective hand over the area under his ribcage. "I got stabbed and the doc, there, saved my life."

"You're referring to the prisoner," Whelan said, glancing over his half-glasses at the stenographer who was working at the end of the table.

"That's right. Doc Avery is in my bloc. He's not like the others. He's a good prisoner. He keeps to himself, keeps quiet, doesn't make no trouble for nobody."

"Now, as I understand it," said Whelan, "there was an insurrection on that bloc."

"That's right," said Mazurek. "Just last week. I came over here today from the hospital. The docs told me I have to take it easy, but . . . I wanted to come."

"All right. Please tell us what happened."

"Yessir. Well, a couple of whackos got a hold of shivs, and when they gave a signal, all hell broke loose. They took me prisoner."

"You were a hostage," said Whelan.

Mazurek nodded and hung his head. "Yessir, they had me. And they were getting a big kick out of telling me what to do. I took all of it I could stand, and then I wouldn't go along with them, so one of them cut me. Sunshine. He tried to kill me. I knew the moment he did it. Wasn't something . . . minor, you know."

"And the applicant . . .?"

"Doc Avery. Yeah, well, he's always quiet, 'cause he knows what these guys are. But he pipes up, right in Sunshine's face, and says, 'Hey, you know Mazurek is gonna bleed to death. You gotta let me stop the bleeding.'

"Those bastards were all shouting, 'Yeah, let him bleed,' but Doc Avery was talking to them real quiet but firm, sayin' if he didn't stop the bleeding, I was gonna end up dead, and they'd all be on death row. So some of them seemed to get that, and they let him get through so he could work on me. He used his own shirt as a bandage. Dr. Quinteros there told me I would have died if he didn't do that, the doc."

Whelan held up a hand to stop his testimony. "We'll let Dr. Quinteros testify about the nature of your injury."

Mazurek shrugged. "Okay. I just want to say to you people

that my wife and daughters and I are grateful to the doc. I owe him my life." Mazurek had been speaking earnestly to the parole board. Now he turned and looked directly at Duncan Avery. Nina felt tears spring to her eyes at the intense sincerity in the man's tough-looking face. "I mean it, Doc," he said gently. "I'll never forget what you did for me."

Duncan nodded slightly.

Whelan turned to the rest of the board and asked them if they had any questions about the incident. A couple of board members asked a few questions about the hostage situation while Nina studied her father. He was paying careful attention to everything they said. You were a hero! Nina wanted to shout. They've kept you caged up all these years, but they have not turned you into an animal.

"Thank you, Officer Mazurek," said Whelan. "We want to thank you for coming forward with your information. We'll hear from Dr. Quinteros now."

A dark-haired young man in the second row stood up and walked toward the center aisle. Meanwhile, Mazurek nodded, and his wife got up and went behind the wheelchair to push him out of the room. Dr. Quinteros gave them both a friendly nod as he assumed the witness seat. Mrs. Mazurek wheeled her husband's chair down the center aisle.

As Mazurek and his wife passed the table behind where Duncan sat, the two men nodded gravely at one another, although there was no physical contact between them. But the woman reached out impulsively and put a hand on Duncan's shoulder.

"Mrs. Mazurek," Whelan said in a warning voice, as the guards in the room surged forward, and then resumed their positions as she quickly drew back her hand.

Whelan waited until Mazurek had been wheeled out the back door of the hearing room before continuing. "Now," he said, shuffling through the papers in front of him, "Dr. Quinteros."

The young doctor sat with his forearms resting on the arms of the witness chair. He was wearing a dark shirt and a tie, but no jacket. The gaze in his narrow black eyes was at once aloof and alert. His face resembled that of an Aztec chief, all angles and planes. His coal black hair had obviously been combed back, but it parted off center and fell in a curve beside his high, sharp cheekbones.

"You are Dr. Andre Quinteros," said Whelan. "You work at the Bergen County State Prison infirmary. Is that correct?"

Quinteros nodded. "Correct."

"Can you tell us about the injury sustained by Mr. Mazurek in the prison uprising?"

Quinteros leaned forward and recounted, in technical terms, the severity of the guard's injury. "Without immediate attention, a tear in the artery like this is life-threatening," he said in conclusion.

"So," said Whelan, "is it your opinion that Mr. Avery here did indeed save the life of Officer Mazurek?"

Quinteros looked gravely at Duncan. "Absolutely," he said.

"Thank you, Doctor."

"Mr. Whelan, I'd just like to add, if I might . . .?"

"Yes?"

"Well, Duncan . . . Dr. Avery . . . often helps me in the infirmary. I think highly of him and I value his opinion. I . . . would miss his help, but I hope you will see fit to grant him his parole."

"Thank you, Doctor, for coming in today. We won't keep you from your work any longer."

The young doctor stood up and smiled at Duncan, and Duncan nodded. Nina watched in mute gratitude as the good-looking doctor started to walk down the center aisle. As he reached the row where she was sitting, he suddenly glanced over at her. Nina was used to catching the eye of good-looking men, but all the same, she flushed as their eyes met. Suddenly, he gave her a brief nod of support as if he had recognized her and knew why she was there. At first she was too surprised to react. Then, recovering herself, she turned in her seat and tried to smile at him, but Quinteros had already exited the hearing room.

Whelan shuffled his papers again. "We have several testimonials as to the role that Mr. Avery played during this prison uprising. We also have the customary reports of his good behavior and a dearth of citations for any kind of infraction of the rules."

Nina knew what was coming next, and she dreaded it.

"Of course, the victim of the murder for which you were convicted and sentenced cannot speak for herself, but we do have someone here to make a statement on her behalf." He looked up into the rows of seats. "Mr. Avery?"

Patrick rose to his feet and walked to the front of the room. He sat down in the empty chair. He was dressed in a perfectly tailored pinstripe gray suit, a dazzling white shirt, and a gray silk tie, which was his work uniform as an investment banker on Wall Street. Patrick made a huge salary at his job, and he liked to flaunt it. He always dressed expensively, drove a Jaguar, and had filled his enormous house with expensive antique furniture and paintings. He was stockier than he had been in high school, but was still fit-looking. His curly hair was prematurely gray, his face tanned and his expression grim.

"And you are . . ." said Whelan, though he knew perfectly well.

"I am Patrick Avery. The victim was my mother, Marsha."

"And the prisoner is your father . . ." said Whelan.

"That's right," said Patrick.

"And, Mr. Avery, can you tell us how you feel about the possibility of your father being paroled at this time, in light of your experience, the loss of your mother."

Patrick smoothed down his tie and the color rose to his face. "I remain firmly against it. I don't believe that Duncan is sorry for what he did, or feels any responsibility. It's admirable that he helped that guard, Officer Mazurek, and kept him from bleeding to death. Apparently, he had no such second thoughts about my mother. He destroyed our family and he took my mother's life away from her. She's never seen our . . ." Patrick voice began to tremble, and he stopped to compose himself. He took a deep breath. "Our children were deprived of their grand-mother. My sister and brother and I were deprived of our mother. I respectfully ask that you deny this man any leniency. He did not show any to us. Our loss is permanent."

There was a murmur, as always, among the board members after Patrick spoke. He made a forceful witness. Whelan motioned for them to be silent, and then Patrick was excused. He did not look Duncan in the eye, but went back to his seat and sat down beside Gemma, who grabbed his hand.

"Now, we would like to speak to the prisoner. Mr. Avery, we have your request for parole here before us. Now, it says that if you were to be granted parole, you would have a place to live with your daughter, Nina. Is that right?" Duncan nodded slightly and looked back, for the first time, at Nina. Nina smiled at him.

Whelan looked in Nina's direction. "Is that right, Miss Avery?"

"That's right, sir. I have a two-bedroom apartment on the Upper West Side of Manhattan. I have plenty of room for him."

"Special permission would have to be granted for you to live outside of New Jersey, but because of the proximity of Manhattan, this would not seem to present any problems in

terms of fulfilling your obligation to meet with your parole officer and so forth. Now, as to work . . . Mr. Avery. You no longer
have your medical license."

Duncan cleared his throat. When he spoke, his voice was
soft and difficult to hear. "A former . . . colleague of mine, Dr.
Nathanson, runs a medical clinic in Newark where I would be
employed as a paramedic. There are plenty of jobs I can do
there that don't require a medical license."

"Yes, I see we have an affidavit from Dr. Nathanson to that
effect. Board members, do you have any questions for Mr. Avery
here? Miss Davis?"

A black woman with her hair skinned back into a bun,
wearing black-rimmed glasses, nodded. "Thank you, Mr.
Chairman. I do have a question. Mr. Avery, as your son who
spoke here has stated, you have never accepted responsibility
for this crime, despite your conviction. And consequently, you
have never expressed any remorse. Now, this lack of remorse on
your part makes me question whether it would be safe to
release you into society again. What can you say to me about
that, Mr. Avery?"

Duncan sighed. "The same thing I have always said, Miss
Davis. I can't accept responsibility for a crime I didn't commit.
Parole or no parole."

"That's it?" she said.

"I'm afraid so."

"You were found guilty, sir," she reminded him sharply.

"It was a mistake," he said.

The woman made a soft clucking sound and shook her
head slightly as she made a note on the paper in front of her.
"I'm finished with him," she said.

"Any other questions?" Whelan asked.

The other board members shook their heads.

"All right," said Whelan. "We need to confer a few minutes

about this. Can I ask all of you to wait out in the corridor? Bailiff, please take the prisoner to the holding cell."

Duncan glanced back at Nina, and she smiled at him with a confidence that she did not feel. It always came down to the same thing—her father's refusal to admit his guilt. But how could he do that, even to be free? He didn't do it. He couldn't say he did. As Duncan was led away, Nina walked out to the corridor.

She went over to the water fountain to get a drink. Patrick walked up behind her. Nina took her drink and straightened up. "All yours," she said to her brother.

Patrick had a drink as well. Then he straightened up also and looked sadly at her. "How you doing?" he asked.

Nina nodded. "Okay, good."

"How's Keith?" he asked, referring to the man with whom Nina shared an apartment. "Still in L.A.?"

"Yeah. HBO ordered four more episodes after they saw the pilot."

"Great. How about you? Are you still doing that Inge play?" Patrick asked.

"No, that closed," said Nina. "But I just got a callback for a Eugene O'Neill Off Broadway."

Patrick smiled wanly. "Another fun evening at the theater." Patrick did not share his sister's taste for serious, family-centered dramas.

Gemma walked over and joined them. She was still incredibly thin and still dressed exclusively in drab colors, although her clothes now had expensive designer labels. Her smooth, parchment-colored complexion was etched with tiny lines, but she still didn't bother with makeup. Gemma's hair was cut short in a fashionably spiky style. She still looked like a college student, although she was now a professor, wife, and mother. Her only obvious concession to their wealth were the various rings she wore and twisted nervously on her fingers. She'd always worn rings, but these sparkled with real gems. Nina reached out to embrace her and felt Gemma's bony shoulder blades poking through her gray cashmere sweater.

"How are the kids?" Nina asked. Patrick and Gemma had twin boys, Simon and Cody, who were seven years old.

Gemma shrugged. "Always fighting."

"Tell them I said hi. How's your class schedule this year?" Nina asked.

Gemma stared at Nina and then at her husband. Patrick had shoved his hands in his pockets and was jingling change. "We *are* out of touch," said Gemma. "Didn't you know that I resigned?"

"You quit teaching?" Nina asked.

Gemma nodded. "A few months ago. One of my mother's colleagues sent me all the research she was working on before she died. I decided to organize and catalog all her work and put it into a book. Try to get it published."

Nina knew that Gemma's mother had died when she was about five. She'd been a scientist who was doing research on genetics in an isolated Andean village when she died in a hiking accident.

Gemma had come to live in Hoffman with her father, an airline pilot, and his second wife, a woman who ran a bridal shop called Your Perfect Day. That marriage had long since ended, and Gemma's father was married for a third time and now lived in Arizona. "Gemma, I think that's wonderful," said Nina. "It's such a great way to honor your mother's memory."

"That's what I thought," said Gemma. She glanced warily at her husband.

"I don't think Patrick agrees."

Patrick jingled the change in his pockets impatiently. "I don't care. If that's what she wants to do, that's fine."

"Not that I can get much done with those boys around," said Gemma.

"You've got full-time help, for God's sake," he snapped. "What am I paying Elena for?"

Gemma flinched slightly and looked around the crowded corridor. "Did you hear from Jimmy?" she asked, changing the subject.

"He said he might come, but you know Jimmy and stress," said Nina.

Gemma nodded. "He seems to be staying straight."

"Still living with the Connellys," said Patrick with exasperation in his voice. "He's thirty years old. I wish he'd find himself his own place to live."

"I talked to him the other night and he sounded okay," Nina said. Jimmy had battled drug and alcohol addiction, but with a lot of help from the family who had taken him in, he had straightened out. Now he was an avid bodybuilder, and had a steady job working at a store that sold flooring. He'd also become quite religious, often attending services three times a week. Nina thought Patrick's judgment was, as usual, unnecessarily harsh, but she didn't say so.

A silence fell among them. Despite their differences about their father, the three siblings had maintained their relationship over the years. It was never easy. They had been separated after the death of their mother and their father's incarceration. Patrick went off to college; Jimmy went to live at the home of their mailman, George Connelly, whom Duncan had asked to look after Jimmy; and Nina was taken in by her mother's aunt, Mary. The house on Madison Street was sold to pay for Duncan's defense. Their father was a topic they simply avoided whenever possible. But today it wasn't possible.

"Look," said Nina. "I don't know what's going to happen in there . . ."

Patrick took a deep breath and gazed up at the ceiling.

"But if they decide . . . in his favor this time . . ."

"That's a big if," said Patrick sharply.

"If they do," Nina continued, "I want all of us, the children, everyone, to try and make peace with one another. Patrick, he's never seen his grandchildren . . ."

"Let's just hope it doesn't come to that," Patrick said coldly.

"Patrick, please," said Nina. "Can't you try?"

Patrick glared at her and shook his head. "I will never understand you, Nina. How can you still believe in him? What does it take to make you see the truth?"

"How can you *not* believe him?" she cried. "How can you judge him like that? If it were me, would you judge me that way?"

"That's different. You're a good person, Nina. I know for a fact that he is not. How could you have sat through his trial and have any doubt? For God's sake, he was sleeping with the woman next door . . ."

Nina thought ruefully of Brandon's mother, Sheila. After the affair was revealed in the newspapers, the Ross family moved away. Sheila came back to testify for the prosecution at the trial, saying that Duncan was in her bedroom, right next door, on the night of the murder. By her account, at least a half hour elapsed from the time Duncan slipped out of her bedroom to the time she heard the sirens on the arriving police cars. She testified that Duncan often talked about how unhappy he was in his marriage.

"Okay," Nina said. "He committed adultery. Nobody's denying that. But it's not the same as murder."

Patrick shook his head. "And at your insistence we spent every last penny from the sale of the house to hire lawyers, and their detectives, to try to exonerate him. And where did it get us? Well, let's see. We found out that he'd seen a lawyer behind Mom's back about getting a divorce."

Nina shook her head. "That's no proof. That doesn't mean he would kill her."

"You're just kidding yourself, Nina," Patrick said. "I'll tell you a fact. We know for a fact that when Duncan 'found' his wife dying, he did not even call nine-one-one. He did not try to get any help for her."

"He was about to when I walked in," Nina insisted. "And what about the money from her pocketbook? They never found it."

"It was probably in Duncan's pocket," Patrick scoffed. "That burglar theory didn't fool the jury. That was just a brainstorm he had, to try to make it look like an intruder. Nina, his prints were on the knife, they'd had a huge fight that afternoon, and she told a woman at the Art League that he had threatened to kill her. How can you believe in him in the face of all that? He's playing you for sympathy. You can't even see it. It makes me hate him all the more."

A court attendant opened the hearing room door and looked around. Spotting them by the water fountain, she gestured for Nina, Patrick, and Gemma to return. Without answering her brother, Nina led the way back into the hearing room. They went back to their opposite sides of the room, like boxers going to opposite corners, Patrick's angry questions still ringing in Nina's ears like landed blows. How could she ever make him understand? Of course, she'd had her moments of doubt about Duncan. Of course, she'd wondered. She was only human. But there was no way Nina could ever convince Patrick to believe in their father, because it came down to a question of faith.

Arnold Whelan waited until they were seated and Duncan Avery was escorted back in. Then he turned to Duncan and peered at him over the top of his half-glasses. Nina's heart felt like it was being squeezed in her chest. She tried to read the expressions of the board members, but they were poker-faced.

Please, God, she thought. Please. He has suffered so much. Please, let him have his life back. Let me have him back in mine while there's still time. "Mr. Avery," said Whelan.

Nina held her breath.

"The board has voted to grant your request for parole . . ."

Nina gasped, and then her heart soared. It was over. He was free! She could hardly believe it. She was going to be able to bring him home and give him back his life. From across the room, she heard a groan, and when she turned to look, she saw Patrick pressing the heel of his hand to his forehead, as if he were trying to quell a migraine or staunch a bleeding wound.

2

NINA placed the bouquet of flowers in the center of the table, and stepped back to admire the effect of her efforts. Everything looked ready. The china, glasses, and flatware in the apartment were strictly utilitarian, but the flowers and the pretty fabric napkins she bought gave the table a festive air. While it would be a tight squeeze, and she'd had to borrow two chairs from the woman who lived in 8-C, they would all fit around it. She looked at her watch, and then out the window at the gloomy November afternoon. It was Saturday, and she had asked her sister-in-law to get her brothers and the children there by five. Gemma had promised that she would do her best. They'll come, Nina thought, although her own jumpy stomach belied her confidence. It'll be fine, she told herself. Stop worrying. But it was impossible not to have her doubts.

She had picked up her father the day before at the Bergen County State Prison, and brought him home to her comfortable apartment. Until recently she had shared it with Keith Ellender, a director she met three years ago when he cast her in an Off-Broadway production of *Lady Windermere's Fan*. Six months ago, Keith was asked to come to L.A. to direct a series pilot for HBO. He wasn't sure he'd be gone all that long. So many pilots never made it into production. But the network liked the results, and Keith was still living in L.A. Luckily, he was glad to have Nina still living in the apartment.

Between the soaps, commercials, and Off Broadway, Nina was busy most of the time, but she didn't make anywhere near enough money to afford an apartment like this. Keith, who was gay, unattached, and over forty, had owned the place, a two-bedroom co-op, for twenty years and wasn't about to sell it. So Nina stayed on. Keith's study, with the pull-out sofa, was vacant, and Keith had given his blessing to her plan to move her father in there for the time being.

It was a luxury to have the space, a luxury to be able to offer her father a place to call home. She couldn't afford even a studio apartment in Manhattan at today's prices. She didn't know what she would have done otherwise, with Duncan getting out on parole. It wasn't something she had ever planned for. Hoped for, yes. But that hope had faded over time.

"How do I look?"

Nina turned around and saw her father standing in the kitchen doorway. He was wearing a new shirt, sweater, and pants she had bought him while he was still in prison. She'd had to estimate his sizes because of all the weight he'd lost. Apparently, she hadn't done a very good job. The pants were cinched around his waist like a dirndl skirt.

"Oh, Dad. I bought them too big."

"It doesn't matter, honey," he said. "They're fine. Believe me. What time are you expecting them?"

"Should be any minute," said Nina.

"The food smells good," he said.

"Well, I hope it will be good." She had cooked all of Duncan's old favorites for dinner last night. He'd greeted each dish enthusiastically, and then pushed the food around, hardly tasting it. When she'd asked him if anything was wrong, he'd insisted that everything was perfect, but she'd known that he was simply trying to reassure her. It was not that he'd seemed anxious or depressed. He'd seemed . . . distant.

The doorbell sounded and Nina jumped. She had been expecting the doorman to buzz her. He must have recognized them. Patrick and Gemma had been there before. She took a deep breath and looked in the mirror. She looked fine, she reminded herself. Her long black hair was pulled up into a ponytail and she was wearing a fitted peacock blue shirt over black pants. She looked casual enough for a family dinner, but a little bit elegant, too. It was, after all, a special night. There were circles under her eyes, but she'd covered them artfully with makeup, and added a bold red to her lips and cheeks. Ready, she thought.

Just as she started for the door, the phone rang. Her father looked at her questioningly.

"Why don't you get the door, Dad?" she suggested gently.

Duncan took a deep breath and nodded. "Okay."

Nina went into the living room and picked up the phone. "Hello."

"Nina."

It was Gemma's soft voice. Nina's heart froze. "Where are you?"

"Nina, I hate to have to tell you this, but I'm afraid we're not going to be able to come."

Nina was silent, but the receiver trembled in her hand.

"An old colleague of my mother's is in Philly at a conference and he's heading back to South America tomorrow. If I want to talk to him for the book, I have to to go down there tonight."

"Why can't you go in the morning?" Nina demanded.

"Because he wants to do it tonight. He's leaving early. Look, it was a last-minute thing. I didn't even know he was in the States. I'm really sorry about this . . ."

"But I have everything ready. What am I going to tell Dad . . . ?" Nina asked. "You promised."

Gemma was silent for a moment. "I said I was sorry."

"What about Patrick and the boys?" Nina cried. "Couldn't he bring them?"

"Patrick has put his foot down. He doesn't want the boys anywhere near your father," Gemma admitted.

"That's the real reason you're not coming," Nina said ruefully.

"No, Nina," Gemma said patiently. "I'm just about to get in the car and drive to Philly."

Sometimes Nina found her sister-in-law's implacability exasperating. She took a deep breath and tried to compose herself. "All right. Never mind . . ."

"I am very sorry, Nina," Gemma said.

"And I suppose Jimmy won't come by himself . . ."

"He called last night to say he couldn't make it. Something about having to run a meeting tonight for his sponsor," said Gemma.

"Oh sure," said Nina.

"I'm sure your father will understand," said Gemma.

"Oh, he'll understand all right," said Nina.

"Boys . . . stop that," Gemma said sharply. "Nina, I've got to go. Please give our . . . my apologies to your dad."

"I will," said Nina. She put the receiver back in the cradle and fell back against the chair. From where she sat, she could see the dining area, with its table crowded with plates and glasses, the candles already lit. She wanted to cry, or to scream, but part of her knew that she had set herself up for this. What kind of foolish optimism had ever made her think that there would be a happy family reunion?

Duncan came into the room looking worried. "Honey," he said, "what's the matter?"

Nina looked up at him. There was no use in trying to pretend. "That was Gemma," she said. "They're not coming."

Duncan nodded and looked away. He pursed his lips slightly, but didn't say anything.

"I'm so sorry, Dad. Gemma has to go meet some guy in Philly who knew her mother. Did I tell you she was organizing her mother's research into a book?"

"No," he said, clearly unconvinced.

Nina sighed. "I feel terrible."

"Don't worry about it. It's not your fault, honey." He didn't ask what would prevent Patrick or Jimmy from coming. He didn't even seem surprised.

It is my fault, Nina thought. I set him up for disappointment. I should never have suggested it. "But I feel so bad," she said.

Duncan nodded toward the foyer. "Never mind about it. Nina, there's someone here to see you."

Caught up in her disappointment, Nina had forgotten that the doorbell had rung. That's right, she thought. "Who is it?"

Duncan hunched his shoulders. "One of your neighbors," he said.

A silver-haired man in a Ralph Lauren shirt with a sweater knotted over his shoulders came into the room. Nina recognized him as someone who lived in the building. She frowned and stood up.

"Miss Avery?" he said.

"Yes?"

"My name is Paul Laird. I live in 10-A. I'm the chairman of

the co-op board. Could I speak to you in private for a minute?"

"I'll be in my room," said Duncan.

"No, Dad, you can stay," said Nina, but he had already retreated.

"Sit down, Mr. Laird. What can I do for you?"

The man sat down on the edge of one of the living room chairs. "This is difficult, Miss Avery, but I'll come right to the point. You are staying here as a guest of Keith Ellender."

"That's right," she said warily. Because she and Keith weren't a married couple, and the apartment belonged to him, the co-op board was privy to all their arrangements.

"It's come to the attention of the board that you have brought your father here to live with you, and that your father is a convicted felon on parole from the Bergen County State Prison."

Nina stared at him and did not reply.

"The policy of the co-op board is inflexible in a matter like this. We absolutely cannot countenance this situation."

"Who told you that? Did Keith tell you?" she cried.

Laird shook his head. "Although Mr. Ellender should have told us, if he knew. Shall I assume that he knows about this situation?"

Immediately Nina realized that she could get Keith into trouble with the wrong answer. They had found out some other way. It didn't really matter how. "No, I . . . this came up suddenly. My dad is just . . . staying with me for a while until he gets back on his feet. He's . . . more like a guest here. I didn't think I needed to . . . ask permission to have a guest."

"Does your father have another address?" Laird asked abruptly.

"Not . . . as of right now," Nina admitted.

"Well, then," said Laird. "it appears that he is living here. I'm sure Mr. Ellender will understand when he hears about this. Naturally, he's going to be informed of our decision. We cannot and will not have a convicted murderer living in this building."

"I can't believe this," said Nina. "You can't do this. There must be a law against this kind of discrimination."

Laird stood up and raised a hand. "Now listen, Miss Avery. I am not here to debate our board's policies. This is not your apartment. You have no rights in this matter. Either your father will have to find another place to live or you both will. You have one week to resolve this. Good day, Miss Avery."

He turned abruptly and walked to the door of the apartment. Stunned, Nina got up and followed him to the door. "This is completely unfair," she said, as he stood in the hallway waiting for the elevator. "My father is no danger to you or anyone else."

"I understand you are upset," he said calmly.

"Upset!" she cried.

"Nina," said her father's voice behind her. "Close the door."

Nina turned and looked at Duncan.

Duncan shook his head. "Just close the door," he said.

Glaring at the man in hallway, Nina slammed the door shut.

"Now come and sit down," said Duncan.

Nina went into the kitchen and turned off the burners under the pots that were bubbling on the stove. Then she returned to the living room. Her father was seated on the sofa. He patted the seat beside him. There was something oddly comforting about the gesture, as if he were resuming his old identity as her parent. Nina sank down in the cushions and folded her arms over her chest. She suddenly realized that she had stopped thinking of him as her father. She had begun to regard him as a kind of invalid who needed her constant help. And she had treated him that way. But now she felt young and frightened, and grateful to be sitting beside him again.

"I heard everything," Duncan said. "I'm sorry this is turning out to be so hard. I was afraid of this."

"It's all right, Dad. It doesn't matter," she said with a bravado she did not feel.

"Yes, it does."

"No," she insisted. "We'll find another place to live. I'll just have to go out and start looking."

"No, Nina," he said, patting her on the knee. "Listen to me. You can't find another place like this. I may have been in jail for a long time, but I'm not blind. I can see how much things cost around here. This is a nice apartment and you like it here. And you're going to stay here."

"I'm not!" she cried like an angry child. "I won't."

"Oh, yes you will," he said. "You're going to stay right here, and I'm going to find a place of my own."

Nina sighed. "Dad, don't be naïve. You couldn't afford anything around here on your own. It's impossible. Even a little broom closet costs the earth . . ."

"I didn't say I was going to stay here," he said. He took a deep breath. "The truth is, I don't really want to live in this city. This place is too much for me. I don't belong here."

"What's wrong with it?" she asked. "I mean, it's big, but the people are great. Most of them . . ."

"There's nothing wrong with it," Duncan said. "This is your home. And I want you to stay."

"But where would you go?" she cried.

"I'll go home, of course."

"Home?" she said, not believing her ears. "You mean . . ."

"I'll go back to Hoffman."

"After what happened there? How could you? Everyone will still remember . . ."

"Nina," he said. "I have to go back there. It's where I lived. It's where I belong. Besides, there are a lot of . . . unanswered questions."

All of a sudden, Nina understood what he meant. He wanted to find out who had committed the crime that put him in prison all these years. Of course he did. "You mean, about Mom, don't you? About who killed her?"

Duncan frowned. "Well, I have to be realistic, Nina. It was so long ago. And even those detectives we hired at the time weren't able to . . . help."

"Oh," she said, disappointed. "I thought you meant . . ."

"I'd like to be able to find out more about it, of course," he said. "I've spent the best years of my life paying for somebody else's crime. And you and the boys . . . you lost your mother. In some ways, there's nothing more important to me. But I have to face facts. It was a long time ago."

Nina looked at him with narrowed eyes. "Do you have a theory about this? I mean, is there someone you suspect? Do you have any idea about who killed her?"

Duncan sighed, and shook his head. "I've thought about it enough. I wish I could say that I understand it, but I don't. Still, I feel like it's important that I be there, where it happened. Otherwise there's no chance," he said vaguely. "And that's not the only thing. My boys are there. And my grandchildren."

"Dad," said Nina, shaking her head. "After what they did today? I mean, I don't even want to see them again . . ."

"Hey, don't talk like that. All these years, you and your brothers managed to keep on caring for one another. I don't want to become a wedge between you. Not now. As for today . . . you . . . we expected too much of them. It's going to take time. That's why I have to go back. I have to be where I *can* see them. Be with them, maybe. Try to get them used to the idea of me being back in their lives." He wove his fingers together and squeezed his hands. "I have to try."

"Jimmy wanted to come," she said, trying to be reassuring. Her father looked so pained. "It's just hard for him. He doesn't cope well with change. But he's not . . . against you."

"Like Patrick," Duncan said grimly.

"There's no getting through to Patrick," Nina admitted.

"But maybe, in time, there's a chance they'll come around to my side. As long as I'm here, there's no chance. I'm sixty years old, Nina. My family is all I have left in this world. What else can I do?"

"Oh, Dad," Nina said. She tried to prevent it, but tears of frustration welled up in her eyes.

Duncan rubbed her back in a circular motion. "Take it easy," he said.

"I feel like I've done everything wrong. I didn't realize you wanted to go back there. I hate going there myself. I avoid it like the plague. I never even asked you what you wanted to do. I just assumed . . ."

"Out of the goodness of your heart," he said. "You wanted to make it easy for me. But there is no easy way for me, Nina. I know that. I accept that."

"It's so unfair," she cried.

Duncan smiled and shook his head. "What a surprise," he said.

They sat in silence for a moment.

"All right, then," she said. "If you want to go back there, I'll go with you."

"Absolutely not," he said. "I told you. You are not giving up this place. I won't be responsible for that. Now that's final, Nina."

There was something about the fatherly authority in his voice that made her smile. "I've missed you so much," she said, wiping away her tears.

"And I've missed you."

"Okay, okay. We'll do it your way," said Nina. "I'll just go and . . . help you get settled. Help you find a place. Will you let me do that?"

Duncan nodded, and put his arm around her. She snuggled under his arm, her errant tears dampening his sweater. She didn't want to say what else she really felt. She didn't want him to know that she was fearful of what he would encounter back in Hoffman. People there believed that he had killed Marsha, and they would not welcome him back. The thought of leaving him alone there frightened Nina. Over the years, some people had told her she was crazy to believe in him. Others just looked at her pityingly. But there would be no mercy in the way they looked at him.

Don't go, she thought. Stay here and be anonymous, with no reminders of the past. But she knew there was no use in saying it. Her face rested just beneath his shoulder, and she could hear, like the echo in a well, the sturdy, persistent beat of his heart.

3

THE next afternoon, while her father stood quietly beside her, Nina purchased two bus tickets to Hoffman. Then, shouldering her bag and warning Duncan to stay close, she began to expertly navigate the maze of concourses and escalators in the Port Authority Bus Terminal that led them, at last, to the platform from which their bus would depart. They joined the short line of people waiting for the bus to begin loading.

"I'm glad you knew the way. I'd get lost in here," said Duncan.

Nina smiled at him. "Nothing to it. From here it's an easy hop to Hoffman. It's a lot more convenient than trying to keep a car in this city."

Duncan nodded, but looked unconvinced. He held his duffel bag against his chest, as if afraid someone would snatch it from him if he held it by the handle. "Do you go back a lot? To see the boys?"

Nina shrugged. "Holidays, sometimes. Although Patrick is such a bully about the holidays. He wants all the food and decorations to look like something out of a magazine, and Gemma just isn't like that. I think it reminds her of Didi. Do you remember Didi, her stepmother, who had the bridal shop? She could spend hours mulling over what color to engrave the matchbooks. Anyway, Gemma gets stressed out. And Jimmy usually stays at the Connellys'. I can't really blame him. I go to visit Aunt Mary, of course. She's in the nursing home right now, recovering from a hip replacement."

Duncan's face colored at the mention of Nina's great-aunt, Marsha's mother's sister. "She was a good woman," he said.

"She still is," said Nina. "Here's the bus."

Nina led the way out the door and up the steps into the idling bus, which smelled of exhaust fumes, fried food, and disinfectant. She walked halfway back, and then indicated that her father should take the seat by the window. Duncan sat down obediently, clutching his bag on his lap. He leaned his forehead against the window and stared out into the darkness of the Port Authority garage. Nina took out her fat Sunday *New York Times*, flipped on the overhead light, and began to read. Once the other passengers were seated, the bus driver closed the doors and, with a rumble, the bus pulled out and began its descent toward the Lincoln Tunnel.

Nina read her paper for half an hour, until the bus reached the outskirts of Hoffman. Then she folded it up and looked out the window. The many deciduous trees that lined the streets of the New Jersey suburb were ablaze, and Duncan gave a little gasp of pleasure at the sight of them.

"Does it look different to you?" Nina asked him.

Duncan shook his head. "It looks like I never left." The bus turned slowly onto Lafayette, the main street downtown, stopping at several corners.

"This looks different," he said. "All these shops are new."

Nina nodded. "Hoffman's become very upscale. I mean, it always was a nice town, but now . . ."

"Look at that. Banana Republic. Tommy Hilfiger. The Gap. What happened to the old hardware store?"

"Everybody goes to Lowe's or Home Depot now, Dad," Nina said.

"What's Home Depot?"

Nina smiled and shook her head.

"And that was the old pharmacy. Now it's an antiques shop."

"Oh right," said Nina, as the bus stopped and opened its doors. "All European antiques. Very pricey. You know who owns that shop? Lindsay Farrell. Do you remember her? She used to go out with Patrick?"

"Oh yeah," Duncan said, peering out. "Pretty girl. Her family had money."

"Yeah." Nina started to say more, but she stopped herself. She didn't want to hurt him. Gemma had confided in her long ago that Lindsay broke up with Patrick after Duncan was arrested. Lindsay's parents were horrified by the scandal. They sent her off to private school in Switzerland, where she ended up staying, getting married and then divorced. Last year she had returned to Hoffman and opened up the high-end shop on Lafayette. Nina had stopped in there once, before she realized it belonged to Lindsay. After that she avoided the place. "It's a nice store," Nina said vaguely.

But Duncan had lost interest in the antiques store. Nina knew why. On the next block was the building where his office used to be. She hated to think of how he would react when he saw it. The office had been taken over by a pair of architects who had completely redone the façade of the building. It bore no resemblance to the office where he had practiced for so long. It was as if he had never been there. He might not even recognize it.

"Is that my . . . ?" Duncan stopped, bewildered.

"They've changed it," Nina said gently, apologetically.

Duncan nodded, but he suddenly looked weary and . . . diminished. They rode in silence for a few blocks. "Nina, where are we getting off?" Duncan asked worriedly. "Isn't Harris Realtors on this block?"

"Not anymore, Dad," Nina murmured. "We're going to the end of Lafayette and around past the park," she said.

"Why are we going there?" he asked. He sounded almost frightened, like a child.

Nina frowned and glanced past him. "Trust me," she said. "I've got a plan."

A FEW minutes later, the bus stopped outside the Milbank Manor Nursing Home. "This is us," said Nina, getting up. "Come on."

Duncan followed her down the steps, but he frowned and halted as Nina started up the walk to the nursing home. "What are we doing here? Isn't this where your great-aunt is?"

"Yes."

Duncan shook his head and refused to proceed.

"Dad, come on. Look. We can't realistically expect to find a place right off the bat. And the only hotel is out by the highway. We don't even have a car. Aunt Mary is stuck here in the nursing home for the time being having physical therapy after her hip replacement. I'm going to ask her if we can use her house and car until we get you situated."

"You can't, Nina," he cried. "For God's sake. She was your mother's aunt. She probably hates me."

"She doesn't hate you, Dad. Come on. You don't have to go and see her. You can wait in the lobby. I just need to talk to her."

Duncan looked around helplessly, as if he no longer knew how to manage his life in this most familiar of places. Nina watched him anxiously. The physical changes in him had happened gradually in prison, so that she had hardly noticed them, but now, in this place where they had once been a family, she saw them starkly. Instead of the confident, robust man she remembered, he was pale and thin, his hair gray, his eyes electric with alarm.

"Dad, you have to trust me," she said. "I'm trying to do the best thing. It will be all right."

Duncan sighed, and followed her up the walk to the building. When they got inside, Nina indicated a little grouping of damask-covered easy chairs in the reception area. "Wait there," she ordered. "I'll be back in no time." Duncan sat down heavily.

Nina signed the guest book, pushed open the double doors, and went down the hallway, edging past trolleys of gauze packages and medications, apologizing to those she passed who were shuffling down the hallway with the aid of walkers. Holding her breath against the smell of decay that seemed to pervade the air, she tapped on the door to her great-aunt's room and heard a feeble voice bid her to come in.

Her great-aunt was propped up in bed by a bunch of pillows and she was staring disinterestedly at the television, which was tuned to an all-news network. Her face lit up at the sight of Nina and she turned off the television.

Nina came over and embraced Mary's frail shoulders, and kissed her on the cheek.

"How are you, darling?" Aunt Mary asked.

"I'm okay," said Nina. She set down her bag and sat in the chair beside her aunt's bed. "How are you?"

"I'm improving," she said. "It's going to take a while."

"You look good, though," Nina said with a smile.

"You're the one who looks good," Aunt Mary said. "I love that emerald green sweater on you."

"You should. You gave it to me," Nina teased her, glancing down at her birthday present, a merino wool V-necked sweater that was a perfect fit. Aunt Mary's presents, like her advice, always reflected how clearly her aunt saw her, and recognized her individuality. It had been an abrupt shock, fifteen years ago, to have to move into the house of a widowed great-aunt whom she hardly knew. But there was no choice. Nina's own family had been ripped apart. Aunt Mary had seemed old to her then, at age sixty. She had gamely offered to take Jimmy in, too, but everyone agreed that Jimmy was too much for an old woman to handle. At Duncan's insistence, Jimmy went to live with George and Rose Connelly. Although they were not friends, George felt a debt of gratitude to Duncan for saving the life of his son, Anthony. George repaid the debt by helping Jimmy to straighten out his life. As for Nina, after a terrible period of adjustment, she had settled into a quiet life with her great-aunt. Aunt Mary had been a teacher, and she liked children, though she'd never had any of her own. She was kind, and fair with Nina, and Nina often thought that it was Aunt Mary's kindness that prevented her own life from descending into a tailspin.

Most important to Nina, despite Aunt Mary's obvious love for Nina's mother, and regardless of whatever her secret opinion might have been, Mary had never spoken ill of Duncan or tried to prevent Nina from seeing her father after he went to prison.

"So," said Mary, "you don't want to hear about my infirmities. Tell me how you're doing."

"I have a favor to ask," said Nina bluntly.

"Shoot," said her aunt.

Nina hesitated. "I told you on the phone about my dad. Getting paroled."

Mary nodded, and gazed at her great-niece.

"Well, I didn't tell you this. The co-op board in my building wouldn't allow him to stay there. And then I found out . . . from him . . . that he wanted to move back here. To Hoffman."

"I don't know if that's a good idea," said Mary sternly. "A lot of people here still have very bad feelings about him."

Nina looked at her directly. "I don't think it's a good idea either, to tell you the truth. But it's what he wants. So he could be near the boys. He was quite determined about it."

"I see," said the old woman.

"I promised to help him find a place and get settled and all that. That's what I wanted to ask you about. There's no one in the house right now, is there?"

Mary looked at her niece, aghast. "You want him to live in *my* house?"

"No. Not live there. No," said Nina. "We just need a place to stay until we find something for him. It's expensive around here. It might take a little while."

Mary nodded, but did not reply.

"I know it's a lot to ask," said Nina, "but I really need this. And you know, you never seemed to be . . . against him. You never seemed to blame him for Mom's . . . You never seemed to believe that he did it."

"I never said that," Mary cautioned her.

Nina frowned. "But you didn't . . . did you?"

Mary looked at her sadly. "I respected your feelings, Nina. That seemed like the most important thing to me at the time. As for your father, well . . ."

"He didn't, Aunt Mary. I wouldn't love him if he had done that . . ."

"Oh, honey," said Mary, shaking her head.

"I don't know what else to do," Nina cried. "I didn't want him to come back here either, but he's so intent on it. I know I have no right to ask for anything from you. You've done more for me—"

"Nina," her great-aunt interrupted her kindly. "Stop that now. I know that you believe in him. And once upon a time, Duncan was a fine young man. For all I know, you're right about him."

"He's not young anymore. And he really needs a hand."

Mary sighed. "If you want to stay in the house and use the car . . . Well, it's your house, too, Nina. You know that's how I look at it."

Nina jumped up and embraced her great-aunt. "Thank you."

"Hey, take it easy," Mary said.

"I'll get him to fix things around the house while we're there," said Nina. "I promise. There won't be any trouble. And we'll be gone just as soon as I get him settled in his own place. You won't be sorry."

Mary took a deep breath and smoothed out the bedcovers over her lap. "Do you think he knows how to tune a piano?" she asked wryly.

Nina beamed. "I'm going to go tell him. He's waiting outside. He didn't want to come in. He thought you wouldn't want to see him."

"All right. That's fine," said Mary. "But, Nina, I want you to hurry up and get him settled. And then get away from him. You can't spend your life fighting his battles. You mustn't."

"I won't. And we'll be out of there before you know it. I promise."

"You have to live your own life, Nina. You need to think about having your own family. What happened to that young man you were seeing? Hank. That shipping executive who came to see you in the play all those times."

Nina sighed. "Hank Talbot. I still see him . . ."

"Nina," said Aunt Mary.

"All he thinks about is how much money he can make. He reminds me of Patrick," Nina protested.

"You said he was fun."

"He *was* fun, at first," said Nina. "Look, don't worry about me. I'm fine. I couldn't be better. Aunt Mary, I've got to go. My dad . . ."

"Go ahead. Go on," said Aunt Mary.

Kissing her aunt again, Nina picked up her bag and flew out of the room, eager to tell her father the good news. When she opened the door to the reception area, she saw that there was a bloodless but cheerful-looking old man dressed in frayed, comfortable clothes and house slippers seated across from Duncan.

"Harry," said Duncan, "this is my daughter, Nina."

The old man peered up at her. "Hello there, Nina," he croaked. He was virtually toothless. "I know your dad for a long time. He used to take care of me."

Nina smiled. "It's nice to meet you."

The doors to the reception area opened again, and a man wearing a bow tie and a blazer entered the lobby. He was peering at a chart through half-glasses.

"Hey, Doc Farber."

The man looked up over the top of his glasses. "Hello, Harry, how're you doing?"

"You remember Doc Avery here?" The old man pointed with a trembling hand at Duncan.

Dr. Farber's smile disappeared and his eyes widened in surprise as his gaze took in the unexpected visitor.

"Hi, Bill," Duncan said.

"Duncan. I heard they let you out," he said gravely.

"The doc here was just givin' me a little free advice." said Harry gleefully.

"This man is not a doctor any longer," said Dr. Farber. "He

disgraced himself and his profession. He has no business giving you or anybody else medical advice. You should be getting back to your room, Harry."

Harry protested, but Dr. Farber buttonholed a passing aide and pointed to Harry. "Help this man back to his room."

"I don't need any help," Harry grumbled as he accepted the orderly's arm.

Without another word to Duncan, Dr. Farber turned and walked back into the ward. Nina used all the acting skills she possessed to keep the embarrassment and chagrin from showing on her face as she looked at her father. His face wore a blank expression. Probably, she thought, a skill he had perfected over years of withstanding the insults of prison life. But blotches of color had risen to his cheeks, betraying him, like the telltale welts from a lash.

4

THEY trudged through the rustling mass of leaves that blanketed Aunt Mary's front yard. "Maybe we can rake these up for her," Nina said. "I told Aunt Mary we'd do a few things around the house." Duncan nodded, but did not reply. He bent down and gathered up a couple of newspapers, still in their plastic sleeves, which had landed near the steps and were camouflaged by leaves. Nina stuck the key in the front door of the rambling, shingle-style house that she had called home during high school and pushed the door open with some difficulty because of the pile of mail that had fallen through the slot and accumulated on the floor. "Come on in," she said to her father.

The house smelled stale and the drapes were shut, so the atmosphere was gloomy. The living room was dominated by a black upright piano, its surface dull and scarred. Aunt Mary had loved to play when Nina lived here. Nina ran her hand across the dusty keys and could see what her aunt meant about the instrument being out of tune. As Duncan entered the house and set his bag down, Nina went around to the windows, pulling back curtains and opening the blinds. Patches of faded butterscotch light began to appear on the worn wall-to-wall carpet.

"There," she said, "that's better. We'll get this place aired out."

"Where do you want these?" asked Duncan, indicating the newspapers he had collected.

"There's a recycling can beside the back door. Put them in there."

Duncan went into the kitchen and looked around.

"Just outside. Open the back door," said Nina.

Duncan did as she asked, and then returned to the living room.

"You can have my old room," said Nina. "It's the one on the right at the top of the stairs. I'll take Aunt Mary's room down here." Although her old room was smaller than her aunt's bedroom and was decorated in girlish pink gingham, it was a little more cheerful than Aunt Mary's room, which had not seen a change of décor or a coat of paint in many years. Besides, she didn't know how her aunt would feel about Duncan staying there.

"Okay," said Duncan indifferently. He looked around the shabby but comfortable living room. The striped wallpaper was faded, and peeling in spots. But the bright watercolor landscapes that hung in a grouping over the sofa still looked fresh and lovely. Noticing Duncan looking at his late wife's paintings, Nina felt a little anxious, but her father's face betrayed no emotion.

Several times Aunt Mary had urged Nina to take some of her mother's paintings with her and hang them in her apartment, but Nina's residences were always temporary. She planned someday to have an actual home, she had told her aunt. A suitable place to hang them.

Duncan walked over to a display of framed photos on Aunt Mary's piano and examined them.

Nina joined him. "Do you remember all these people?" she asked.

Duncan nodded slowly. "Oh sure. Your mother's family. I knew most of them. Your grandparents. There's your uncle John. And of course, these . . ." Aunt Mary had all the Avery children's pictures framed and on display. Duncan picked up Nina's high school graduation photo, which was larger and more prominent than those of her brothers. Nina hadn't really looked at that photo in a long time. She was struck by the look of sadness in her own eyes.

"I had the one you brought me in my cell," he said. "I looked at it every day." He set the photo back down carefully and then picked up another, smaller graduation picture displayed beside it. It was a black-and-white photo and the girl pictured in the photo had raven hair like Nina's, but there was no sorrow in her eyes and she had a bright, vivacious smile.

"She probably looked like that when you met her," Nina said gently.

Duncan stared at it for a moment and then replaced the photo of his late wife on the surface of the piano. "Shall we go and see Jimmy?" he said.

Nina was a little taken aback by the abrupt change of subject. "Uh . . . I don't know. I have to call him."

"Does he know we're arriving today?" Duncan asked.

"No. It was so sudden. I didn't have a chance to call him. I'll call him now."

"I'll take my bag up," said Duncan, heading for the stairs.

"Okay," said Nina, feeling vaguely troubled. She glanced back at the photo of her mother, a high school girl smiling with such innocence and hopefulness, completely unaware of the violent, bloody way her life would end. People always wished they knew the future, she thought. It was better not to know. How many people would really want to go on if they knew what the end would be? With a sigh, she went into the kitchen and sat down next to where the phone was hanging on the wall. She dialed her brother's number and waited while it rang.

JIMMY was having his AA meeting at the Presbyterian Church Fellowship Hall. He had told Nina to meet him there. Nina indicated a slatted park bench in front of the church, and she and Duncan sat down. There was a gaslight beside the bench that was beginning to illuminate as the light of day faded. "This way we can see him come out when the meeting's over," she said.

Nina shivered and jammed her hands into the pocket of her fleece-lined jacket. She glanced at her father, who was only wearing a gray windbreaker. He did not seem to notice the falling temperatures as afternoon turned to evening.

"Aren't you cold?" she said.

Duncan started as if she had awakened him. "What? No. No, not really. I mean I'm used to it. It was always cold in . . . . there. They always claimed there was nothing they could do about the lack of heat. Except in summer, of course, when we'd swelter. You'd get so you barely noticed it."

"I guess so," she said.

"So, Jimmy's sticking with the sobriety," Duncan said.

Nina nodded. "It's been almost . . . ten years now."

"And he's got a job," said Duncan.

"Yeah. He works at Hoffman Flooring. He's been there for a while."

"He turned his life around," said Duncan. "It's hard to believe."

"I know," said Nina. "Considering the way he was."

"What happened to that Mears kid he hung around with?" Duncan asked.

"I don't know." Nina said. "I asked Jimmy and he said that Mears had to leave town. Something about a kid dying of a drug overdose. Mears was involved somehow."

"Was he charged?"

"I really don't know, Dad. I don't think so. I don't think there was any real proof."

Duncan shook his head. "There was something evil about that kid."

"Yeah," Nina agreed. "Things started to turn around for Jimmy once he got away from him and got into rehab."

"I'm so glad," said Duncan.

Nina saw the door of the Fellowship Hall open. "I think it's over."

They got up from the bench and crossed the street as people began to stream out, passing them as they approached the building. They exuded the smell of cigarette smoke and coffee in the crisp autumn evening.

Nina edged past several people and walked into the Fellowship Hall. A broad-shouldered man with a wide neck was emptying ashtrays and collecting used Styrofoam coffee cups.

"Jimmy," she said. "Come on. Dad's waiting."

Jimmy looked up at her sheepishly. His once unruly black hair was now cut close to the scalp in military fashion. His muscles bulged beneath a faded short-sleeved golf shirt. "Just cleaning up," he said.

"Couldn't somebody else clean up tonight?" she demanded.

"Just give me a minute," Jimmy said, and Nina had the overwhelming impression that he was stalling for some reason.

"Hey. Is this a private party?" said a voice from the doorway.

Nina turned around and saw her father leaning into the room.

Jimmy piled the empty ashtrays on the table and wiped his hands on a dish towel. "Hi, Dad," he said faintly.

Duncan came into the room and walked up to Jimmy, lifting his arms as if to clasp him in an embrace. Jimmy stuck out his hand and Duncan took it, reluctantly. Jimmy shook hands and nodded, meeting Duncan's gaze only briefly.

"How are you, son?" Duncan asked.

"I'm doing okay. How about you?"

Nina could see her father's eyes glistening. "Okay," he said.

Jimmy sighed and then pursed his lips and blew out a breath. "So. Nina says you came back here to look for a place."

"Yeah, I wanted to be near you and your brother. I've missed you kids so much. I want to try and make up for some lost time."

"Yeah," said Jimmy with forced enthusiasm. "Maybe we could do that."

"How about we start with dinner tonight? I can afford to take you out somewhere fancy like the Bun and Burger. As long as you don't order dessert," Duncan said, smiling.

Jimmy grimaced. "Actually, Rose told me to . . . invite you to the house."

Duncan nodded, pressing his lips together. "Isn't that nice? What do you say, Nina?"

"Sure," she said, although she would have much preferred for the three of them to be alone. She could tell by the look in his eyes that Duncan was weary and felt the same way. But he was not about to decline the invitation.

"All right, then," said Duncan. "Lead the way."

GEORGE and Rose Connelly's house was a modest bungalow with a small, neatly tended yard and a bright standing lantern that threw out a welcoming arc of light. A foot-high statue of the Virgin Mary, set inside a pale blue starry niche, stood in the front garden near the steps. A bouquet of red artificial roses in the vase near her feet were a jarring note in the otherwise browning shrubbery of autumn.

Nina parked behind Jimmy's Saturn and she and Duncan followed him up the front steps. He opened the door and called out, "Hello. I'm home." The front of the house had a dark glassed-in porch with canvas-covered porch furniture. But it was bright inside the house, and an appealing smell wafted out to the darkened porch.

"Come on in," said Jimmy, leading the way through the open front door. "You can have a seat." He gestured toward the matching taupe sofa and love seat perpendicular to one another against the living room walls. Above the sofas were a bevy of framed family photos, many of them including Jimmy, and an assortment of acrylic landscapes in tubular aluminum frames. There was also a framed picture of a haloed Jesus.

Despite Jimmy's suggestion, Nina and Duncan remained standing. Rose Connelly came out of the kitchen wiping her hands on a dish towel. She was a short, stout woman with a blond perm. She was wearing a Western-style denim shirt with pearl snaps up the front and pink flowers embroidered across the yoke.

Jimmy reached out and put a protective arm around her shoulders.

"Hi, sweetie," she said.

"Mom, you remember my father, and Nina."

Rose smiled at Nina. "Hello, dear." Then she nodded at Duncan. "Dr. Avery," she said.

"Hello, Rose. You're looking well," said Duncan.

"Something smells great," said Nina, trying to ignore the strained smile on Rose's face and her own unease at hearing Jimmy call this woman "Mom."

"I made a stew for dinner. I hope that's okay. Go get

George, honey," she said to Jimmy. "He's out in his workshop. Sit down, sit down."

"This is so nice of you," said Nina, slipping off her coat and holding out her hand for Duncan's jacket. "Where can I put these?"

"Just lay them on the glider on the sunporch. Dr. Avery, can I get you a drink? We have beer, or wine coolers."

"Uh, no," said Duncan. "I'm not allowed to have alcohol. Conditions of parole. And call me Duncan. Please."

Rose nodded, but Nina saw something stiff and disapproving in Rose's expression. Rose had always been warm and friendly to Nina when she visited in the past. There was a distinctly different atmosphere to this visit. Nina deposited the coats on the porch and came back into the living room, seating herself beside Duncan on the love seat. Rose sat in a wooden Windsor-style armchair across the room, beside the gas fireplace.

"So, Jimmy tells me that you two are staying at your aunt's house?" Rose asked politely.

"Just temporarily," said Nina. "We need to find a more permanent place for Dad. Do you know of anybody who has an apartment?"

"Around here? No, oh no," said Rose quickly, frowning as if Nina had suggested the impossible. "There's nothing."

Nothing, Nina thought? Rose Connelly had lived here for years. Surely she would know someone with an apartment to rent. If she wanted to help. Nina reminded herself not to take offense. Rose and her husband, George, had done her family a great favor.

"How is Anthony doing?" Duncan asked.

The harsh expression on Rose's face softened. "He's doing fine. Healthy as a horse. Knock on wood," she said, tapping on the arm of her chair. "Graduates from college this year. He's going to go to medical school," Rose said proudly.

"That's wonderful," said Duncan. "If there's any way I can help, any advice about managing the work . . ."

Rose's smile disappeared. "That won't be necessary," she said coolly. "Oh, they're here," she said, relief in her voice as she looked through the archway into the dining room.

George Connelly came in, trailed by Jimmy. Their former postman was graying, but still trim, and wore the same jovial expression that Nina remembered from childhood when he would greet her by name at the front door as she ran to get the mail.

Duncan stood up as George entered the room and extended his hand. "George."

George brushed Duncan's hand away and gave him a quick embrace, clapping him heartily on the back. "Good to see you, Doc," he said.

Duncan looked at Jimmy, who fidgeted uncomfortably under his gaze, and then back at George. "I'm glad I can thank you in person for all you've done for my boy."

George shook his head. "It's been our pleasure, Doc. We love this boy like our own son." He gazed at Jimmy, who smiled shyly at the ground.

Duncan nodded. "Of course, he's imposed on your hospitality for rather a long time. I never meant for him to become a permanent fixture under your roof."

"I don't really think of that as a problem," Rose said sharply.

"Jimmy will always have a home here," George said in a soothing tone. "Rose, that dinner smells so good. Can we eat?"

ROSE served the meal in dutiful silence while Duncan and George talked about fishing. George had a skiff he kept on a trailer down by the river. Duncan always claimed that he never had time to fish, but even when George was their mailman, he and Duncan would have long conversations about what was biting and the relative merits of different kinds of bait.

"We might still get a day or two in before the boat's got to come out of the water for the winter," said George. "The three of us can go. You, me, and Jimmy."

Nina glanced at her brother. He had been silent through much of the meal, and his face was contorted with anxiety. He was clearly suffering, as she was, from the tension that would descend on the table whenever the conversation flagged.

Almost as soon as they set down their forks, Nina suggested that they should be getting home. They got up from the table and thanked Rose for her dinner. She remained seated, insisting politely that it was no trouble. George got up to bid them farewell and Jimmy accompanied them to the door. The three of them stood in awkward silence on the darkened sunporch.

"Well, we'd better be going." Duncan reached out and put his arm awkwardly around Jimmy's shoulders. His voice was husky when he spoke. "I just want you to know that I'm proud of you, Jim. I know addiction is a hard battle. I'm proud of the way you took your life in hand."

"Working in a flooring place," Jimmy demurred. "It's not like being a doctor."

"Hey, it's honest work," said Duncan. "I think it's great. I think you're great."

Jimmy shook off Duncan's embrace. "Stop it, Dad. Just stop it."

"Jimmy," said Nina in a warning tone.

Even in the dim light of the porch, Nina could see Jimmy's eyes glistening, and there was a pained expression on his face. "I can't handle this."

"Handle what?" Duncan asked, perplexed. "All I said was that I was proud of you."

"You don't even know me," Jimmy cried. Without a word of farewell, he turned and rushed back inside the house.

5

DUNCAN sat silently beside her in the car. Nina glanced at his stony profile and fumed at the memory of her brother's behavior. "I'm so sorry about that scene with Jimmy," she said, breaking the silence. "He's kind of a high-strung guy. I'm sure he didn't mean to be so . . ."

"Stop apologizing, Nina. You don't owe me any apologies."

"This is why I didn't want you coming back to Hoffman. I mean, everywhere you turn you're running into this kind of thing. People can be so cruel."

Duncan snorted. "You have no idea, Nina. You could never imagine, in your wildest dreams, how brutal and inhuman people can be to one another," he said in an expressionless voice.

Nina knew he was talking about his life in prison. "How did you stand it?" she asked cautiously. "Especially knowing you were innocent. It must have been horrible. I can't even imagine how horrible," said Nina. "And after all you went through . . .

Jimmy acts like he's the one who's suffered. Honestly, it makes me want to scream."

Duncan was silent for a moment. Then he said, "Your brother really seems to have made a home with the Connellys."

"Yeah, maybe too much," said Nina. "Patrick's afraid he's going to live there forever."

"He calls her Mom," said Duncan.

"I noticed," said Nina. She drove along in silence for a moment. Then she said, "Why *did* Jimmy go to live with the Connellys, Dad? I mean, we hardly knew them. Mr. Connelly was our mailman. I never really understood how he ended up there."

Duncan did not answer right away. For a moment Nina wondered if her question had registered. She glanced over at his brooding profile. "Dad?"

Duncan shook his head. "The Connellys wanted to help because of Anthony. They were grateful and they wanted to help. And I thought . . . I could see what strong people they were. Good people. I knew it would take a lot of strength to get him away from . . . the drugs. I thought I could trust them to do . . . what was best for Jimmy."

"Well, in all fairness, I'd say you were right about that," she admitted.

"Your mother always blamed Jimmy's problems on me, you know. She said I was a terrible father."

"That wasn't true," said Nina loyally.

"I don't know," Duncan said wearily. "Maybe it was."

NINA had left the lights on, so the house glowed cheerfully as she pulled her aunt's old Volvo into the driveway. She got out of the car and inhaled deeply of the autumn night. "It does smell good here, doesn't it?" she said to her father, who had emerged from the passenger side.

"You can't imagine," he said.

"Let's go in. I'm tired. I don't know about you."

Duncan frowned. "I think I'm going to take a little stroll."

For some reason, the idea of him out walking alone in the dark filled her with anxiety. "It's kind of late," she said. "It's dark."

"I'm not afraid of the dark," he said.

"I know, but . . ."

"Nina," Duncan snapped. "Don't be my jailer. Please. I don't need any more of that."

Nina shook her head. "I'm sorry, Dad. You're right. I don't know what's the matter with me."

He shoved his hands in the pockets of his windbreaker and started off down the driveway, the leaves crunching and rustling around his feet. Nina turned and went into the house after he had disappeared from view.

The house felt damp and chilly, so she turned up the thermostat, and she switched on the TV so the noise would keep her company. Everywhere she looked there were little jobs to do. Obviously, Aunt Mary had been letting the housekeeping slide because of her age and her bad hip. Nina dusted off the piano keys and closed the instrument's lid, straightened up a pile of magazines, and took a bunch of old newspapers into the back room for recycling. She looked in the empty refrigerator and sighed, knowing she needed to go to the store the next day. But first things first. She had to check her messages, to see if her agent had any news for her. She fished her cell phone out of her satchel on the kitchen table and punched in the numbers to reach her voice mail.

"Yeah, Nina," said the gravelly voice of Len Weinberg, who had been her agent since the start of her career. "You got

Monday and Tuesday free like you wanted. But you've got three auditions after that. Wednesday morning you have an audition for Seasons Cosmetics and you have to be in the chair by six a.m."

Six a.m., Nina thought. She'd have to take the bus into the city Tuesday or she'd never make it on time. As she listened to the rest of Len's message, she wandered back into the living room and flopped down on the couch, gazing absently at the talking heads on the news. All of a sudden, she saw her father's face pictured on the screen. It was a recent photo, taken during a jailhouse interview after he won his parole. She put down her phone, grabbed the remote, and turned up the volume.

"Authorities here in Hoffman have learned that the convict-ed wife killer, who was once a respected physician, has moved back into their community. The news has some people worried. We talked to the chief of police, who had this to say."

An image of a stocky red-haired man filled the screen. His tie was tight against a stark white collar. Under his solemn face, the footage was captioned "Chief Eugene Perry, Hoffman Police." Nina did not recognize the new chief from the time of her mother's murder. "I'm aware of Dr. Avery's history," Chief Perry said. "It's nothing for people to be concerned about. He does not pose a threat to the community."

The reporter was returned to the screen. "The chief is con-fident that they have the situation in hand," he said, "but there are others here in Hoffman who are not so sure."

The reporter's face was then replaced by tape of some middle-aged woman shopping on Lafayette Street saying, "You're darn right I'm worried about it. I mean, a man that vio-lent living here in our community. I didn't know the man, but I remember when it happened . . ."

Oh my God, Nina thought. Who told them? We've been here one day. Already they've got him plastered all over the news. How can he get any peace? I knew he shouldn't come back here.

The camera switched back to the reporter, who was saying, "This is Ed Fitler, reporting from Hoffman, New Jersey, where an anxious town is trying to adjust to the homecoming of a convicted killer."

Fuming, Nina snapped off the TV and stalked over to the window. There had to be a law against that. How could they put that stuff on TV for everybody to see? She peered up and down the street, as far as the trees allowed her to see, but there was no sign of her father.

She could picture him walking along out there, kicking through the leaves, his hands in his pockets, taking a little pleasure from his freedom. What if somebody saw him out there and recognized him? And decided they didn't want him on their street? People could be so irrational and vicious. They might come chasing after him. They could hurt him. Kids were known for things like that. Adults, too. She couldn't just leave him alone out there. She grabbed up the keys and her jacket and ran out to the car.

Nina slowly trolled the quiet, lamplit streets of Hoffman. She drove up and down the streets looking for a thin man in a windbreaker. Where could he have gone? she wondered, as she peered up driveways and along sidewalks. Once the twilight joggers and dog walkers were finished, nobody walked around this town. Anyone who saw him might take him for a burglar. Anyone who recognized him might take him for something worse than that.

Nina drove along the northern perimeter of the Madison Creek Nature Preserve, and then slowly turned down their old street. Before she even got around the corner she had a feeling she was going to find him. It made kind of a perverse sense that he would go there. And sure enough, as she rounded the corner, she saw, under the light of a streetlamp, his lonely figure, standing on the sidewalk staring up at the house. The house where she grew up. The house where her mother was murdered.

Nina rolled up to the curb and lowered her window. Duncan turned around with a start and then recognized her.

"Nina. What's the matter?" he said irritably, bending down and looking into the open window.

"Dad, I thought I better come pick you up."

"Why?" he demanded.

She didn't want to tell him about the newscast. It would probably be in the local paper on Aunt Mary's doorstep the next day. That would be soon enough. But he was looking at her impatiently. "Why?" he repeated.

"I was just . . . worried. You'd been gone so long. What are you doing all the way over here?"

"Nina, leave me alone. I know you mean well, but you are hovering over me and I can't stand it. You have to stop it. I'm not some child. I'm your father. I'll come back when I'm ready."

Nina looked past him at the house where they had once lived. Through the branches of the trees she could see lights glowing in every window. It had taken a long time for someone to buy the house. Everyone knew what had happened there, and once prospective buyers found out, they never returned. The people who finally bought it got it at a bargain basement price. But there it stood, looking warm and homey, as if no family had ever been torn apart and scattered to the winds because of what happened in that house. She felt tears rise to her eyes again, but she blinked them back.

"Fine," she said coldly. "Do what you want." She turned away from him and began to roll up the window. She half hoped that he would knock on the window, try to stop her, apologize for his curtness with her. But Duncan did none of those things. He stepped back onto the sidewalk and watched as she pulled away.

I'm only trying to help you, she thought. It's not as if I like being here. Everything here reminds me of all that. Of everything that happened. If you don't want me to help you, fine. You can handle everything by yourself, fine.

Dark thoughts jangled in her mind as she drove back to Aunt Mary's house and pulled into the driveway. She got out, slamming the car door, and marched up the walk toward the front door. Halfway up the walk, she noticed that there was something on the front door that had not been there when she left. A piece of paper had been attached there, although its corners fluttered in the evening breeze. Her heart suddenly started to pound and she approached slowly, looking around to see if whoever left the paper was still around.

Don't panic, she thought. Maybe it's a take-out menu, or somebody came to fix something and left a message for Aunt Mary. But she knew it wasn't that. Nobody brought around take-out menus at this hour. Nobody came to do repairs. She stepped up to the door and looked at it. The message was written in capital letters in black, and it was easy to read: WIFE KILLER. GO BACK TO JAIL WHERE YOU BELONG.

Nina tore it off the door, her face flaming. She turned and looked around her, wondering if whoever had posted it there was still watching the house, waiting to see what their reaction would be. Somebody knew that her father was in this house. Somebody cruel and vindictive. The street was quiet and peaceful, the image of slumbering suburbia on a mild autumn evening, she thought bitterly. The kind of place where no one would think dark thoughts, or plot against his neighbor.

6

NINA went to bed before her father returned, but she couldn't fall asleep.

She switched on the bedside lamp and lay in her aunt's sagging double bed, looking around at the dingy corners of the bedroom, wondering how long it had been since the curtains had been taken down and washed, or the room had been painted. I can fix this room up for her, Nina thought. I'll clean it and paint it so that when she comes home it will be fresh for her. Nina occupied herself with these plans until she heard the front door open and then close again. Quickly she switched off the lamp so that Duncan would not think she was waiting for him.

When Duncan came down for breakfast the next day he looked exhausted. After a night's sleep, Nina felt better and was back in his corner. She had hidden the posted message in her room so that he would not see it. Whoever the sick bastard was who had hung it on the door, Duncan did not need to know about it.

"What do we need to do today?" he said, as he slowly ate a bowl of cold cereal.

"Well, I've decided to give Aunt Mary's room a freshening up. It will be a nice surprise for her when she comes home. So, I need to go to Lowe's and buy some paint. Maybe you could help me move the furniture away from the walls and take down the curtains."

"Sure," he said absently. "You want your old room? I can sleep on the couch in the living room. That's fine for me."

"No, no. I can sleep in the sewing room. There's a sofabed in there. But we do need to start thinking about finding you an apartment. What else do you need to do?" she asked.

Duncan grimaced as he chewed. "God, I need to go to a dentist. My teeth are a mess."

"Today?" she said.

"No, today I need to go to Motor Vehicles. Get a temporary license and apply for my new license."

"Are you allowed to do that?" she asked.

"Oh yeah," he said. "I can't vote. I can't drink. But I can drive," he said.

"All right. We'll do that."

"I was hoping," he said.

"What?"

"Maybe I could see my grandchildren."

Nina tried to hide her surprise. After that humiliating boycott of dinner at her apartment, she wondered why he would want to set himself up for rejection again so soon. Duncan seemed to notice her reluctance.

"What's the matter? You know I want to see them. That's one of the reasons I came back here."

Nina grimaced. "I know but . . . Gemma's probably working. I don't want to disturb her," she said.

"Oh, I don't expect an invitation. I meant . . . you know, get a look at the kids. I haven't even seen Patrick's house. Could we drive by it? Maybe the kids will be playing outside. I just want to see them."

"I . . . guess we could," said Nina, embarrassed by the pleading note in his voice. "And we should go downtown and get you something else to wear. Something that fits."

"You're the boss," he said, and she knew that was his way of trying to say he was sorry for snapping at her the night before. She wasn't going to tell him that she could never hold it against him. Not after all he had suffered. He was entitled to his anger, she thought. Even if he took it out on her.

THEY completed their business for the day and drove out to Old Hoffman, the part of town studded with fields and horse barns, where its wealthiest citizens resided. On their way they passed the entrance to the country club.

"Is Patrick a member?" Duncan asked.

Nina was caught off guard by his question. When Patrick moved to this neighborhood he learned that he was permanently blackballed from the club because of his father's crime. And Patrick had been furious—not at the country club members for their narrow-mindedness, but at Duncan, for causing him further deprivation.

"Nina?"

"Uh . . . no."

"No? Does he still play golf?" asked Duncan.

"Yes . . . but . . . I think . . . Gemma was uncomfortable there. She's not really the country club type," Nina said quickly. That certainly wasn't a lie, Nina thought.

As they rounded the curve to Patrick's house they passed the driveway leading to the house where Lindsay Farrell's parents lived. It was a little odd, she thought, that Patrick had bought the next property over from theirs. Had Lindsay moved back in with her family when she returned to town? Was she now living right next door to Patrick?

"This is it," said Nina. "The next one on the left. It's hard to see it through the trees." Patrick's house was covered in fieldstone and blended into the gray bark of the surrounding trees in the November landscape. In front of the house was a large pond with mallards gliding on its silvery surface.

Duncan peered out the window. "Wow," he said. "How much money does your brother make, anyway?"

"A lot. He mints the stuff," said Nina, as she pulled to the side of the road and let the car idle. "It's beautiful inside, too. Patrick picked out everything."

"What about his wife?" Duncan asked. "Isn't that usually the wife's job . . . ?"

"Oh, come on, Dad," Nina teased him. "Times have changed. It's whoever wants to do it these days. Anyway, Patrick's very particular. He has very . . . exacting taste. He likes everything to . . . look . . . a certain way."

"Are they a good couple? Are they happy together?" Duncan asked.

"Patrick and Gemma . . . ?" Nina thought about her brother and his wife. When Marsha was killed and Lindsay dumped him, Patrick's self-confidence faltered. He leaned on his tutor and their relationship seemed to become much closer. Despite her coolness and reserve, Gemma had proved loyal. She had stuck by him through the trial, through college, when everyone else abandoned him. Nina used to think their marriage was kind of romantic. She imagined that Patrick had been won over by Gemma's loyalty and realized finally that Gemma's indifference to fashion concealed her natural attractiveness. But Nina's illusions had faded. Once Patrick had been proud of Gemma's exceptional intelligence. Now he always seemed to find fault with her. And Nina knew they argued a lot. On her rare overnight visits she had heard them, and realized that they sounded distressingly like her parents used to sound. But all couples argued, she told herself, trying to think positively. "I guess they manage," she said.

"There they are!" Duncan cried.

Nina looked where he was pointing and saw a pair of chubby little boys chasing one another across the immaculate yard.

Before she could tell him to stop, Duncan had jumped out of the car and rushed toward the ornate wrought-iron fence that surrounded the property. He leaned against it and peered through the trees at the twins.

Nina got out of the car. "Dad, you shouldn't let them see you."

"Which one is which?" he asked. "Can you tell them apart?"

Nina squinted at the two boys and then nodded. "The one in the dark green sweatshirt is Cody. He's a little bit smaller than Simon."

Duncan shook his head. "My grandsons," he breathed, as if he could hardly believe they were real.

Shadows were beginning to fall across the yard and Nina looked at her watch. It was late in the day, and she didn't want to be there when Patrick returned.

"We better not hang around here, Dad," she said. Duncan looked wistful leaning against the fence, drinking in the sight of the twins at play.

The boys ran shrieking after one another in the direction of the house and then Simon put on a burst of speed and caught up with Cody, grabbing the hood of his sweatshirt and pulling him down to the ground. They began snarling and tumbling over one another like pudgy bear cubs, shouting insults. Simon sat down on Cody's stomach and they had a brief, inadudible conference. Then Simon freed his twin and they raced in the direction of the pond.

"They're awfully close to the water," said Duncan. "Are they allowed to be out there alone like that?"

"They're okay. Dad," said Nina. "Come on. You've seen them. We better go. Patrick will not be happy if he finds you here."

But Duncan was not listening. "Nina, look. They're right at the edge of that pond."

Nina looked up and down the road, watching anxiously for Patrick's silver-blue Jaguar to come racing around the curve.

"How do you get in here?" Duncan said. He began to search the fence for an opening. He found a latch and lifted it.

"Dad, don't go in there. If Patrick comes home and finds you here he's going to be angry. I know him."

A splash and a horrible cry went up from the yard. The ducks squawked and rose from the surface of the pond with a flapping of wings. Duncan was already through the gate and running down the lawn. Nina looked toward the pond and saw Cody in the water, shrieking and gasping. His face was bright red and he was sobbing. Nina hurried down the lawn after her father. Duncan reached the water's edge and put a hand out to the boy. "Take my hand," he demanded.

"Hey," Simon protested. "Who are you?"

The back door of the house opened and Gemma burst out, looking alarmed. She was followed by a short, heavyset woman with brown skin and a sullen expression on her round face. Gemma ran toward her sons and reached them just as a muddy Cody, still wailing, spurned Duncan's offer of a hand and stood up in the knee-high water where he had landed. The other woman reached the edge of the pond and stood with her hands on her ample hips, shaking her head and muttering in Spanish.

"Cody," Gemma cried. "Are you all right? What is going on?"

"He pushed me," Cody shrieked, pointing at Simon.

"I did not," Simon protested. "He fell in. This guy scared him and he fell in." Simon pointed at Duncan, who stood, pale and trembling, in his gray windbreaker.

Gemma turned and started as she recognized her father-in-law. "Dr. Avery."

"Hello, dear," Duncan said.

"Call the cops on him," Simon insisted.

The older Spanish-speaking woman sighed and extended a hand to Cody. Grasping her brown hand, Cody clambered out of the pond. The woman began to chatter disapprovingly at him in Spanish.

Gemma turned on the woman. "Elena, you were supposed to be watching them. I told you I was going to be working. What were you thinking?"

The older woman frowned at Gemma and shook her head sharply. Clearly angry, Gemma launched into rapid-fire Spanish. She spoke like a native after spending her early years in South America. She questioned the older woman, who glared at her and replied in a wounded tone. Gemma shook her head and pointed toward the house. "Go in the house with Elena, both of you. Cody, change out of those clothes and don't leave them on the floor of your room."

They walked a few steps and then Cody pushed Simon out of the way and took off running. Simon yelped and started after him. Elena, with a withering glance at Gemma, lumbered up the lawn after them.

Gemma shook her head. "This is why I'm having so much trouble getting the book together," she said. "Elena was supposed to be watching them." Gemma watched her sons as they disappeared into the house. The back door of the house slammed and Gemma turned to Nina and Duncan, looking ill at ease. "I didn't know you were coming for a visit."

"It's not exactly a visit. My father wanted to see the twins," said Nina.

"Why didn't you just come to the door?"

Patrick, Nina wanted to say, but she didn't. "Dad just wanted to have a look at them. They're cute, aren't they, Dad? He's been looking forward to this."

An awkward silence descended. "Well," said Gemma. "Shall we all go inside?"

Nina didn't want to put Gemma in an impossible position. Obviously, she had her hands full between the twins and her work. Plus Patrick could be home at any minute. "No. We need to go."

Gemma smiled tensely, twisting her rings. "All right. If you have to."

Nina turned to her father.

Duncan stood with his hands in his pockets, gazing at the surface of the pond.

"Dad?" she said.

Duncan frowned. "It's dangerous to let those boys play by themselves so close to the water," he said.

Gemma's smile faded. "I didn't let them," she protested. "The housekeeper was supposed to be watching them while I was working. That's her job."

"Besides, the water is knee-high on them," Nina said, exasperated.

"That's all it takes," Duncan persisted, peering intently at Gemma. "Just a minute's carelessness and your life is ruined."

"Oh, for heaven's sakes," Nina said, scowling. She turned very deliberately to her sister-in-law. "Gemma, I'm sorry we bothered you. We're going to go now."

"It's all right," said Gemma.

"No, it's not," said Nina. Without another word to her father, Nina began stalking up the lawn toward the gate.

"Hey," Duncan said, following behind and catching up to her at the car. He jerked the car door open. He was the one scowling now. "There's no need to be rude to me, young lady."

Nina turned on him. "Rude to you? You're the one who was rude. To Gemma."

"Hey, let me tell you something, Nina. You don't know everything. I understood that conversation. She told us that the housekeeper was supposed to be watching them, but the house-keeper said it was her afternoon off."

"They were speaking Spanish," Nina said impatiently. "Since when do you speak Spanish?"

"For your information, Nina, the doctor at the prison was Spanish-speaking. He taught me," said Duncan. "Dr. Quinteros. He was at the parole hearing."

For a fleeting moment, Nina recalled the handsome doctor catching her eye, offering her reassurance. It seemed like a life-time ago. She turned on her father. "Spanish or no Spanish, it was a misunderstanding. Why are you believing the house-keeper over Gemma? It seemed to me that woman had a bad attitude."

"Maybe she had a right to have that attitude. Listen, Nina, those are my grandsons. I don't want anything . . ."

"Yes, those are your grandsons," Nina cried. "And in case you haven't noticed, their mother is one of the few people who's been nice to you. You haven't got all that many people being decent to you. You might try not alienating the few peo-ple who are."

"Don't tell me how to act," Duncan said, pointing a finger at her.

Nina felt far beyond the point where she would accept a scolding from her father. Not after all that had happened. "Fine,

Dad. You stop embarrassing me and I'll stop telling you how to act," she blurted out.

Duncan looked at her ruefully. "You know, if I'm becoming a burden to you, Nina, you can go on back to your own life and not worry about me. I can manage."

"Just get in the car and don't be ridiculous. You can manage," she scoffed. "You've done a great job of managing so far."

The minute she said it, Nina wished she hadn't. It had sounded terrible and she hadn't meant it. She was just tired, and worried about him. But she could tell by the injured look in Duncan's eyes that now he felt betrayed by her, too. He opened the car door and climbed in without a word. She hadn't meant to hurt him or insult him. She wanted to tell him that, but somehow she knew he wouldn't want to hear it. It was already said, and it was too late to take it back.

7

THEY spent an uncomfortable evening speaking to one another only when necessary. But the next morning, when Nina began taking her aunt's room apart, Duncan appeared in the doorway and started pushing furniture away from the wall. As she bundled up the curtains and started to carry them out to the washer, Duncan said, "Where's the paint?"

She pointed it out to him, and left him opening the can on the newspaper and stirring it with a wooden stick. When she returned, he had already begun cutting in the color around the windows. "Thanks, Dad," she said.

"No problem," he said. They worked side by side making desultory conversation until Duncan asked if he could turn on the radio, and the music, along with the sun outside, breaking through the gray clouds, made the day seem brighter.

Before she knew it, Nina was looking at her watch and realizing it was time to clean up and get ready to leave. All day, she had kept an ear cocked for the phone, waiting to hear from some of the realtors they had met, hoping someone would have a lead on an apartment for Duncan. But no one called while they were painting. As one realtor had explained to them the day before, it was a problem of limited supply and great demand. Hoffman was so close to New York City that every available space seemed to be rented, or available only for a huge price. Nina could tell that the search would have to be continued when she returned from New York.

She needed to catch the bus back to the city, and that afternoon Duncan was scheduled to begin his first shift at the clinic in Newark. Armed with his temporary license, Duncan planned to drive to work. For her part, Nina had to be back in her apartment to pick out her clothes and get to sleep early so she would look her best for her auditions, which began early the next morning.

"Are you sure you don't need some more money?" she asked her father an hour later as he drove her to the bus stop on his way to Newark. It was strange to see him behind the wheel again, to be a passenger beside him.

"I've got enough money. God, there's so much more traffic than there used to be," he said. He had been driving carefully, almost too slowly.

"You have to keep moving, Dad," said Nina.

"I know that, Nina."

"Sorry," she said.

For a few minutes they rode in silence. Then he said, "Good luck with your auditions."

"Thanks. I'll only be gone a few days. If somebody calls about an apartment, make an appointment for us to see it over the weekend. And don't forget, you have to meet with your parole officer Thursday morning at ten. There's food in the refrigerator and if you need anything, you have my cell phone number and my service number. I call the service all the time . . ."

Duncan shook his head. "Nina, stop it. How often do I have to tell you?"

They had pulled into a parking spot on Lafayette Street right near the bus stop. Nina hated it when he used that tone with her. She knew he was annoyed with her. But all she was trying to do was let him know she was in his corner. And now the peace between them that they had reestablished that morning suddenly felt fragile. She glanced in the sideview mirror, trying to see if the large green and silver bus was in view.

"I will miss you, though," he said apologetically.

Instantly, she felt better. Relieved. "I'll miss you, too," she said. She glanced again in the sideview mirror and looked across the street at Lindsay Farrell's store. With a little jolt of surprise she realized that there was a familiar car parked at the meter in front of the store. A silver-blue Jaguar. How many of those could there be in this town? she thought.

Duncan glanced at his watch. "Honey, I'd better be on my way. I don't want to be late on my first day."

Nina was not about to mention her suspicions to her father. "No problem," said Nina. "I'll wait under the shelter. The bus will be along soon."

"I'm sorry to leave you like this," Duncan said.

"It's okay. Don't worry." Nina leaned across the seat and kissed him on the cheek.

He nodded absently and glanced again at the map of Newark. She knew he was anxious about finding his way to the clinic. "Good luck with the job," she said, as she got out of the car and took her bag from the backseat. "And, Dad, I'm sorry about what I said to you yesterday out at Patrick's. I didn't mean it."

He smiled sadly at her and squeezed her hand. "Nina,

you've been a lifesaver to me. No man could have a better daughter."

She squeezed his hand back, not trusting herself to speak. She slammed the car door shut and waved at him. "See you soon. Friday at the latest."

Waving and looking carefully in all directions, he pulled away from the curb and merged with the traffic. Nina sighed, and sat down on the bench to await the bus.

She thought about running through her lines for the table reading she was doing tomorrow afternoon, but she knew she wouldn't be able to concentrate. Instead, she sat watching the people going by on the busy street. And staring at the blue Jag. After about five minutes, the door of Lindsay Farrell's shop opened, and a man and a woman emerged. The woman was slim but voluptuous, wearing a short purple leather skirt and matching spiked heels, with a brilliant red silk kimono top embroidered with brilliant, jewel-colored butterflies. It was Lindsay Farrell. Lindsay's platinum hair was still long, but in a fashionable asymmetric cut. She looked even more dazzling than she had in high school.

Lindsay was resting one long elegant hand on the jacket sleeve of the man she was with—Patrick. Patrick was speaking to her earnestly, inclining his salt-and-pepper head toward her so that their faces almost touched. She was nodding solemnly as Patrick spoke. They brushed cheeks and Patrick walked around the car, getting into the driver's seat of the blue Jag. Lindsay waved as he revved the engine.

Nina quickly bent over and rummaged in her bag. She stayed that way until she could see that the parking space was empty. But when she zipped the bag and straightened up, she caught sight of Lindsay, still standing outside the store, hands on her hips, head at an angle, gazing curiously in her direction.

All of a sudden she heard her own name. "Nina?"

Nina feigned confusion and looked around, as if wondering where the voice might be coming from. She finally looked at Lindsay, but allowed no recognition to show in her face. Lindsay checked out the traffic and then strode across the street in her stiletto heels toward the bus stop. Two male drivers stopped to let her pass and stared. They were each rewarded with a flash of her dimpled smile. Lindsay stepped up on the curve and stood right in front of Nina.

"Nina," she said. "Don't you remember me? Lindsay Farrell."

Nina looked at her blankly, and then pretended a delayed recognition. "Oh, sure," she said slowly. "Lindsay."

"That's right," Lindsay said. "That's my shop across the street. Your brother, Patrick, was just here. Didn't you see him?"

"I didn't notice," Nina lied.

"He loves antiques. He has a really good eye."

A really roving eye, Nina thought disgustedly. "What are you doing here? I thought you left Hoffman," Nina said blandly.

Lindsay shook her head. "I did. I lived in Europe for a long time. But I had to come back. Messy divorce. I had to regroup. Anyway, I opened an antiques store. A girl's got to support herself somehow. You know how that is. I heard you're still single." There was a grating hint of condolence in her voice and in her huge blue eyes.

"Right," said Nina, smiling thinly.

"Patrick told me they let your father out of jail. Is that why you're here?" Lindsay asked.

It's none of your business, Nina thought angrily. Was it possible that Patrick was betraying Gemma with this vapid bimbo? It couldn't be. Patrick had been lucky to get away from her in the first place. He had to know that. Whatever Gemma might lack in terms of warmth or sociability, her loyalty was unquestionable. How could he even think about hurting her like that?

"Nina?"

"Oh yes, my dad. I'm really happy about it," said Nina.

Lindsay tossed her silvery blond hair and it gleamed in the fading autumn sunlight. "Really? Patrick doesn't seem to feel that way."

Nina glanced down the street and, to her immense relief, saw the bus approaching.

She stood up and slung her bag over her shoulder. "He's entitled to his own feelings," she said. "Sorry. I have to run. My bus is here."

"Taking the bus?" Lindsay asked sympathetically.

"I'm a New Yorker," said Nina. "We don't do cars."

If Lindsay made a reply, it was drowned out by the hydraulic whoosh as the bus doors opened and the vehicle sank down to an accessible level against the curb. Nina got on board without a backward glance. By the time she had given the driver her ticket and found a seat, she could no longer see any sign of Lindsay Farrell on the street.

As she was getting ready for bed, performing every beauty ritual she knew, the phone rang. Immediately, Nina thought of Duncan as she grabbed it.

"Nina, I finally got you. It's Hank."

Nina felt instantly uneasy. Hank Talbot. The man Aunt Mary had asked her about. Nina and Hank Talbot had had a brief fling in the summer after he saw her in a play and inundated her with flowers. She remembered telling her aunt about him enthusiastically when they met. And it had seemed promising at first. He was good-looking, successful, and divorced, and for a short time she enjoyed being with him. But gradually she realized that he couldn't sustain interest in any conversation that didn't center on himself. Some men made her feel like an earthbound alien, and Hank Talbot turned out to be one of them. Her aunt was right—she wanted to love someone, to have her own family. But sometimes she thought she would never make that kind of connection with anyone. She couldn't pretend to love a man when she didn't. Even though Hank seemed to scarcely notice it when she began to back out of the affair, she still felt a little guilty. And now, hearing his voice on the phone, she felt pressured as well. "Hi, Hank."

"It's hard to catch up with you these days. Of course, I've been out of town so much. I was in Europe for almost a month."

"Oh really," she said, recalling that, after the first fusillade of flowers, she had come to dislike it when he tried to impress her. "Where in Europe?"

"Paris, actually. They couldn't handle things in the Paris office. They needed me there to straighten them out."

"Paris. My favorite city," she murmured.

"You should have come with me," he said lightly.

Nina stifled a sigh. "I've been . . . real busy." She had never told him about her father when they were dating. She wasn't about to tell him now.

"Well, I'm back in town for a while, and while it's not the Tour d'Argent, I've heard about a new place that's supposed to be pretty good," he said. "You interested?"

Nina grimaced. "I'm really only back for a couple of days myself and then . . . I'll be out of town again."

"Playing the boonies?" he said with an edge to his voice.

Her guilt about dumping him faded. She heard a click on the line. "No. Um. It's a personal thing. Hank, listen, I've got to take this. I'm expecting an urgent call. But thanks for . . . the invitation."

Before he could reply she pressed the flash button, and felt relieved when she heard the familiar voice of Keith on the other end of the phone. She pictured him in his poolside rental in Westwood, wearing preppy clothes and schoolboy glasses, with his East Coast pallor and thinning blond hair. The proverbial fish out of water.

"How did the return to Hoffman go?" he asked.

"A little rocky," Nina admitted. "My father's so vulnerable. Everything is strange to him. And people say such nasty things. It scares me a little."

"I'm really sorry about the co-op board," he said.

"It's all right. He's where he wants to be."

"Why don't you bring him out to L.A.? He can enjoy the weather and the palm trees. We'll take him to some clubs, give him the VIP treatment at the studio."

Nina felt irritated with Keith. She knew that his ability to grasp other people's problems was limited. "Keith, he's on parole. He's not on vacation. He can't go larking off anywhere he pleases."

Keith sounded chastened. "Right," he said. "I wasn't thinking."

Nina felt the injury in his silence and realized she'd overreacted. "Thanks anyway," she said apologetically, "for the thought. I know you're only trying to help. So, tell me, how's the series going?"

"Fine," he said, instantly recovered. "Better than they'd hoped. They want me to stay. The network ordered seven more episodes."

"Stay?" said Nina anxiously. "For how long?"

"Well, as long as . . . need be. The show is being very well received. This could turn into something . . . permanent."

"Permanent?" she said. She knew that she would miss his friendship if he stayed in L.A. But, guiltily, she realized that her first concern was the apartment.

"Don't worry," he said, as if he were reading her mind. "I'm not going to give up the co-op. You can stay there as long as you like."

"I wasn't thinking about that," she lied.

"Yes you were. I would be, too, if I were you. But you know, Nina, you ought to think seriously about coming out here. This is where the work is, and now I'm in a position to help."

"I know," she said. "And I know you would."

"You've got to do it while you're still young. Besides, it would be fun. We could do the town together. I'll introduce you around."

"I've thought about it," said Nina. "Believe me. But . . ."

"But what?"

Nina sighed. "I can't leave right now. Everything is too tentative."

"With your father," Keith said flatly.

"He needs me right now," she said.

"God, Nina. How much more are you going to sacrifice for him? Hasn't he done enough to ruin your life?"

"Hey," she protested angrily. But then she told herself not to take his remark seriously. In a way, it was typical Keith. He didn't allow entangling alliances to drag him down. How could Keith be expected to understand that Duncan was a man teetering on a tightrope? How could she explain to Keith that she had to be there, to have her arms outstretched, in case her father fell?

IN the morning, when she arrived at the Seasons Cosmetics audition, the casting director frowned as he looked from Nina's glossy head shot to her haggard face. She had had trouble sleeping, which always had a bad effect on her appearance. The circles under her eyes looked like dark smudges against her white skin, no matter how hard she tried to cover them. She sat in the chair as the casting director and his assistant circled her, examining her.

"Great hair," he said, lifting up a shiny black length of it as if it were a horse's tail. The assistant murmured agreement. "I like the purple," he said, inserting one finger under the shoulder strap of her short formfitting dress. The casting director bent down to eye level and studied her facial features as if she were a large doll. "Good cheekbones, great lips." He stood up and put his hands on his hips. "But, honey, I think those eyes of yours have seen a few too many sunsets, if you know what I mean. Cosmetics is a young girl's game."

Nina knew better than to be offended. Accepting rejection gracefully was the first thing an actor learned to do, although it never got any easier. "Thanks for seeing me," she said.

I don't care, she thought, as she pulled on her jacket and headed out the doors of the white loft to the elevator. I'm not a model. I'm an actress. But she knew that residuals from TV commercials could be lucrative, and it was hard to convince herself that it was for the best. She really could use the money. Especially now that Keith was thinking about settling down in L.A. He could change his mind any day about keeping the apartment. It would be just like him to change his mind completely, and if he did, how could she argue with him? He didn't owe her a thing. If she had more money, she could help her father get a nice place—maybe something big enough for both of them.

That's not what you want, she reminded herself. You're supposed to be getting on with your life. But how was she supposed to do that? Ignore Duncan's problems and isolation? Her father deserved some happiness now. Some measure of comfort after all those years in prison.

Around lunchtime, she went to the table reading of a new play that was being held at a church in Chelsea. The actual production would be Off Broadway, and she fell in love with the part the director gave her to read. He seemed pleased with her, but he had several other actresses to see. He promised to get back to her.

That afternoon she had another commercial audition. This one was held at the ad agency. She rushed home beforehand and changed into a gray designer pantsuit that she bought half-price at a discount store. It looked businesslike, but fit her perfectly, showing off her figure to good advantage. The product was a new kind of floor cleaner, and the part was a housewife, which didn't require quite as much in the way of glamor as the cosmetics audition. She read for the director, who liked her. He called in the account manager and she did it again. The two men put their heads together and nodded.

Please, she thought, let me get this one.

"Miss Avery," said the director. "The product manufacturer is going to be in town tomorrow for lunch. We want him to meet you before we make our final decision."

Final decision. That sounded promising. But lunch tomorrow? Nina thought. She wouldn't get back to Hoffman until almost dark tomorrow night. Worrying about her father, she hesitated. What if he was lonely and got discouraged? What if the cretin who put that sign on Aunt Mary's door decided to come back and harass him? What if they defaced the house or, worse, tried to hurt him? Doomsday scenarios crowded her mind. And then she chided herself. Her father had been alone in prison for fifteen years. He could certainly handle one extra day on the outside without her. Besides, he'd be furious if he thought she gave up this job just to rush back to Hoffman.

"Sure," she said. "I can be here. I'd love to meet him. What time?"

8

OVER an early lunch, Nina met the product manufacturer, a cheerful, down-to-earth businessman from Des Moines. He announced right there that he thought Nina would be ideal to represent his floor wax, and so the deal was concluded with handshakes, and contract discussions were directed to Len Weinberg. There was even some optimistic talk of multiple commercials, and Nina left the meeting feeling happy and hopeful.

She rushed back to the apartment to change and pick up her bag, and she was able to get to Port Authority and make the three o'clock bus to Hoffman. She stared impatiently out the window, wondering how everything was going with her father. Last night, when she realized she would be spending another night in New York, she had called her aunt's house, but there was no answer. Maybe he had met up with an old friend, she told herself, and gone out to dinner. She had tried calling several times, and then forced herself to stop. He had been so adamant about her not hovering over him that she knew he would be angry when he finally answered and she pounced on him. But she felt as if she were holding her breath all the time she was away from him, and she felt an immense relief when the bus reached the stop nearest Aunt Mary's house and Nina was, at last, deposited on the sidewalk.

Maybe we'll go out to dinner tonight, she thought, as she walked up the sidewalk through the dry, shifting leaves. Somewhere really nice. She thought about the places she knew around here. Patrick had taken her and Jimmy out to a steak house that was chic, but the food was hearty and unfussy. Maybe they could try that. She wondered briefly what Duncan would wear to such a place. She had kept some of his clothes when they sold the house. She'd packed his shirts, ties, and jackets in boxes and stored them in Aunt Mary's basement. He'd be too thin for the jackets now, but he could wear the gray windbreaker with a shirt and tie. Nina came around the corner and began to approach the house. She could see that there was an unfamiliar car parked in the driveway and that her aunt's old Volvo was gone. As she came up the front walk she saw a man standing on the front doorstep, ringing the doorbell. He was a dark-eyed, olive-complected man wearing a black open-necked sport shirt and a burgundy jacket.

"Can I help you?" she asked suspiciously, coming up the steps behind him.

"Are you Nina Avery?" he asked.

Nina frowned. "Yes. Why?"

"Is Duncan Avery your father?"

Nina was instantly on her guard. "Why? What do you want to know for?"

"My name is Bill Repaci. I'm your father's parole officer," he said. The man pulled a plastic folder out of his jacket pocket and showed her his ID badge with his picture on it. "Your father had an appointment scheduled today."

"I know," said Nina.

"He never showed up. I'm here looking for him."

Nina did not want the man to see how much his words alarmed her. She reached into her bag and pulled out the keys to the house. "Let's go inside," she said, putting the key in the lock with a trembling hand.

She opened the door and turned on the lights. The house looked normal. Just as she'd left it.

"Sit down, Mr. . . ."

"Repaci," said the man, and he remained standing.

Nina put her bag down. "I've been in New York the last few days. I just got back. Did my father let you know we . . . he was living here?"

Repaci nodded. "He called me about it. He explained the situation and I said it was all right, subject to the committee's review, of course."

"I can't imagine that he would forget about his appointment this morning."

Bill Repaci shook his head. "We spoke about it on the phone yesterday. He said he would see me this morning just before he hung up."

"He's probably at work right now," said Nina.

Repaci shook his head again. "I went over there when he didn't show up at my office. He didn't show up at work today either. Or call."

Nina stared at him. "He didn't?"

Repaci looked at her grimly. "Nope. He was there yesterday, and the day before. But today, nothing."

Nina's knees suddenly felt as if they were going to give way. "Excuse me, I . . ." She sat down on a nearby chair.

Repaci finally sat down on the couch. "You all right?" he asked.

"Before I left, I . . . I told him not to forget his appointment with you. And he knows . . . I mean, he needs this job. He knows that."

"You had no indication that he might not . . . you know, that he was thinking of bolting . . ." said Repaci.

"No, absolutely not," said Nina vehemently. "I'm sure he didn't . . . bolt. There has to be some explanation."

"Look, miss, I've been doing this for a long time. I've seen this kind of thing happen. Some guys get a little taste of freedom and it's like . . . they can't deal with just having a little. They can't tolerate the restrictions . . ."

"He's not like that," Nina insisted. "He's very . . . disciplined. He's a doctor. He's . . . he's able to cope with things."

"He's been in prison for a long time," Repaci observed. "That changes a person."

"No," Nina insisted, standing up and walking toward the kitchen. "Not my father. There has to be some explanation. Let me call . . . my brother. Can I do that? Can I call my brother? Maybe he's seen him."

"Be my guest. But I've got to report this to the board and to local authorities."

Nina, who was fishing in her bag for her cell phone, looked at him in alarm. "Oh no. You can't . . . Oh, please, Mr. Repaci. I know there's some reasonable explanation."

"Parole has these restrictions for a reason," he explained patiently. "Your father has already been given unusual leeway. He was allowed to move to New York. Then back here. And then he doesn't show up for his second appointment. And he blows off work. Parole violators don't get second chances, miss. Parole *is* the second chance."

"But he's waited so long. If they take this away from him . . ."

Repaci stood up. "Ma'am, I am not here to argue with you. If you want to call your brother, I'll wait to see if he knows anything."

"Right," said Nina, numb. Where would Jimmy be? She tried to think about his schedule, but her mind wouldn't focus on it. All she could think about was her father, and the possibility that they would put him back in prison for his negligence. She found the phone, punched up her directory, and called the carpet store. After two rings, she recognized the voice that picked up and said, "Hoffman Flooring."

"Jimmy," she blurted out. "It's Nina. Have you seen Dad? Do you know where he is?"

Jimmy sounded wary. "No. Isn't he at his job?"

"Jimmy, his parole officer is here. He didn't show up for his appointment and he didn't go to work today."

There was silence at Jimmy's end of the phone.

"Do you know what that means?" she demanded. "They could send him back to prison. We need to try and find him. I don't even have a car. He took the car. Can you come over right away? Please, Jimmy, I need your help."

Jimmy was silent again for a moment. Then he said, "Where are you? At Aunt Mary's?"

"Yes," Nina said.

"All right. I don't know where he is, but I'll come over. Okay?"

"Okay. Thanks, Jimmy," she said. "Think about where he might have gone. And hurry," she said.

She hung up and shook her head at Repaci. "My brother hasn't seen him," she said.

Repaci nodded grimly. "All right," he sighed. Putting a hand on each knee, he pushed himself up and off the sofa. "I'm going to head back to my office and start making calls."

"Please," Nina pleaded. "Just give us a little time. My brother and I will find him. Could you just give us a little window here? He's been in prison for so long. Please, Mr. Repaci."

Repaci looked at her with narrowed eyes. "Didn't he go away for killing your mother?"

Nina lifted her chin defiantly. "He was innocent," she said.

Repaci snorted. "Really?"

Nina felt his remark like a slap in the face, but she didn't flinch. She had to be careful not to alienate this man in any way. "Just give us an hour or two. What difference could an hour or two make?"

Repaci raised his eyebrows. "Look, I appreciate your loyalty to your father. But he was convicted of a violent crime. An hour or two can make all the difference in the world." Repaci looked at his watch, and then handed her a printed business card. "I'm heading back to my office. You call me there if you find him. Maybe you can find him before the cops do."

Nina took the card with a trembling hand.

Repaci headed toward the door. He stopped on the doorstep and looked back at her. "I'm sorry for your trouble. I know you've done all you could. Some of these guys—there's no helping them."

9

THE minute the parole officer left, Nina called the clinic. The receptionist confirmed what Bill Repaci had said. Duncan had neither come in nor called to make an excuse. The receptionist was not sympathetic. "Dr. Nathanson is very annoyed," she said. "He was giving your father the benefit of the doubt by hiring him here."

Hanging up, Nina began to look through the house. Maybe he'd left a note somewhere, or written something on the calendar. But when she looked at it, she saw that the calendar was marked only in Aunt Mary's neat handwriting. The Garden Club, birthdays, surgery. There was none of her father's impatient scrawl on it. The surface of Aunt Mary's desk was likewise undisturbed.

Maybe in his room, she thought. She ran up the stairs to the bedroom that had been hers as a teenager. It still had the pink gingham curtains and bedspread her great-aunt had bought for her all those years ago. The bulletin board still held class pictures, her dried corsage from the prom, and a Bulldogs pennant from Hoffman High School. There was little indication that her father was staying there. The bed was neatly made, and the only sign of him was his book on the bedside table and his few clothes hanging in the closet. On the floor of the closet was his canvas duffel bag. Nina hesitated, hating to invade his privacy like the prison guard he had accused her of resembling, but this could be an emergency. I'll be careful, she thought. He'll never know. She crouched down, unzipped the bag, and cautiously reached in. Lying right on top of the pile of his belongings was all the printed information he had received about the conditions and terms of his parole as well as emergency phone numbers and a calendar with the dates and times of his appointments listed for him by Mr. Repaci. Everything was in perfect order. Nothing had been noted or changed about the day's date. Nothing appeared to be amiss, except for the fact that he hadn't shown up.

Nina looked around, feeling helpless. Where are you? she thought. She replaced the papers in the top of his bag right where she found them, hoping he would not notice that they had been disturbed. She went back downstairs to the phone, which was hanging on the wall against the once cheerful, now faded wallpaper in the kitchen. Below the phone was a Formica shelf that contained take-out menus, an address book, and a pad of Post-it notes, along with an assortment of pens. Below the shelf was a trash basket. She looked down into the basket and saw a discarded bright yellow Post-it note. She didn't remember throwing it in there. Wait a minute, she thought. She reached in and retrieved it. The names on it were in Duncan's handwriting and were impossible to decipher—thanks to years of writing prescriptions. But she was able to make out the numbers. She hesitated, not knowing what she was going to say when someone picked up the phone. Improvise, she thought, and she dialed the first number.

"Dr. Bergman's office," said a pleasant voice.

"Oh hello," said Nina. "My name is Nina Avery. I'm . . . uh . . . my father, Duncan Avery . . . I'm having some trouble locating him. I saw . . . Dr. Bergman's number and I wondered if maybe he'd come in there today for an appointment."

"No . . ." said the woman from the doctor's office. "Although I do have him here for Monday at ten. He's scheduled to have a checkup and a complete set of X-rays."

"X-rays!" Nina cried. "X-rays of what? Is he sick?"

"Of his teeth," said the woman on the phone. "Dr. Bergman is a dentist."

"Oh, of course," said Nina, relieved. "That's right. He was saying that he needed a lot of work done on his teeth."

"Yes, well, he's due in Monday."

Nina thanked her and hung up. She studied the Post-it note again, but still could not make out the writing. There was a second number. It was a local call. The first had been pretty easy to deal with. She had to try. She dialed the number, hoping the person who answered would give her a clue.

After two rings, a recorded message came on. "The number you have reached, 555-4726, has been disconnected."

Whose number? Nina wondered.

The doorbell rang, startling her. Jimmy, she thought, looking at her watch. It's about time. Nina hung up the phone and walked to the front door, ready to give her brother a mild scolding for taking so long.

Instead, when she opened the door, she saw a uniformed patrolman and a portly redheaded man of about forty wearing a well-cut suit on the doorstep. The man in the suit looked vaguely familiar to Nina.

"Mrs. Mary Norris?" he said.

"Um, no, that's my aunt," said Nina.

"Is your aunt here, miss?"

"No, she's in the hospital. Can I help you?"

"Your name, miss?"

"My name is Nina Avery. Who are you?"

The redheaded man turned rather pink in the face. "Miss Avery," he said. "I'm Chief Perry of the Hoffman Police." He took out his badge and showed it to her.

Suddenly, Nina remembered. The police chief who was interviewed on the news about Duncan moving back to Hoffman. "Oh yeah," she said.

"Does your aunt own a 'ninety-five gray-green Volvo?"

"Yes," said Nina. "Why?"

"Are you related, by any chance, to Duncan Avery?"

Nina's heart was pounding, but she gripped the doorknob and tried to appear calm. "He's my father," she said.

The police chief sighed. "May I come in?" he asked.

Nina nodded and stood aside. Before the detective and the patrolman could even enter the house, Jimmy's Saturn pulled up beside the squad car in the driveway and Jimmy got out.

"Nina, what's going on?" he called out.

"Who is that?" the chief asked.

"It's my brother." Nina shook her head and turned to the police chief. "What's going on?" she said.

Chief Perry looked at Jimmy, who was trudging across the front lawn. "Let's wait for your brother," he said. "This concerns him as well."

Jimmy walked up to them. "What is it?" he asked.

"You two might want to go inside and sit down," Chief Perry said.

"Never mind that," said Nina. "Tell us why you're here."

Chief Perry sighed again and looked from Nina to Jimmy. Then he shook his head. "I'm sorry to have to be the one to tell you both this. We got a call about an hour ago from a fisherman down by the river. He thought he saw somebody slumped over in a green 'ninety-five Volvo that was parked down there. He was a little reluctant to go over and look. A couple of officers responded. When they opened the door to the car, they found your . . ."

"No," Nina cried. "No!"

"Your father. I'm terribly sorry, Miss Avery. I understand he just got out of jail, and I'm sure you were hoping—"

"What happened to him?" Jimmy demanded.

"He'd been shot in the chest. We found a gun in his hand. It appears that he took his own life."

"Oh my God," Jimmy whispered, all the color drained from his face.

"No," Nina cried. "That's crazy. You're wrong. That's not my dad. He doesn't even have a gun. He's not allowed to have a gun on parole."

Chief Perry nodded. "That's true. But if he wanted to get one—well, you have to realize that he had certain connections from being in prison. He was forbidden to associate with former felons by the terms of his parole. But if getting a gun was his intention—well, guns are not hard to come by, Miss Avery. Especially if you're determined . . ."

"Suicide," Jimmy whispered.

Nina was shaking her head. "It's probably not even him. What made you think it was him?"

"We found his driver's permit in his wallet," said Chief Perry firmly.

"This isn't true. Somebody stole it from him. This is a mistake!" she cried.

Chief Perry looked at her sadly. "This has got to be so tough," he said, and there was genuine empathy in his gaze.

"Where is he?" Nina demanded. "I want to see him."

"No, Nina, don't," cried Jimmy.

"Look," said the chief. "I know you need to see your dad, and as it happens, we need you to see him to make a positive identification. They've moved the body to the morgue. I'll take you over there. The car is still down by the river. We can have it towed back here once our lab guys go over it. If that would suit you."

"Stop talking like he's dead," Nina protested.

"This is my fault," Jimmy said. "I'm sorry, Nina." Tears trickled out of the corners of Jimmy's eyes and down his face.

"Take it easy," the chief said. "I know it's a shock. Come on. Let's go. The sooner we get this over with . . ."

"Stop it, Jimmy," Nina insisted. "There's some explanation. This is all a mistake."

NINA stood in the chilly hallway at the county morgue and stared numbly at the blank slider that covered the window in front of her. All she could think about the whole way over in the car, and during the walk up the echoing stairs and through the empty corridors of the building, was why she had thought it was so necessary to go back to New York for these last two days. If she had been here . . . If she had only been with him when he needed her . . .

Nina shook her head as if to ward off the possibility that the dead man was her father. She hadn't seen the body yet. There was a still a chance it wasn't him. There was no reason to think the worst yet. But she couldn't deny, even to herself, that suicide was one of the unspoken fears that had plagued her the most. Why did I leave him alone? she thought. How could I leave him alone when I knew the kind of disappointment and rejection he'd been facing? How could I have run off to New York like that and left him to handle everything on his own? Please, God, don't let it be him. If it isn't him, I promise, I won't leave him again.

"Are you ready?" Chief Perry asked.

Jimmy, who had recovered his composure, touched her arm. "Nina, why don't you skip this part? I'll do it. You go sit down."

She shook off his consoling hand. "I'm ready," she said.

Chief Perry pressed a buzzer beside the window, which sounded on the other side of the wall. "All right," the chief said. "It'll be over in a minute."

The slider was pushed open and Nina gasped, clapping her hand over her mouth at the sight of the dead man lying on the table. She stepped back, colliding with Jimmy, but she did not look away.

"Jesus," said Jimmy

Duncan's face was gaunt, his mouth hanging open. His skin looked rubbery and had no life to it, no color except for a grayish green tinge. Nina could see his bare shoulders just above the drape that concealed the rest of his body and the mortal wound. His shoulders were white, and his bony clavicle and slack, sinewy biceps made him look frail, old.

"Is that your father, Duncan Avery?" Chief Perry said.

Nina heard the voice from far away. She had to answer. She had to admit to them, to everyone, that this was her father. Duncan Avery. All those years of waiting and hoping and suffering, all for what? For this. She wanted to say that it wasn't him, that it wasn't over. She wanted that to be true more than anything. Maybe if she just denied it. Nina opened her mouth to reply, and then the whole world went black.

• • •

WHEN she woke up, she was lying on a sofa in a little waiting room that had been fitted out for the families of the morgue's occupants. Jimmy sat hunched on a chair beside her, gazing at her worriedly. Chief Perry was across the room, talking quietly on a cell phone.

"Nina, are you all right?" Jimmy asked.

The image of her father's face in death filled her mind's eye. She closed her eyes again, wishing she could blot out the reality of it. Tears slid out from under her eyelids and down the sides of her face.

Chief Perry folded up his phone and deposited it into his jacket pocket. He came over and stood behind Jimmy, cocking his head to get a look at her face. "You gave us a scare," he said.

Nina gave up and opened her eyes. She was awake. There was no use in pretending it was all a bad dream. She felt her tears trickling down onto her neck, into her hair. She wiped her eyes and struggled to sit up.

"He's at peace now, Nina," said Jimmy earnestly. "We have to take comfort from that."

"No," Nina pleaded. Jimmy leaned over and put his arms around her. She wept against his broad chest. "No. No."

Chief Perry waited a respectful interval until Nina pulled away from her brother and began to fumble in her coat pocket for a tissue. The chief handed her his pristine, folded white handkerchief. "I'm terribly sorry," he said

"Thank you," Nina sniffed, blotting her tears.

"We have some loose ends," said the chief. "When you go home, can you look around and see if there was a note?"

Nina sniffed again. "Wasn't there one in the car?"

"We haven't been able to find one."

Nina looked at Jimmy and then back at the chief. "No note?"

"Often there's no note," said Chief Perry.

"And he didn't have a gun," Nina said.

"Well, actually he did," the chief said.

Nina shook her head. "He didn't own a gun. Maybe it wasn't suicide. Did you consider the possibility that someone else might have killed him?"

Chief Perry looked at her patiently. "Like who?"

"I don't know," Nina cried. "But I can't believe he would have done this without even a word . . . no explanation."

Chief Perry cleared his throat. "Look, I didn't know your father, but . . ."

"There are a lot of people in this town who seem to hate him," Nina insisted. "Everywhere we turned, people were cruel to him. Somebody posted a hate message on our door. It could have been someone like that. You're just accepting that he did this without any reason."

"I'll want to see that hate message," said Chief Perry somberly. "If the wound was not, by some chance, self-inflicted, the autopsy will tell us that. But I have to tell you that I saw the fatal wound, Miss Avery. Point-blank range is what we're talking about."

"Still," said Nina stubbornly. "There's a possibility . . . When will you know about the autopsy?"

"In the next few days," he said.

"And the gun. Don't forget about the gun."

"That gun will be difficult to trace. It's an old Colt automatic. There were a lot of them issued years back to police, to military men. You can buy them anywhere."

"And there's something else," Nina said. "I just remembered this. He made a dentist's appointment for Monday. You mean to tell me that a man who was going to kill himself would make an appointment to have his teeth fixed? Is that rational?"

"It doesn't matter," said Jimmy dully. "None of it matters."

Chief Perry shook his head. "Suicide is an irrational act. You're not going to turn it into something reasonable." He pulled up another chair, sat down, and leaned forward. He frowned and pressed his lips together, as if struggling with what he was about to say. Finally, he sighed. "Look, you seem like a couple of good kids and I know this is horrible for you. Suicide always leaves the survivors with so many questions. But in a case like your father's, it's not that unexpected.

"You have to remember that for fifteen years your father was living for the day when he would have his freedom. Planning what he'd do, how he'd spend his time. But men in that position, that your dad was in, they sometimes find that freedom isn't at all like they'd hoped it would be. Would you say that was true of your dad, Nina? Were there a lot of disappointments?"

Nina folded her arms over her chest and would not meet his gaze. "I suppose," she said.

"Their old life has disappeared," Chief Perry continued gently. "They're greeted with suspicion, sometimes out-and-out hatred. They have no money. The best years of their lives are behind them. They can't find work because they have to explain where they've been for the last fifteen years. And nobody wants to hire a felon. Family and old friends reject them. They're afraid to meet new people because the subject is gonna come up. Everywhere they look is loss. It's more than a lot of people can bear."

"He wasn't like other people," Nina insisted. "He was strong."

"No," said Chief Perry. "He wasn't like a lot of prisoners on parole who had nothing to begin with. Your father had a big life. He was a doctor, he had money, he had a family. For him, the fall was that much greater."

Nina didn't want to hear it. She didn't want to give in to it, because if she did, she was closing the door on any possibility of doubt. And once she accepted the idea that Duncan had taken his own life, she could not avoid the next logical conclusion. "Then it's my fault," she said. "For leaving him alone. He kept saying he was all right. But I could see what was happening to him . . ."

"Oh, you mustn't think that," Chief Perry said kindly. "You know as well as I do that day-to-day life can be boring and frustrating under the best of circumstances. Imagine a man like your father. The experience was probably crushing."

"You didn't know, Nina," said Jimmy miserably. "How could you have known?"

Just then the door to the lounge opened. Nina looked up and saw Patrick.

"What are you doing here?" Nina demanded.

"I called him," said Jimmy.

"He *was* my father. Nina, are you all right?" Patrick asked.

Chief Perry stood up and offered his chair to Patrick. "I'm gonna leave you folks. When you're ready to leave, Officer Burrows is out there. He'll escort you home."

Nina glared at her brother as Patrick sat down in the vacated chair. He frowned at her. "I'm sorry, Nina. I'm not that surprised, but I'm sorry all the same. I guess it was all too much for him."

"Especially the fact that you wouldn't even speak to him," she cried.

"You can't blame me, Nina. After what Duncan did . . ."

"Don't call him Duncan. Show him some respect, for God's sake."

"Please, we shouldn't be arguing over this. It's over. It's finally over. Can't we just let go of it?" Jimmy pleaded. " I don't want to fight with the two of you anymore. Can't we try to get along? Dad would want us to get along."

Nina didn't want to agree. It seemed like agreeing would be betraying her father's memory. But she also didn't want to argue. Not with her brothers. Not now.

Patrick reached out and put his hand over Nina's. "Jimmy's right. It doesn't do any good. Nina, I just want you to know that I admire you for what you did for . . . him."

"Oh sure," she said.

"No. I mean it. You did everything humanly possible for him. Your love was unconditional. He was very lucky to have you . . ."

Nina felt the tears finally rising to her eyes. A tidal wave of regret was welling up inside her. Spilling over. "It wasn't enough," she croaked.

"Don't ever think that, Nina," Patrick insisted. "You didn't deserve this. None of it. None of us did."

10

THE funeral was held on Monday, and was completely private. Despite Jimmy's protests, not even the Connellys were invited. In this instance, Nina found herself allied, for once, with Patrick. She didn't want to know who would or would not show up to pay respects to her father. She didn't want to talk to a single reporter or answer a single question. She was relieved that despite everything, Patrick was going to participate in laying Duncan to rest. He insisted that there be no eulogy and, reluctantly, Nina gave in. It would have made a miserable day even worse if Patrick had refused to attend. As it was, Patrick invited his sister and brother to come back to his home after the brief graveside service. He had arranged for a lunch to be catered for them. "It will be just us," he said.

Aunt Mary's Volvo was in the shop being detailed to get rid of the bloodstains on the front seat, so Nina rode with Jimmy in his Saturn. As they rounded the curve leading to Patrick's property, Nina could see the stone house, flanked by billows of slate gray storm clouds. The surrounding trees swayed and a few still bore isolated leaves the color of bronze or claret that had stubbornly resisted the autumn winds.

"He wanted to see the twins so I brought him up here the other day," said Nina.

"Yeah, I heard," said Jimmy.

Nina turned from the window and looked at her brother. "You did? Who did you hear it from?"

Jimmy did not reply.

"Did you talk to Dad?"

Jimmy's large frame shifted uneasily in the seat. "Yeah."

"When?"

"I went to see him the other night. When you were in New York."

"You did?" Nina asked. "Why? I thought you didn't want to see him."

"I changed my mind. I felt bad about . . . I just wanted to clear the air with him," said Jimmy. "Is that allowed?"

"Of course," said Nina, ignoring his sarcasm. "It's just that you never mentioned it. Did he give you any idea of what he was going to do? Was he depressed?"

"How do I know?" Jimmy said defensively as he turned down Patrick's winding driveway. "I'm not a shrink. He didn't say he was going to kill himself, if that's what you're asking."

"But he must have told you something," Nina demanded.

Jimmy pulled up behind another car parked in Patrick's driveway, a white minivan. "We caught up on some things. That's all. What does it matter anymore?" Jimmy asked. As soon as the Saturn stopped in the drive, the driver's door to the minivan opened and George Connelly got out. He was wearing a plaid tweed jacket and a tie. He gave Jimmy a smile and a wave. Rose Connelly came around the front of the van carrying a cake plate with aluminum foil over it. Jimmy jumped out of the car and rushed to embrace them.

With a sigh, Nina got out of the car also. She forced herself to smile. "Hello, Rose, George," she said.

Rose, balancing her cake, gave Nina a hug. "I'm so sorry, dear."

"Thank you," said Nina.

"Patrick invited us to lunch," Rose said. "Wasn't that nice of him?"

"Very nice," said Nina. She stepped back to let them pass. Jimmy walked between them, with George's arm draped protectively over his shoulders. For a minute, Nina felt as if Jimmy was shielding himself with the Connellys. Shielding himself from her questions, which obviously made him uncomfortable.

Gemma, dressed all in black, stood at the open front door as they approached, twisting her sparkling rings nervously. Patrick stood behind her.

"I brought a little something," said Rose, indicating her cake.

"That's nice," said Gemma.

"Not that we really need anything," said Patrick. He led the way into the dining room, pointing out a lavish buffet that was set out on a glowing antique sideboard. The room was lit with dozens of candles, which made a welcome contrast to the gloomy weather outside. In the den the TV was blaring and Nina could see the twins through the door, lying on the carpet, transfixed. Elena sat on the sofa, peering out warily at the arriving guests.

"Turn that off, boys," Patrick called out. "Come in here and eat. Go ahead, everyone. Help yourself."

"Patrick ordered enough food for an army," Gemma said. "Here, Nina, this came for you." She pointed to a lavish flower arrangement that was set on the highly polished surface of the dining room table. "There's a card."

Nina opened the card. "Thinking of you," it read. Love, Keith.

"Who are they from?" Gemma asked.

"Keith," said Nina. She had called him in L.A. to tell him the news.

"That was thoughtful of him," Gemma said.

"Yes, very thoughtful," Nina said.

The twins came barreling into the dining room, squealing, and Patrick squatted down and scooped them into his arms, burying his face in their necks. Gemma leaned over and rubbed Patrick's shoulders.

Jimmy loaded up his plate and put it down at the table between Rose and George. "Mom, Dad, can I get you a plate?" he asked.

"No, no, honey," said Rose. "You sit down and eat. We'll get ours in a minute." She patted the chair between them and smiled tenderly at Jimmy.

Standing alone by her flower arrangement, Nina felt a headache starting over her left eye. She felt someone tap her gently on the arm. She turned around and saw Elena, wearing a Great Adventure sweatshirt over her stretched-out stirrup pants, standing beside her.

Timidly, the woman handed Nina a laminated Mass card with a picture of an Aryan-looking haloed Jesus on the front. She said something to Nina in Spanish. Nina caught the word *padre.* Nina did not understand the language, but when she looked into the older woman's eyes she could see they were filled with sympathy. "Thank you," said Nina. *"Gracias."* Nina smiled, and clasped the woman's rough hand in her own. The older woman nodded, and headed back toward the den as Gemma reappeared at Nina's side.

"That was so nice of her," said Nina, showing Gemma the Mass card.

"She got one for Patrick, too," said Gemma. "Well, we're all the family she has here. I mean, she has people back in Panama, of course . . ."

"Speaking of family, how's the rest of your family?" Nina asked. "What do you hear from your father?"

Gemma stared across the elegant, candlelit dining room. Her forehead wrinkled slightly. "Um . . . I heard from him . . . last year. The new wife was pregnant at the time. She's probably had the baby by now. Didi calls me once in a while. Although she never got over the fact that I eloped." Gemma smiled weakly.

"I'll bet not," said Nina wryly, remembering Gemma's stepmother and her fixation on wedding matters. "It must have been strange for you growing up in that house. I mean, you were so brilliant. Did they appreciate that about you?"

Gemma frowned again, this time in puzzlement. "I don't know. Well, it doesn't matter. Patrick appreciated me."

We all rewrite history to suit ourselves, Nina thought. She didn't remember Patrick appreciating Gemma until he was accepted to enroll at Rutgers. But if Gemma remembered it differently, it didn't hurt anything. "He should appreciate you," Nina said loyally.

The doorbell rang, and Gemma frowned. "I'd better get that. Nina, will you have some lunch?"

Nina nodded and picked up a plate from the buffet. She wasn't hungry, but it would be rude not to eat after Patrick and Gemma had gone to all this trouble. What she really wanted to do was to kick off her black heels and trade her fashionable boatneck black sheath for a comfortable bathrobe. But, headache or not, there were rituals one had to observe. She held her plate against her chest like a shield and looked without appetite at the lavish plates of food. She picked out a few items and carefully forked them onto her plate. She was conscious of a sudden hush that had fallen on the room. When she turned around, she saw Lindsay Farrell standing in the doorway.

Lindsay looked like an acolyte of St. Lucia in her long ivory-colored gabardine trench coat, her cheeks pink, her blond hair dazzling in the glow of Patrick's Venetian chandelier. Just beyond Lindsay's shoulder, Nina could see Gemma's narrow face, her eyes wide and anxious.

"Patrick," said Lindsay.

Patrick, who was seated at the table wolfing down his lunch while George Connelly was speaking to him, looked up, and started in surprise.

"Lindsay," he said. He stood up to greet her, smoothing down his tie and kissing her, European style, on both cheeks.

"I knew the service for your dad was today," said Lindsay. "Since I'm right next door, I wanted to stop by. Hi, Jimmy, Nina. I'm so sorry for your loss. How are you doing, Jimmy? Long time no see."

Jimmy looked up at Lindsay warily. His face was still slack with surprise at the sight of her. He did not stand up. "Fine. Thanks."

"Glad you're here," said Patrick smoothly to Lindsay. "Can you stay for lunch?" He pointed to the extravagant buffet.

"Oh, Patrick," Lindsay exclaimed. "I never saw that Provençal sideboard in place. It looks magnificent in here."

Patrick beamed. "Come in the living room. I want you to see what I did with that pair of Italian commodes you found for me."

Lindsay demurred. "I don't want to take you away from your family at a time like this. Really, I just came to offer my condolences. Oh, and these chocolates," she said, lifting a small gilded gift bag. She turned to Gemma. "Gemma, I'll bet your boys like chocolate."

Gemma looked at the bag as if it were on fire. "Not that kind," she said.

"Jesus, Gemma," Patrick muttered, taking the gift bag and setting it on the table.

Gemma looked helplessly at her husband. "They don't, Patrick. They like Hershey bars."

Lindsay glanced into the den and gave the twins a wave, which they ignored. "I can see that," she said.

Patrick took Lindsay by the elbow. "Come see the commodes," he said.

Gemma looked at her other guests. "Keep on eating," she said with a frantic note in her voice. Everyone dutifully turned their attention back to their plates to avoid looking at Gemma. She began to collect platters of food from the buffet, piling them on top of one another and carrying them toward the kitchen.

Hearing the clatter, Patrick returned to the dining room. "Gemma," he demanded. "What do you think you're doing?" Lindsay stood in the door of the dining room, looking at them curiously.

Gemma stood very still, a crooked tower of food-filled plates teetering in her arms. "I'm clearing up," she said in a small voice.

"It's not time to clear up," he said through gritted teeth. "I'll tell you when it's time to clear up."

There was a silence in the room as Nina and Jimmy kept their eyes trained on their plates. They had a history of pretending not to notice marital quarrels, no matter how they escalated. But the discord between Patrick and Gemma had sabotaged whatever small measure of camaraderie had existed in the room.

All of a sudden, Rose Connelly pushed back her chair and stood up. "Gemma's right. We shouldn't leave all this food lying out. It could spoil. I'll help you put it away, Gemma."

Patrick turned and glared at Rose, but she seemed impervious to his displeasure. She picked up a plate of tomatoes and mozzarella garnished with ribbons of basil and headed for the kitchen. Nina saw her opportunity. She stood up. "I'll help as well," she said. Ignoring Patrick, and the thudding in her head, she followed Rose's lead and picked up a couple of dishes. All she could think of was how soon she could leave.

11

IT was only four o'clock when Nina arrived back at Aunt Mary's house, but it seemed to her as if the day had been interminable. What do my brothers and I have in common anymore? she thought. We are survivors of the same family. Our lives have been twisted by the same horrible events. We are a constant reminder to one another of how our family jumped the track, crashed, and burned.

She entered her aunt's house and only turned on one light in the living room. She felt slightly sick to her stomach, and even the light from the one lamp hurt her eyes. She slumped down on the couch and pressed her eyes with her fingertips. Gemma had tried to force her to take Keith's flower arrangement when she left, but she'd refused it, saying she had nowhere to put it. The truth was that she didn't want it. It was a nice gesture on Keith's part, but it only served to remind her of how alone she felt, now that her father was gone. A flower arrangement was no substitute for a shoulder to lean on. What she needed on a day as grim as this one was someone to be there with her, to go to the bathroom and get her a cold washcloth for her head, to make her some tea.

She thought back over her relationships, the love affairs she had had. She'd had passionate flings, and two long-term romances, but she always seemed to hold back a part of herself from the men she cared for. Sometimes the troubles the men in her life fretted over made her feel impatient, and that always signaled the end of the relationship. But how could she commiserate about a contract that was not renewed or a promotion that wasn't offered when she thought about her father, an innocent man in a prison cell in Bergen County? John, a guy she'd lived with for two years, once told her, in a moment of sarcasm, that his problems never seemed to measure up to hers.

The pain in Nina's head jabbed her. She couldn't stay awake and deal with it. She needed to sleep, and let it pass. She kicked off her black high heels and shuffled in her stocking feet to the downstairs bathroom. She took two extra-strength painkillers and, not bothering to change out of her dress, returned to the living room, where she fell across the couch, praying for oblivion and relief.

THE sound of the doorbell woke her, and Nina sat up, disoriented by the dim light in the room and the fact that she had been asleep. Her watch read 7:00 and for one confused minute she didn't know whether it was morning or night. And then it came back to her. The funeral. The lunch at Patrick's. Her headache. She frowned, and thought about her head. It seemed . . . better. Thank God. But she was hungry and thirsty. And there was someone at the door. Automatically, she rose to answer it, and then she thought, Why? There was no one she wanted to see. She didn't want to hear any halfhearted condolences or self-satisfied homilies about people living and dying by the sword. She'd seen it all in the newspaper and heard it on the television. Nina sank back down on the couch cushions. Go away, she thought. Whoever you are.

The doorbell sounded again.

Just stay put, she told herself. It's bound to stop.

The bell rang again. The caller was persistent. Maybe they had seen her through the sheer living room curtains when she first sat up. She realized that it was no use wishing them away. Someone knew she was here and was not going to leave until she responded. She got up, shoved on her black shoes, and walked to the door, straightening her black knit dress and calling out irritably, "Just a minute." She looked in the vestibule mirror and saw how pallid her face looked. She'd worn her hair up in a chignon to the funeral, but now it fanned out, coal black and tangled, around her face and down her back. She ran a hand through it, pinched her cheeks to give them some color, took a deep breath, and opened the door.

The man on the doorstep was looking out at the lamplit street. When he heard the door open, he turned to face her. It was a stranger.

"Nina?" said the man.

Nina frowned. She felt as if she recognized him but couldn't place him. His black hair fell in a curve against his high cheekbones. His skin was the color of polished amber and his black eyes studied her narrowly.

"Do I know you?" she said.

He shook his head and smiled. "No," he said. "I just feel as if I know you. My name is Andre Quinteros. I'm a . . . I was a friend of your father's."

"Oh my God, of course," she said, blushing. " I knew I'd

seen you somewhere. You testified at the parole hearing. You're the doctor from the prison. Dr. Quinteros."

The man nodded. "I heard about Duncan. I'm so sorry."

"Thank you," she said.

"I know this is a bad day for you but . . . I wondered if you might have a few minutes. There's something I wanted to talk to you about."

Nina frowned. "I am not . . . exactly at my best right now."

"I know," he said. "I hate to trouble you, today of all days, but I really . . . I think it's important."

Duncan's supporters were few, and here was one who had come to pay his respects, she thought. "It's okay, come in," said Nina distractedly. She stepped back from the door and Quinteros followed her into the house. "How did you know where to find me?" she asked.

"Your father called me when you came to stay here."

"He did?" Nina said, surprised. She realized that she had been monitoring Duncan so closely that she thought she knew everything he did. Obviously, she was mistaken. She hadn't known about his visit with Jimmy. Or his keeping in touch with this doctor. In so many ways, she had been ignorant of his intentions. "I didn't know."

"Yeah. We talked for a while."

"What did he say? Did you . . . ?" Nina shook her head. "I'm sorry. I'm being rude. Sit down. I'm still a little out of it. I just woke up. I got a terrible headache after the funeral and I just . . . had to lie down."

"How's the head now?" he asked.

"It was better when I woke up. But now it's starting to hurt a little bit again."

"Have you eaten?" he asked.

"Oh, no," she said. "I . . . I'll look for something later. I have no idea what's here."

"You probably haven't eaten anything all day," he said.

"I couldn't really manage it at lunch," she admitted.

"I haven't eaten either," he said. "Come on. I'll buy you dinner."

Nina started to protest and then she stopped herself. This was not a stranger. This was someone who had been a friend to her father. Suddenly it seemed as if this was exactly what she needed—to be with someone who had known her father and cared about him. "That would be great," she said. "I'll get my jacket."

NINA slid into the booth opposite Quinteros. The waitress passed by and handed them two enormous menus with red faux-leather covers and gold tassels along the spine. Nina opened her menu and shook her head. "Diners and traffic circles," she said. "Two great New Jersey institutions."

"I hope you mean that in a nice way," he said teasingly.

"Absolutely," said Nina. "I am a Jersey girl, born and bred. God, I don't know how to choose here."

"I love their pastrami," he said.

Nina frowned at him disapprovingly. "You're a doctor?"

Quinteros smiled. "I've got to get it while I can. When I move back to Santa Fe I'll miss it. They don't do deli out there."

"Move back?" Nina said.

"Well, my fiancée lives out there. So does most of my family."

Fiancée, she thought, surprised by a fleeting feeling of disappointment to know that he was taken. "I've heard it's a beautiful place, Sante Fe."

"It is," he said.

The waitress returned and looked at them questioningly,

holding her pad at the ready. "I'm told the pastrami is great," Nina said with a smile. "With pickles." She caught sight of herself in one of the myriad mirrored surfaces in the huge diner. She looked completely drab and washed out. Exactly the way she felt.

While Quinteros placed his order, Nina watched him thoughtfully. He was not much older than thirty, she suspected, but he had what she would call an "old face"—the face of an old soul. Even when he smiled, his eyes turned down as if he were sad.

The waitress left, and Nina sat up against the cushioned back of the booth. "So, Dr. Quinteros . . ."

"Please, Andre," he said.

"Andre and Quinteros. That's kind of unusual," she said.

"My mother is from Quebec," he said.

Nina nodded. "And you work at the prison."

Quinteros squinted and calculated. "Three years now."

"Why the prison?" she said. "If you don't mind my asking. I mean, not only is it far from where you plan to live, but I've logged a lot of time there. It's a depressing place to be."

Andre nodded in agreement. "It is. It's dismal. I won't be sorry to leave it behind me. But I was idealistic when I finished my residency. I thought I could do some good. Provide better care than the inmates were used to."

"Very noble of you," said Nina, unable to disguise a hint of skepticism.

"No. It's not noble . . . I had a brother in that prison," said Andre. "Herve, the youngest."

"Had? He's out now?"

"No, he died in custody, actually. About six years ago."

Nina was taken aback. "I'm sorry," she said sincerely. She recognized his offhand tone, as if it didn't hurt him to say the words. She had perfected that tone herself.

"He lived in Newark. He was busted for drugs," said Andre. "He got into a fight with another inmate and somewhere in the scuffle he got a ruptured spleen, but nobody knew it. His abdomen was distended. The doctor at the prison examined him and said he had gas. Gave him laxatives."

"Gas? The doctor didn't know the difference?"

Andre shrugged. "Didn't know. Didn't care. He was a hack. An alcoholic. It didn't much matter to him. Herve died in his sleep the next night."

"Oh my God," said Nina. "That's awful."

Andre nodded. "As a matter of fact, your father tried to intervene. He recognized the misdiagnosis. They put him in solitary for speaking up and making trouble."

Nina shook her head. "He never told me about that."

"Well, he wasn't the one who told me, either. I heard about it from one of the inmates when I went to work there. But it always made me feel a little bit . . . indebted to your father."

"Thanks. That means a lot to me. More than you know. Thanks for telling me that," said Nina. For a moment they were silent. Then Nina said, "How old was he? Your brother."

"Nineteen," Andre said. "Don't get me wrong. He was no angel. He had a bad drug problem. But his death . . . Well, it devastated my parents."

"I can imagine," Nina said.

Andre smiled. "A lot of people thought Herve deserved to die. They don't know what prison is like."

Nina nodded, grateful to be with someone who did know. She fell silent, thinking of visiting days at the prison. Aunt Mary always made sure she had a ride if she couldn't drive Nina herself. Some of the people from Aunt Mary's church used to drive her, and Nina would muster some small talk with whoever was at the wheel on the way. But the ride back was interminable. The drivers never knew what to ask her about her visit with

Duncan, and she tried not to notice them casting furtive, pitying glances her way.

"Two pastrami sandwiches." The waitress had reappeared and placed their sandwiches down in front of them. Andre picked up a half and began to eat it.

Nina stared at the plate. It looked good, and it smelled good, but she still didn't feel much like eating.

"Go ahead," he said, noticing her reluctance. "Get started on that. You need to eat something."

"You're the doctor," she said, and she picked up half the sandwich.

For a few minutes they ate in silence, and Nina could feel the food actually starting to settle her stomach. Her strength seemed to return to her with each bite. Andre watched her, and when she had finished a half, he set down his own sandwich and wiped his fingers, as if to indicate that it was all right to talk again.

Nina wiped her mouth with a napkin. "So. You said my father called you. What did he want? Did you have any inkling that he was planning . . ."

Andre frowned. "To kill himself?"

Nina nodded.

"No. Actually, that's why I came to see you. When I read it in the paper I was shocked. To say the least."

Nina stared at him. "Everyone says I'm crazy, but I've had my doubts about it."

Andre seized on her remark. "What kinds of doubts? What do you mean?"

"I don't know," she said. "There seem to be a lot of people in this town still hating him for what happened to my mother. Maybe somebody . . . hated him enough to want him dead. Or . . . I don't know. He always maintained his innocence. Maybe he tried to find out something about the murder and he stirred up a hornet's nest. It's probably not rational but . . . but I've thought that."

Andre picked up a plastic-wrapped straw and tapped it on the Formica tabletop. "I have my doubts, too," he said.

Nina's heart started to hammer. "Tell me why you say that."

"Well, I knew your dad fairly well. He used to work in the infirmary with me and we would talk. I was teaching him Spanish," said Andre with a smile. "He was a very intelligent man. He'd become fluent, actually."

"Yes, he told me," said Nina.

"We talked about a lot of things. He talked about you a lot. He adored you . . ."

Nina blushed, and part of her wanted to hear more about what her father had said about her, but she was not about to be distracted from her more urgent concern. "What makes you think he didn't kill himself?"

"He was looking forward to getting out . . ."

Nina interrupted him. "Chief Perry said people don't realize how tough it's going to be. He said it was not uncommon for ex-prisoners to become very depressed when they finally understood what their life had become."

"I'm sure that's true," said Andre.

"My father had been a doctor. He'd once had money and prestige. Chief Perry said that would make it all the worse for him."

Andre frowned and tapped the straw.

"What aren't you saying?" She could see he was struggling with what to say next. "Do you know something about this that I don't?" she persisted.

Andre spoke carefully. "I think you should find out from the police if they have any evidence at all that his death was not a suicide," said Andre. "The autopsy may reveal new information . . ."

Nina cocked her head and tried to catch his eye, but he avoided her gaze. "That's what the police chief said. But you sound as if you already know . . ."

Andre was silent for a moment, frowning, as if he was struggling with a decision. Then he sighed. "Nina, your father *had* been suffering from clinical depression. While he was incarcerated. It was severe at times. In fact, in treating him we had him try a variety of medications." Andre looked directly at her. "He never mentioned it to you?"

Nina stared at him and shook her head. "No. I mean, who could blame him for being depressed. But no. He never said a word."

Andre frowned again. "I was hoping he might have shared this with you."

Nina felt disoriented by this new information. "So you're saying . . . Wait a minute. You're saying . . . Are you saying that he *did* kill himself?"

"No," Andre said sharply. "Just the opposite. Your father had it under control. And after a few false starts we found a medication that really helped him. By the time he learned about his parole, he was in very good . . . mental health. He told me that every day, every moment was precious to him. He was absolutely determined to make the best of every moment he had left in his life."

Tears welled in Nina's eyes at the thought of her father keeping his despair from her, not trusting her with it, for some reason. "Why didn't he tell me?"

"Don't take it the wrong way. He probably didn't want to worry you. You'd spent so many years being supportive of him. He didn't want to burden you any further. There was no need. I'd arranged for him to renew his prescription with Dr. Nathanson at the clinic where he was working. He was doing fine, Nina."

"But maybe once he had to actually cope with his 'so-called' freedom, he stopped doing fine," she said.

"Your father was a very strong-willed person," Andre said.

"Or he stopped taking his medication."

Andre frowned. "Well, that's a possibility, Nina. Certainly. That's one of the reasons I came to see you. I think it would be a very good idea to find out. Once they have the autopsy results, they will have a toxicology screen, and they will know exactly what he had in his system. I think it would be a good idea for you to speak to a detective and find out what those results were."

"But . . ." Nina shook her head slowly. "But if the police find out he was . . . clinically depressed, they'll be more certain than ever that he committed suicide."

"Let's face it. You and I both know that the death of a convicted murderer is not very high up on the cops' list of concerns. They may just want to close the file on him. The public, the newspapers are not going to care what happened to Duncan Avery. They'll think your father got what was coming to him," he said.

Nina sighed. "You're right about that."

Andre leaned forward and held her gaze with his own. "So you have to be his advocate. Here." He reached into his jacket pocket and pulled out a pad and a thin gold pen. He scribbled something on the pad. "This is the chemical name for the medication he was taking. If you have your doubts, take this to the police and ask if this chemical turned up in his system at the autopsy. If this compound was there, in his blood . . ."—Andre tore off the piece of paper and handed to her—"that means Duncan was still taking his medication faithfully. And if that's the case, I'd be willing to bet anything that your father did not kill himself."

12

A YOUNG uniformed officer wearing a humorless expression confiscated Nina's bag and searched it while his more pleasant-looking colleague instructed her to pass through the metal detector arch and wait on the other side. Fortunately, she did not set off any alarms, and her bag was handed back to her with a brief order to direct her question to the sergeant on duty. Nina had not been in the police station since the days following her mother's murder, and it was clear that in the ensuing years the town of Hoffman had spared no expense in outfitting the police department for the security demands of the new century.

Nina approached the sergeant's desk and waited while the sergeant spoke to someone on his headset about a prisoner transfer. As she looked around the police station, once so familiar to her, she thought about her meeting the night before with Andre Quinteros. Part of her was angry at her father for not telling her about his depression. Another part kept mulling over what Andre had said about him. That he was not suicidal. Not at all. That seemed to validate her own impressions, but still, she had been so shaken by Andre's information that she could hardly sleep all night. She couldn't even remember if she'd said good night to Andre when he dropped her off at her door.

"Miss? Can I help you?"

Nina started, and then realized that the sergeant was speaking to her. She asked him if she could speak with Chief Perry. The sergeant frowned, as if this were unlikely, but he took her name and pressed the intercom. He spoke quietly into his headset and then turned to Nina. "Go through there," the sergeant said, pointing to a door on his left. "Down the hall, third door on the right."

Nina put her hand on the doorknob, waited for the buzzer, and entered the squad room. She kept her eyes lowered as she hurried toward the office to which she had been directed. She knew it was probably paranoia, but she felt as if all the officers in this station recognized her and knew about her family's notorious history. As she approached the door to Chief Perry's office, she saw that it was open, and that there was a trim white-haired man in casual civilian clothes leaning against the doorframe, talking to the occupant. He looked over at her as she approached, and all at once, Nina recognized his small bright eyes and lined face. It was the detective who had been the chief investigator on her mother's case. He had always treated Nina and her brothers kindly, even though he was busily building a case against their father. "Detective Hagen?"

The man smiled but looked puzzled. "Hello, young lady," he said.

She realized that he did not recognize her. The last time he'd seen her she was a teenager.

"You don't remember me. Nina Avery."

The old man's twinkling eyes widened with surprise. "Oh

my goodness, Nina," he said. He reached for Nina's hand and shook it. "How are you, dear?"

"I'm fine," she said. "And you?"

"Aw, I'm doing okay. Just talking a little golf with the chief here. What brings you here?"

Chief Perry joined them in the doorway. "Hello, Nina. Come on in. I'm glad you're here. Frank, it was good to see you. Don't you be a stranger now."

Nina frowned. "Don't you . . . aren't you still working here, Detective Hagen?"

"No, I'm retired. They put me out to pasture," Frank Hagen said, aiming for a jovial tone but unable to suppress a wistful note. "Nina, about your dad . . ."

Chief Perry interrupted. "I'm just about to discuss that with Miss Avery in my office," he said firmly. "Come in, Nina."

Nina entered and sat down in the chair in front of Chief Perry's desk as he walked around it, smoothing down his tie as he sat.

Frank Hagen hesitated, and then said, "Right. Well, you people have business, and the wife's got storm windows on my To Do list today."

"Frank, can you close that door on your way out?"

Hagen nodded and raised a hand as he reached for the doorknob. "Yessir."

Perry sighed as the door closed and the latch caught.

"How long ago did Lieutenant Hagen retire?" Nina asked politely.

Perry raised his eyebrows. "Let me see. It's been about three years." Chief Perry gave Nina a quick, grim glance. "I hope I can make the adjustment a little better when it's my time to leave. He can't quite make the break, you know? He keeps coming around and trying to interest me in golf, and it's really not my game."

"I understand," said Nina.

"So, what can I do for you, Nina?"

"I'm here about my father's death," said Nina.

"What about it?" Perry said.

Nina took a deep breath, and pictured Andre's face in her mind. The certainty in his eyes. "I have been . . . thinking. I was not completely satisfied with the idea that my father took his own life. And then I was talking to my father's physician and he asked me about the autopsy report."

Eugene Perry cleared his throat. He peered at Nina. "What about it?" he asked.

Nina took the slip of paper that Andre had given her last night out of her pocket. "Dr. . . . um . . . Quinteros wanted me to find out if my father had been taking this medication that was prescribed for him at the time of his death. This is the chemical name for the compound he was taking."

"Well, why don't we look," said Chief Perry amiably. He took the slip of paper and put it on the desk beside him. He shuffled through the papers on his desk and pulled out a file. "What was the medication for?" asked the chief.

Nina took a deep breath. If she told him the truth, would he just dismiss her questions out of hand? She had to risk it. "Actually, he was taking medication for depression. Dr. Quinteros said that if he hadn't quit taking it, it would show up in his toxicology screen."

Chief Perry shook out the earpiece on a pair of half-glasses and put them on. He frowned, scanning the densely printed paper, and ran his index finger down a column of figures. Then, stopping his finger on the page, he glanced again at the slip of paper. "Yup," he said. "Here it is. Your father was taking this medication."

Nina felt a buzzing in her veins. She leaned toward the chief. "Then I'm afraid I have to question your conclusion that my father killed himself. Dr. Quinteros will tell you. It's highly unlikely if he was taking his medication."

Nina expected the chief to be resistant, to scoff at this idea, but instead he shook his head. "As a matter of fact, that's just further confirmation of what we already know," the chief said.

Nina sat back, surprised. "What do you mean? What do you already know?"

"It seems that . . . Look, Nina, I don't know whether this is going to seem like good news or bad news to you." He closed the autopsy folder and set it back down on his desk. Then he took off his glasses and fiddled with the earpiece. "The coroner's report indicated that your father was . . ." He hesitated, and then spoke in a rush. "Nina, we now know that your father was not the one who fired the fatal shot. He may have been trying to disarm the killer when the shot was fired."

Nina was stunned. This information caught her completely off guard. "The killer?"

Chief Perry shifted uneasily in his chair. "Yes. Someone else shot your father. He didn't commit suicide."

"But I thought . . ." Nina was nonplussed. "Are you sure?" she said.

Chief Perry nodded. "Yes. We know that now."

"He definitely did not kill himself?"

"No. According to the autopsy . . . no."

Nina could hardly believe that the chief was admitting this to her. "I can't believe it."

The chief looked mildly surprised. "You said you had your doubts about suicide."

"I know. I did, but . . . " .

"I told you we wouldn't know for sure until after the autopsy."

"Why didn't you say something?"

"You didn't really give me a chance. And besides, you had a

perfectly reasonable question about his tox screen and I wanted to answer it for you."

"When did you find out about this?" Nina said.

The chief frowned. "I've known this for a couple of days. But frankly, I wanted to wait to tell you until we had some more . . . answers."

"What kinds of answers? Do you know who did it? Who killed him?" she asked.

"Well, I can't tell you too much, but we have a . . . a theory about the suspect. I'm directing the inquiries that are being made and I would prefer to keep certain things quiet right now."

Nina had begun to tremble, and she felt lightheaded. "What inquiries . . . ?" she said. "Nobody has asked me anything. Are you sure you are really investigating this? Because I would expect your men to come and question me. You have to find out who did this, Chief. Just because my father was . . . convicted of a crime is no reason to shortchange him . . . or me . . ."

"Nina," the chief said sharply. "I told you. We're investigating."

Nina was brought up short by the rebuke in his tone. But she gazed at him defiantly. "Somebody has to fight for him," she said.

Chief Perry shook his head. "Look. I want you to know that I find your loyalty to your father very . . . absolutely admirable."

Nina stared at him, disarmed by the compassion in his voice.

He glanced at the framed family photo on his desktop and sighed. "I'm a father myself, Nina. You make me wonder about my own children. Would they stand by me in hard times the way you stood by Duncan Avery?"

"I just want the truth," she said.

"I know. And you're right. I've kept certain things from you. Call me an old . . . fogey. I have a daughter and I was thinking about her. There are certain things I wouldn't want my daughter to know about me in the same circumstances." Perry sighed. "I used my judgment. I thought it would be better to wait until we had some facts, some . . . some proof, before we made you suffer through another humiliation."

Nina's face flamed. "What are you talking about?"

Chief Perry adjusted the perfectly straight knot in his tie and frowned at the ceiling before he spoke. "The spot by the river where your father was found. It's secluded, and it's well known for . . . what you might call assignations of an illegal variety."

"What kind of illegal activity?"

The chief's freckled complexion flushed pink. "I'm talking about prostitution. Over the years we've had a number of arrests for prostitution in that area."

"Prostitution!"

Perry nodded. "We're proceeding on the assumption that your father may have met his death as a result of a rendezvous, shall we say, that turned ugly. It's not uncommon for women in that profession to carry a concealed weapon."

"A prostitute," Nina scoffed. "That's absurd."

Chief Perry looked at her sympathetically. "I know you don't want to think of your father that way, but he was a normal man. A man who'd been kept away from the company of women for many years . . ."

"That's disgusting," said Nina. "You're just determined to make it seem as if he was to blame . . ."

"Nina. We got your aunt's records from the phone company. One of the last calls your father made was to the number of a known prostitute. A hooker with a drug problem whom we've picked up multiple times . . ."

Nina stared at him.

"This is what I didn't want to tell you. We're looking into it, but . . ."

"Maybe he called a wrong number. It could be any-thing . . ."

"Well, as it happens, her number was disconnected because she hadn't been paying her bills . . ."

The disconnected number. Nina suddenly remembered the number from the Post-it note, which she had dialed when she was searching for Duncan.

"We questioned the woman's neighbors. Someone recog-nized Duncan. I guess he went there when he couldn't get her on the phone. A neighbor saw them going off in his . . . your aunt's car. We still haven't been able to locate her. We're work-ing on that."

"Who is it?" Nina demanded.

"I can't tell you that, Nina. But we'll get to the bottom of it. We are investigating and we will continue to investigate until we apprehend a suspect. All right?"

Nina gave a shuddering sigh and shook her head. "I don't know. I don't know what to think. I was so sure . . ."

"Sure of what?" the detective asked.

Nina shrugged. "I thought maybe he . . . I don't know."

"If you have any information that could help us, now's the time to tell me about it," said the chief.

"It's just that . . . he always said that he was innocent. He wasn't the one who killed my mother. I just thought he might have gone looking. You know, stirred things up trying to find Mom's killer . . . I thought it was about that."

Chief Perry gazed at her sadly. "Your mother's killer went to prison, Nina. Your father knew that better than anyone."

13

PARKED in the nursing home lot, Nina sat behind the wheel staring through the drizzling rain at the building, knowing she should go inside and visit her great-aunt. She knew she had neglected Aunt Mary, and she felt guilty about it. But today, despite her guilt, Nina was too depressed to get out of the car. She couldn't make herself do it. She couldn't put on a cheerful face for anyone. Not even Aunt Mary. Not after news like that. Her father had been killed by a prostitute?

What a sordid way for all of this to end, she thought. She did not want to know this about her father. But she couldn't stop thinking about it. For the first time, she felt absolutely furious at Duncan. She knew her anger was inappropriate, that she was blaming the victim, but she couldn't help it. This would be the last chapter of his life story. It was horrible, and unfortunately, as Chief Perry had pointed out, not that difficult to imagine. This was the image of her father she would never be able to erase from her mind, no matter how hard she tried.

Nina glanced at the door to the nursing home, which had swung open. A middle-aged aide in flowered scrubs was wheeling an ancient-looking woman out the door. The aide stopped the wheelchair on the sidewalk under the portico, which was bordered by lavender mums, still blooming. The patient, tiny and wizened, wrapped in a shawl, looked up hopelessly at the drizzling skies.

Despite her own troubles, Nina felt a little pinprick of sympathy. There are worse problems than yours, she reminded herself sternly. Quit feeling sorry for yourself and go visit your aunt. She was there for you when your world collapsed. Nina forced herself to open the car door and step out into the rain.

TWO hours later, Nina dropped her purse on the piano bench and slumped down on the sofa in her aunt's living room. The nursing home visit, greeted with delight by Aunt Mary, had made Nina feel better for a little while, too. But now, back in the gloomy house, she felt the depression descending on her again. What now? she wondered.

Nina's skin prickled as she pictured herself surrounded, hounded by reporters after the police arrested a hooker and charged her with killing her john, Duncan Avery. She knew how it would be. They would ooze fake sympathy, reminding Nina of her faith in her father—the naïve girl who believed that her father could do no wrong.

The only way to escape the curiosity seekers was to go back to New York and disappear into the anonymity of the city. There was probably little time to waste. The arrest could come at any moment. Nina forced herself to get up from the sofa and climb the stairs. She had moved back into her old bedroom, since her father was gone and the clutter from the nearly finished paint job in her aunt's room remained. As she got her clothes out of the closet, she looked down and saw Duncan's bag, still sitting where she had left it on the closet floor, the packet of parole information still visible.

She had brought her father to this house. It was her responsibility to rid the house of any last vestiges of his presence. With a sigh, she pulled his few shirts and the one pair of pants that hung neatly in the sacheted closet off their hangers. She folded them and laid them on the bed. She looked at the book he had left on the nightstand. It was a well-thumbed copy of *Man's Search for Meaning* by Viktor Frankl with a bookmark in it, as if Duncan had been in the process of rereading it and had just set it down. Yeah. Set it down to go in search of a blow job, she thought disgustedly, as she tossed the book on the meager pile of clothes. She noticed that there was a prescription vial on the nightstand also, made out to Duncan Avery. She'd seen it before, but she hadn't thought much about it. Now she recognized it. It was the prescription Andre had told her about. Should I keep this? she wondered. It wasn't as if anybody were ever going to use it. She held the vial over the fabric-covered pink wastebasket and hesitated.

Then she was struck by the meaning of what she was doing. Why in the world are you sorting through these things, she thought, as if some of them were worth packing and saving and others weren't? What, after all, was the point of saving her father's meager belongings? There were already boxes of his books and clothes in Aunt Mary's basement where she had carefully stored them so long ago. What was the use of putting even more stuff down there? Fill up the duffel and throw it directly into the trash.

The realization was satisfying in a bitter sort of way. Clutching the vial, she walked over to the closet and picked the duffel bag up off the floor by the handles. As she lifted it up, the duffel bag felt unexpectedy heavy. What's he got in there? she wondered, carrying it to the bed and setting it down on the bed-spread beside the pile of clothes.

She reached into the bag, rummaged through its contents, and her hand fell on something metallic and cold.

Nina knew what it was before her hand unearthed it and pulled it out of the open zipper. She knew, but she could hard-ly believe it. She was holding a gun. Her father had a gun in that bag. Nina sank down on the edge of the bed, and stared at the pistol in her hand.

She knew nothing about guns, except that they were dead-ly, and that her father was not allowed to possess one. But he did, she thought. Why? Why would he do something so dan-gerous and illegal? There would be no answer, she thought. She would have to live the rest of her life wondering what Duncan Avery was really all about.

Her thoughts traveled back to his trial, and the prosecutor painting a verbal picture of Duncan as a man who appeared dig-nified and respectable, but who gave in frequently to his illicit desires. Sex and violence sprang from the same source, the D.A. said. Didn't it make sense that this man of uncontrollable impulses might have become violent with his wife, a woman he wanted to be rid of?

No, Nina thought. No. She had to draw the line some-where. She couldn't give in to those doubts now. Her faith in her father's innocence had sustained her all these years. If she started to doubt him now, she would only be hurting herself. Duncan was beyond being hurt. No. She couldn't allow this lat-est discovery or the information about the sordid end of his life to call into question everything she had relied on all these years.

Nina stuffed the gun into the canvas duffel bag and piled his clothes on top of it. She zippered the top and carried it down to the kitchen, ready to take it to the trash, where it belonged. There was a big plastic trash can out by Aunt Mary's garage. She would have to pick her way through the puddles in the backyard to get to it. But as she opened the kitchen door and looked out at the dark sky and the rain, she had a sudden, sickening thought. You weren't allowed to throw guns into a trash can. What if some kid found it and killed somebody with it? No, that's why they had those occasional days when people could turn in their firearms to the police with no questions asked.

Jesus, Dad, she thought. You just keep making my life difficult.

Nina sighed. She would have to keep her ears open for one of those occasions and bring the gun to the police station. She definitely did not want to have to answer any questions about it. Meanwhile . . .

She had to put it somewhere. It might as well go down in the basement with his other belongings. With a sigh, Nina closed the back door and walked over to the door to the basement. She flipped the switches at the top of the stairs. The light over the stairs came on, but the basement itself remained dark. Must have burned out, she thought. For a moment she hesitated. She hated going downstairs in the dark. But she knew where Duncan's other belongings were stored. In an area along the near wall. She could reach that without a light. She walked down the stairs and peered, by the light of the staircase bulb, into the dank basement. She could see the cardboard boxes she had left there years ago. With a sigh, she carried the duffel bag over to the stack of boxes.

Her eyes unexpectedly welled with tears as she placed the shabby duffel bag on top of the boxes she had saved for her father when he first went to prison. There would be no further use for any of these things, she thought. He would not be needing them. Maybe once she got rid of the gun, she would give the rest to Goodwill. If they would have it, she thought.

A shrill ring cut through the quiet of the house, and she

jumped. It was the phone upstairs. Oh, no, she thought. What if the police have found that woman? Dammit, I didn't get out of here fast enough, she thought. There was no way to tell who was on the phone. If only there were some way to screen the calls. Aunt Mary had none of the modern conveniences. No answering machine. No Caller ID. Nina stood at the foot of the basement steps, uncertain whether she should run to find out or try to escape the inevitable by letting it ring. As she was pondering her options, the ringing stopped.

Nina breathed a sigh of relief and began to mount the cellar stairs. I'm going to get my stuff and leave, she thought. I'll splurge on a cab to the bus stop.

As she reached the top step and entered the bright kitchen, the phone began to ring again, as if the caller had taken a brief respite and then redialed. Why don't you get an answering machine? Nina wondered, thinking impatiently of her aged aunt. It's the twenty-first century, for God's sake. The phone continued to ring, implacable and demanding.

Leave me alone, she thought, glaring at it. Whoever you are. But she knew there was no escape. If the news was out, she would have to face it. You can do it, she thought. You have a lot of practice being steely. Nina hesitated and then picked up the phone angrily. "What?" she said sharply into the receiver.

"Nina, it's Andre."

For a moment, she felt both relieved and chagrined. She had promised to call him but she had forgotten. She'd forgotten everything but the discovery of Duncan's gun, and the latest information from the police. And now here was Andre on the phone, wanting to know if he had been right. "Hello," she said.

"I hope I'm not bothering you," he said warily.

"No, no," said Nina, feeling instantly apologetic. "I was afraid it might be a reporter on the phone, so I almost didn't answer."

"You need to give me your cell phone number," he said. "Here, I've got a pencil. Give it to me."

Reluctantly, Nina complied. "What do you want?" she asked in a dull voice.

"I just wanted to know—did you go to see the police?"

"Yes," said Nina. "I went. And you were right. He was taking his medication. It wasn't a suicide. My father was murdered."

She heard a sharp intake of breath on the other end of the line.

"But it turned out they already knew that. They even know why," she continued, trying to sound matter-of-fact. "It seems he was murdered by a prostitute. You know, Andre, it was just like you said. He wanted to live every day to the fullest." Her effort to make light of this news fell flat.

Andre did not reply.

She took his silence as a rebuke, and suddenly she felt angry at her father's doctor for urging her to seek out this information, which had proved so humiliating, even though she knew logically that she would have found out anyway, eventually.

"Frankly, I think I might have preferred to believe it was a suicide. Is there anything else?" she demanded.

"Have they made an arrest?" Andre asked.

"Not yet. They're trying to track the woman down. Andre, look, I'm not in the mood to talk, if you don't mind . . ."

"So what makes them think it was a prostitute?" he said.

"She was seen by a neighbor getting into his car outside her house. The neighbor recognized Duncan," said Nina wearily, and realized that she had just referred to her father by his first name, as Patrick always did. "And what else? They found him in a place where people—you know—go to do that sort of thing . . ."

"That's it?" he said. "That's all they know?"

"I don't know. Maybe they have other evidence. I didn't really want all the disgusting details. Look, I appreciate that you came by and tried to be . . . supportive but—"

"But they're sure it was murder. Someone shot him."

Nina tapped on the phone. "Yes. Hello, did you hear me? I have to go."

"Nina, listen . . ." His voice was interrupted by clicking sounds. "Can you hold on a minute? I'm still at the prison," he said.

Before she could reply that she didn't want to hold on he was gone and there was silence on the phone. Nina held the receiver to her ear and closed her eyes. She didn't want to talk anymore. She wanted oblivion. She wanted sleep. She pictured Andre's angular face, his sensual lips and keen dark eyes. He was a very attractive man. He seemed full of life. Maybe at some other time in her life she would have made an effort to get to know him, but not now. What was the use? He was engaged and he was moving back to Santa Fe. And she—she was depleted, depressed. Anything he had to say to her would be about Duncan, and she didn't want to think about Duncan anymore.

Andre came back on the line. "Nina, are you there?"

"Yes," she sighed.

"Crisis averted," he said. "Look, I want to see you, but I can't get there tonight."

"I'm tired, Andre. I'm whipped. I don't really want to talk about all this."

"I know you're tired," he said kindly, and the compassion in his voice made Nina suddenly feel like weeping. "I'm sure you're exhausted."

Her tone softened. This was not the enemy. This was someone who had tried to help. "Oh, Andre, I'm sorry to be so cranky. It was just so awful. The police chief was trying to spare my feelings. He didn't want me to know about my father—you know—meeting his demise in such a . . . degrading way. I can't help feeling . . . It sounds stupid, but I feel . . . like my father betrayed me."

"He didn't betray you, Nina," Andre said calmly. "They've got it all wrong."

14

ANDRE'S words were like a surge of electricity that traveled through the phone wires and jolted her. "Wrong? What do you mean 'wrong'?" Nina cried.

"It's very simple," he said. "The medication he was taking, Nina . . ."

"Yes. What about it," she said irritably.

"It had an unfortunate side effect that's common to a number of antidepressants. It rendered him impotent."

"What? How do you know that? I mean . . ."

"Believe me. I know it for a fact. We discussed it very frankly. Physician to patient. He'd tried some of the other medications that had no sexual side effects, but he got the best results with this particular compound. I asked if it wasn't too high a price to pay and he assured me he could live with it. In prison, of course, it actually made his life somewhat easier. He knew that if he wanted to resume sexual relations, he was going to have to go off the drug for a while."

"But he didn't go off it," she said.

"Exactly," said Andre. "If he planned to seek the services of a prostitute, he knew enough not to take his medication."

Nina held the phone to her ear, but her face felt slack, numb.

"Are you there?" he asked.

"Yes. Are you sure?" she asked.

"Absolutely. We talked about it very frankly."

Nina was silent for a moment. "So you're saying . . .? Then the police must be lying about this. There's no way he would have been with a prostitute."

"No, hold up there. I didn't say that. He may very well have contacted this woman. I'm just saying that he wouldn't have solicited her for sex."

"Why else, then?" Nina cried. "And why would she want to kill him?"

"Look, I don't know, Nina. I don't know all that much about your dad's life. As much as we talked, he never revealed all that much to me. He was kind of a secretive person. Don't take that the wrong way. It's just the way he seemed to me."

Nina sighed. "Oh no. I know exactly what you mean. He was a very private person. I'm sorry. This is not your problem."

"Well, not so fast. I may not know too much about Duncan's comings and goings, but I can tell you this. Often when a guy gets out of this place, the ones who are still inside ask him to deliver messages to their girlfriends or their wives. Sometimes they give a guy money to buy something for her. That kind of thing."

Nina's head was spinning. "Do you think he might have done that?"

"I don't know. It's possible," said Andre.

"So why would the woman want to kill him?"

"Nina, we're not talking about your most rational citizens here. They might have argued about something. The boyfriend might have promised her that Duncan was bringing her a gift—some gift that he didn't actually have for Duncan to deliver. I've heard of that happening. Then the girlfriend blames the poor sucker who comes around for stealing it and the boyfriend looks like a hero. Or Duncan might have delivered bad news and this woman just went off and killed the messenger. I don't know why. I'm just speculating."

"No, of course you don't," Nina said. She was silent for a moment, thinking about what he had told her. Then she took a deep breath. "You know, you've already . . . gone out on a limb for me, Andre. For my father . . . I don't have the right to ask you for anything else. It's just that . . ."

"What?" he asked.

"Could you . . . I mean, you're right there at the prison. Is there any way you could find out if any of the prisoners asked him to do them a favor like that? Asked him to go on some kind of mission?"

Andre sighed.

"I'm sorry," Nina said. "I feel horrible even asking you . . ."

"No, no, it's all right. I know how to find out. It just might take a while to get the answer. And I have to leave tonight for Santa Fe."

"You're going?" Nina asked. "For good?"

"No. I'm not moving till the New Year. But I haven't seen . . . Susan . . . my fiancée . . . in a few months. She asked me to make a trip out. So . . ."

"Never mind," said Nina. "You've got your hands full."

"No, I can put some feelers out here at the prison. If I find out anything I'll call you."

"I would appreciate that so much," she said, relieved.

"It's no problem," he said.

"I'll . . ." She had started to say, "I'll miss you," but then she realized how silly that sounded. She hardly knew the man. "I'll

.always be grateful to you," she said, and the words sounded stiff and insincere to her own ears.

"It sounds as if you feel a little better," he said.

"I do," she said, realizing as he mentioned it that her heart felt considerably lighter than when she had answered the phone. "I know it's ridiculous, but I do."

"Good," he said. "I'm glad."

"When the chief told me about the prostitute, it made my father's death seem like the punch line of a bad joke. I could just imagine everyone nodding their heads and saying, 'Duncan Avery, killed by a hooker. It figures.' "

"Do you mean 'everyone,' or do you mean your brothers?" Andre said.

Nina closed her eyes and smiled. "Touché. My brothers would be the worst. But now—I know it's crazy—but I feel almost as if you've told me my father was still alive. That's stupid, isn't it?"

"Not to me," he said.

I really will miss you, Nina thought. But she didn't say it.

NINA slipped into the back of St. Catherine's Church just as the priest was beginning to bless the host. She searched the sparsely filled pews and caught sight of Jimmy's broad leather-jacketed back, his head bent. Beside him, Rose Connelly worked her rosary. Nina exhaled. She had gotten there in time.

After she had finished talking to Andre, she had called Patrick's house, only to learn from a harried Gemma that he was working late and refusing all calls. Jimmy, on the other hand, had already left Hoffman Flooring when she tried to reach him there. She called the Connellys next, and George told her that Jimmy and Rose had gone to five o'clock Mass and that she could catch up with Jimmy if she hurried. She had rushed out of the house and driven to Lafayette Street, where the old stone church anchored a prime corner on the otherwise commercial street. She parked at a meter, and it wasn't until she reached the neo-Gothic oak doors of the church that she remembered that there was a parking lot in the rear. She never had occasion to drive here. She hadn't spent much time at St. Catherine's as an adult. When they were children, their mother would shepherd them off to church. Jimmy had never wanted to get out of bed in time for Mass. Now, here he was attending midweek, his head meekly bowed. Her brother had changed indeed. In many ways, she thought sadly, he was a stranger to her now. He and Patrick both.

She looked around at the soaring arches of the church, the gorgeous rainbow of colors in the windows, and for a moment she recalled how she had once loved to be here, to sit between her mother and her brothers and listen to the familiar, comforting words of the liturgy. A lifetime ago.

The priest completed the Mass, and the scattered worshippers murmured, "Thanks be to God," and began to rise from their seats. Nina hurried down the side aisle and reached the end of the row just as Rose, followed by Jimmy, was exiting her pew.

"Hi, Mrs. Connelly, Jimmy," she said.

"Nina," Jimmy said, surprised. "I didn't know you still came here."

"I was looking for you. I have to talk to you, Jim."

Jimmy frowned. "I have to drive Rose home," he said.

"It won't take long," said Nina.

Rose was taken aback. "What's so urgent? Can't you come to our house?"

"Yeah, why don't you just come over?" Jimmy asked.

"You can talk there," Rose said.

"It's important," Nina said stiffly to her brother. "Can't you spare a few minutes?"

"Mr. Petrocelli has to clean up the church, you know," Rose said. She pointed toward the lone usher, an old man in a threadbare suit who was going through the pews, folding up the kneelers.

"Okay. I won't be long, Mom," Jimmy said. Nina forced herself not to grimace. It wasn't as if their real mother had died when they were babies. Marsha Avery had raised them. Loved them. And yet Jimmy had given this other woman her honorific.

"All right," Rose sighed. "I'll walk across the street to the Acme. I need a couple of things. I'll meet you at the car." Rose gathered up her coat and her pocketbook, and headed up the center aisle toward the arched doorway of the church.

Nina sat down in the pew and gestured for Jimmy to sit beside her. Jimmy resumed his seat and looked at her quizzically.

"It's about Dad," she said. She saw him flinch, but she ignored it. She felt her heart beating fast as she blurted out the news. "Jimmy, Dad did not kill himself."

Jimmy's eyes widened. "What are you talking about?"

"I mean it," she said. "The police chief told me himself. They know it for a sure. He did not kill himself. He was shot by someone else."

Jimmy stared at her. Nina could see a vein throbbing in his forehead. His skin had turned a pasty white. "Who?" he breathed. "Do they know?"

"They think it was a hooker, but . . . I think they must be wrong about that. They didn't have all the facts. A doctor who works at the prison told me that Dad was taking a medication for depression and that one of the side effects is impotence. Well, suffice it to say, he wasn't looking for a prostitute." Nina could tell from the alarmed, bewildered look on her brother's face that she was racing, rambling, and not making enough sense. "Anyway, the important thing right now is that it wasn't suicide. He was killed by someone else and the police are going to have to start investigating all over again. They don't know who killed him yet, but they *are* going to find out. I'm not going to let up on them until they do."

"Jimmy," came a voice from the darkness at the rear of the church. Nina turned her head and saw Rose trundling down the aisle toward them, wearing her coat and shouldering her pocketbook. Catching Nina's glance, she shook her head. "My memory. I swear, if I don't write it down . . . I got halfway to the store and I remembered that Jimmy needed batteries, but I couldn't remember what kind . . ."

Nina turned and looked at her brother. His eyes were wide and he was clutching at the knit shirt stretched over his broad chest. "Jimmy, what's the matter?"

"I don't know," he gasped. "I don't feel good."

Rose had reached them now, and she let out a cry at the sight of Jimmy's distress. She put an arm around him and spoke loudly in his face. "Jimmy, what is it? Tell me!"

Jimmy clutched the sleeve of Rose's coat. "Mom," he whispered. "Chest pains."

"What?" Nina cried, her own heart flooded with panic. "Oh my God. Oh my God. Where's my phone?" She began to rummage frantically in her pocketbook. "I'll call nine-one-one."

"No," Rose said to her sharply. "That's not necessary. Jimmy, this is not your heart. It's one of your panic attacks. Do as I say. Take a deep breath and try to relax."

Jimmy gazed into her eyes as if he were drowning and Rose held the life preserver.

"Are you sure?" Nina whispered.

"Positive," said Rose calmly, patting Jimmy's back reassuringly. "He used to have them all the time when he was giving up the drugs. It's okay, honey," she encouraged Jimmy. "Think about palm trees. Breathe. You're going to be okay."

Jimmy shook his head and began to inhale. Some color returned to his broad face. "Okay, it's okay. I'm better now."

"See?" said Rose gently. " I told you it was nothing serious."

"Thank goodness," said Nina. "He really scared me."

"I'm an old hand at this," Rose sighed. "Jimmy, where are the keys? Come on. I'll drive us home."

"Are you sure you're all right, Jim?" Nina asked. "I shouldn't have sprung that news on you like that. I didn't mean to upset you."

"You didn't. I'm all right. I don't know what happened." Jimmy's color was returning, although he trembled when he went to stand up.

"I figured you'd be relieved to know it wasn't suicide," said Nina. "I was. And you being a Catholic . . ."

"Sure. It's . . . a big relief. Really. But now—well, you know. Here we go again," he said.

Nina bristled. "Here we go again?"

"Nina, can we talk later? I . . . I need to get home."

"That's right," said Rose briskly. "That's the best place for you. Come on, sweetie. I'm gonna get you to your own bed, where you can lie down. That's all you need. Just a little rest."

"I have a meeting tonight," he said, leaning against Rose, who put an arm around his waist. Jimmy did not turn back to look at Nina.

"We'll get you to your meeting," said Rose. "Leave everything to me."

15

FOR a few minutes, Nina remained in the pew, too unnerved to move. Mr. Petrocelli came up to the pew and looked at her apologetically.

"I need to lock up," he said.

"Oh, all right. I'm sorry," said Nina. She got up and walked to the door of the church, and stepped out into the evening. The lights went off behind her, and the church became dark and tomblike, but the rest of Layfayette Street was still bustling with commerce. Even though it was dark, it was also November, and all the stores were open late for Christmas shopping.

Nina started to walk down the street, thinking about Jimmy's extreme reaction to her news. It was as if the very mention of their father threw him into a tailspin. Obviously, all he wanted to do was put it behind him. If she was honest with herself, she knew Patrick would be equally, or even more, hostile to this news. In her brothers' hearts, Duncan had died a long time ago.

"Hey, look out, lady," said a man dressed in an elf costume. He was giving away fudge samples outside a candy store and Nina had nearly collided with him.

"Sorry," she mumbled. What kinds of holidays would she have this year? I don't want to spend them with my brothers, she thought. I don't want to sit around with their families and pretend to be a part of it. How unbearable that would be. It was a far cry from what she had envisioned for herself. She had been making holiday plans in her mind ever since the news of Duncan's parole. Plans to give her father a celebration that would make up for all those years he had spent in prison. And now . . .

As she walked down the street to the car, she passed Farrell's antiques store and saw, with a mixture of surprise and outrage, that the silver-blue Jaguar was once again parked in front of it.

Patrick, you lowlife, she thought. She hesitated, and then made up her mind. She had wanted to talk to her brother. In her bitter state of mind, it seemed that this would be the perfect opportunity.

A bell tinkled as Nina opened the door to the antiques shop. A Nordic-looking young man in a fitted blue dress shirt with a white collar was waiting on a couple who were inspecting an ormolu clock. He looked up at Nina as she came in the store. "-I'll be with you shortly," he said in a European-sounding accent.

"I'm not . . ." she began to protest, but he had already turned away. Nina wondered if the salesman could tell by the way she was dressed that there was nothing in this store that she could afford, even if she were here to shop. The elegant store was lit with ornate crystal chandeliers. Savonnerie rugs were spread out beneath a wealth of objects and furniture, large and small, their surfaces a welter of gilt and crystal, enamel and shining wood. The whole place exuded luxury and good taste.

Nina pretended to look around at the furniture while she made a circuit of the store, although she was actually looking to catch a glimpse of her brother with Lindsay Farrell. It angered her when she thought of how judgmental Patrick had been about their father. "He was sleeping with the woman next door," Patrick had reminded her at the parole hearing. "How can you believe in him?"

Look who's talking, Nina thought bitterly. She glanced at her watch and almost immediately the young blond man approached her, assessing her with his glacial blue eyes.

"Is there anything I can show you while my other customers are deciding . . . ?"

"Actually," said Nina, "I'm looking for Lindsay. Is she here, by any chance?"

The blond man glanced toward the back the store. "I believe she's in the office. Let me go check for you."

"Oh, Arne," called the woman across the sales floor, stroking the ormolu clock posessively. The salesman looked back at her.

"That's all right," said Nina. "You take care of them. I'll find her." She began to walk toward the back, holding her satchel bag close to her jacket so that she wouldn't accidentally brush up against some priceless object and knock it over. At the back of the store there was an open doorway with a hall. One of the frosted glass doors down the hall was illuminated by a light behind it. Nina hesitated and then knocked.

There was some shuffling behind the door, and then it was opened by Lindsay Farrell, her skin glowing, her huge blue eyes looking impatient. Tonight she was a vision in a formfitting pink and gray tweed Chanel-style suit with a deep V neck that showed her cleavage. Beneath the short skirt she wore silvery stockings on her killer legs.

"Lindsay," said Nina. "I was looking for you."

Lindsay looked vaguely uneasy. "Nina," she said.

"Could I just talk to you for a few minutes?" Nina asked.

"I'm busy right now," said Lindsay.

"It won't take long," said Nina. Glancing over Lindsay's shoulder, she recognized the graying good-looking man emerging from the private bathroom. "Hello, Patrick," Nina said.

Lindsay looked down at the pointy toes of her gray calfskin stilettos and then opened the door wide. Patrick was rolling down his shirtsleeves, and his jacket was draped on a chair back. He looked up and faced his sister. "Nina. What are you doing here?" he asked, clearly surprised to see her. He began to pull on his jacket. "I thought you went back to New York."

"I was looking for you. I called Gemma and she told me you were working late. Then I saw your car parked outside," she said pointedly. Nina's heart was in a tumult. She couldn't say what she wanted to say. She wanted to accuse her brother of betraying Gemma. But it wasn't as if she had found him in bed with Lindsay. She knew what she was seeing, but she felt utterly tongue-tied when it came to accusation. "I have to talk to you," said Nina, looking from her brother's florid face to the glamorous antiques dealer.

Patrick sighed and turned to Lindsay. "I'd better go. I'll see you later," he said. He turned back to Nina. "Come with me," he said, putting a hand under her arm.

Nina shook him off. "Don't tell me what to do. Don't touch me."

Patrick glared at her and dropped his hand. "Fine. I'll follow you."

"You two can talk right here," Lindsay said. "I have customers to attend to."

"I don't want to run you out of your office," said Patrick.

"Really," said Lindsay, pulling the door open. "It's no problem. Be my guest." Before Patrick could protest any further,

Lindsay went out and pulled the door shut after her. Patrick turned and looked at his sister.

Nina returned his gaze balefully and stood behind the gilt-edged armchair with a needlepointed back and seat where his jacket had recently been draped. "I hope you know what you're doing, Patrick."

Patrick walked around and sat down behind the gleaming burlwood escritoire covered with accounting books that served as Lindsay's desk. He drummed his fingertips on the edge of the desk and did not look at her. "What couldn't wait, Nina?"

Patrick's relationship with Lindsay is none of your business, Nina thought. Just tell him what you came to say and get this over with. She took a deep breath. "All right. I suppose you're going to tell me that you don't care about this, but I thought you should know. The police have now determined that Dad did not commit suicide. It was murder, as I suspected." She could not keep herself from adding that last little dig.

Patrick's ruddy face paled visibly but otherwise he showed no expression. "Really," he said flatly. "Who killed him?"

"They don't know that yet. But they're investigating . . ."

Patrick stared into space without speaking.

Nina studied her brother's face. "What are you thinking?" she asked.

Patrick turned his head and looked at her. "I guess I wasn't the only one who hated him," he said.

"Oh, Patrick," said Nina in disgust. "He was your father, for God's sake. Somebody murdered him. Don't you have the . . . the decency to care?"

Patrick leaned across Lindsay's desk and gazed earnestly up at his sister. "Nina," he said. "Suicide, murder? What difference does it make? He got what he deserved. You have got to let go of this crap about Duncan. You know I don't want to hear about it. You know that."

Nina shook her head. Why had she thought it might matter to him? He was as hard-hearted as ever. She wanted to hurt him back, to make him squirm. But at the last minute, she wasn't able to be as harsh as he was. Her accusation came out sounding feeble. "Yeah, I can see where your mind is. Nice work, Patrick."

"You don't see anything . . ." he started to say in a warning tone.

But she did not wait for him to finish. She left the office, slamming the door. Lindsay, who was changing the shade on a lamp whose base was a porcelain shepherdess, looked up as Nina emerged from the office.

"Nina?" she said. "Is everything all right?"

Nina avoided her gaze. "Just great," Nina said.

"Look," Lindsay said, looking around cautiously. "I don't know how much Patrick has told you . . ."

"Patrick doesn't confide in me," Nina snapped.

"But I know he feels close to you," Lindsay persisted. "And I'm sure you know that Patrick is . . . um . . . very unhappy. And I don't think it's a good idea to live that way. Not if you can help it." Lindsay peered at her with narrowed eyes. "Has he said anything to you about his plans?"

Nina resisted the urge to slap her. "I don't care about his plans," she said indignantly. "If you want to know about Patrick's intentions you'll have to ask him yourself. I have a lot more important things to worry about. Now, if you'll excuse me, I need some air."

"He is your brother," said Lindsay.

"Don't remind me," said Nina. Turning her back on Lindsay, she made her way through the store as quickly as she could without upending some valuable piece of merchandise. She could feel the curious gaze of the salesman and his customer following her. She didn't care. Poor Patrick, she thought.

Patrick wasn't happy? What about Gemma? Gemma had stuck with Patrick through thick and thin and this was her reward. A husband who wasn't happy and was busy making other arrangements. Why should I be surprised? she thought. How quickly had he turned on his own father? Betrayal came as naturally to Patrick as breathing. Nina pulled the door to the antiques store closed with more force than she should have, and heard the sound of the crystals on the sparkling chandeliers tinkling in her wake.

16

THE stores on Lafayette Street were just beginning to open, their awnings whipped by the wind, when Nina hurried, on foot, toward the police station the next morning. She had to wait while the security officers pawed through her overnight bag, only to be disappointed to learn from the sergeant on duty that Chief Perry was at a regional meeting and would not be back in the office until much later in the day. Was there someone else who could help her? the sergeant asked.

Nina thought about it for a minute. She didn't want to have to explain the whole thing to a stranger. Perhaps she ought to stay in Hoffman until the next day. But then she chided herself. She had an appointment she had to keep. When she had checked her messages the night before there was an urgent summons from Len, her agent, telling her that the ad agency was ready to begin production on the floor wax commercials and she needed to get back to New York.

In a way it was a relief. Nina was glad to have a reason to go back. She didn't even feel like herself in this town, and she definitely needed to get to work and start making money. But she wanted to tell Chief Perry what she had learned about her father's medication, and the resulting improbability of his having had a rendezvous for sex.

"Miss?" the sergeant prodded.

Oh hell, Nina thought. This job might be lucrative, depending on how successful the commercial proved to be. At any rate, it was a job and she had to take it. It wasn't as if her father's death had left her an heiress. He didn't even have life insurance. Her discussion with Chief Perry would have to wait. If they found the prostitute in the meantime, they would learn about Duncan from her.

"No, I'll come back," she told the sergeant. She walked glumly out of the station and back into the biting wind of a day that was gray and more like winter than autumn. She buttoned her leather jacket and wound her long rose-and-teal-colored challis scarf more tightly around her neck. As she walked down the steps to the sidewalk between the parking lot and the station house, she heard someone calling her name and looked up.

The man who hailed her was wearing a wool cap, but when he took it off and smiled at her, she saw that it was Lieutenant Hagen. The retired guy, she thought, ready to spend another day hanging around the working guys. "Hello, Lieutenant," she said gently, deliberately using his old title. A gust of wind whipped her black hair in front of her face but she pushed it away with a gloved hand as Hagen, dapper in a corduroy jacket and neatly pressed pants, approached her on the sidewalk.

"Nina, I'm glad I ran into you," he said. "I wanted to talk to you the other day, but you were busy with the chief. I want you to know I was very sorry to hear about your father's death. I mean that sincerely."

"Thank you," said Nina politely, although she couldn't help thinking about the fact that this man had been instrumental in putting her father in prison. It was his job, after all, she reminded herself. She didn't hate him for it. "That's nice of you to say."

"Yeah," said Hagen, jamming his hands in his pockets. "It's kind of strange."

Nina glanced up Lafayette Street to see if there was any sign of the bus. She didn't want to miss this one. She'd have to wait an hour until the next. "What is?" she asked distractedly, afraid the retired detective with not enough to do might be getting ready to wax philosophical.

"About your dad. He came to see me, you know," Hagen said.

Nina held her windblown hair back and stared at him. "He did? When?"

"Well, it must have been just after he got back to town here. A lot of cops have unlisted numbers, but I had teenagers so I keep mine in the book. Anyway, he looked it up and gave me a call. After he identified himself, I wondered for a moment if he was into some kind of revenge thing . . ."

"What did he want?" Nina interrupted.

"Well, he assured me that he meant me no harm, so I talked to him. He started right in on how he never was the one who killed your mother. I told him, you know, Doc, this is all water under the bridge. But he was really fired up about it. He wanted to talk about the investigation."

"He did? What about it?" Nina asked.

Hagen nodded and put his cap back on, shivering. "Damn, it's freezing out here. I'd ask you to come into the station, but it's not really my place to invite people inside anymore." He glanced at his watch. "I'm meeting a buddy of mine here for coffee soon or I'd . . ."

Nina interrupted him. "What did my father want to talk about?"

Hagen pressed his lips together and shook his head. "He wanted me to review the files. I told him I didn't have the files, that they were in the station. I said to him, you know, why are you bothering about this? I mean, you're a free man now. You've done your time. Why waste your time on this? But your father was determined to . . . uh . . . look into the matter. Clear his name, he said." Lieutenant Hagen nodded, and peered into the distance. "Wanted to clear his name."

Nina shivered, only partly from the chilly breeze. "But he told me he wasn't optimistic about that because it was all so long ago," she said.

Hagen shrugged. "He said he had some brand-new information."

"What information?" Nina demanded.

"I don't know. He didn't say. Anyway, I got to thinking about it and I thought, you know, he had no real reason to want to dig the whole thing up. He was out of prison. It wasn't a question of trying to regain his freedom . . ."

Nina kept picturing her father's weary face, and remembered so clearly that he had said there was little chance of turning up anything new after all these years, after all the professional detectives had failed. So what had changed?

"I thought it over and I finally decided to try to help him. I mean, you can never tell. You try to make sure you do your job right, but mistakes are made sometimes. It's been known to happen."

Nina stared at him. "You think you made a mistake in my father's case?"

Hagen held up his veiny white hands. "Not as far as I know. But we all know about cases where it happened. Anyway, I did go to my buddy in Records. I've still got a lot of friends here. My buddy let me take a look at the file."

"Did you find anything there that he thought might be helpful?" Nina asked eagerly.

Hagen shook his head sadly. "No. After I went over all the notes and photos and whatnot, I tried to get in touch with your dad. But then I heard about . . . you know, that he . . . um . . . shot himself. I felt bad about it. But I guess it wouldn't have made any difference. I didn't realize he was so down."

Nina stared at him. "He didn't kill himself," she said. "Don't you know that? The police determined that it was murder."

Hagen was indignant. "Who said that?"

"Chief Perry told me," said Nina with satisfaction. "The other morning when I ran into you. I had begun to doubt the whole suicide idea, so I came in to talk to Chief Perry about it. That's when he told me that the autopsy showed it was actually murder and not suicide at all."

"Nobody told me that," said Hagen ruefully. The old man had a flinty, indignant look in his eye. Even though he was officially out of the loop, he clearly felt entitled to inside information. "That was my case," he said.

Nina had a feeling that she might be able to win him to her cause. She was happy to tell him what she knew. "They're looking for some prostitute they think killed him, but I happen to know that my father wasn't in the market for the services of a prostitute. He was taking a medication that made him . . . that rendered him impotent."

"Oh jeez," said Hagen, wincing sympathetically. "Jeez. I didn't know about any of that. Your father didn't say a word. How about that?"

Nina studied Hagen's aging face. He looked uneasy, and as if he felt guilty. "Well, he didn't tell me either. His doctor told me."

"Hmmm. How about that?" Hagen repeated ruminatively.

Nina glanced up the street again. Still no sign of the bus, but she knew she had to hurry. "I have to go. I'm in a hurry right now, but the next time . . . when I'm back here I'd like . . . if it would be all right . . . Do you think I could see that file—the one on my mother's investigation? I'd really like to see it."

Hagen avoided her gaze. "Yeah. Well, it's kind of grisly stuff. You need a strong stomach . . ."

"Detective Hagen, I found my mother's body. I walked into that kitchen and stepped in the blood . . ."

"You're right, you're right," he said.

Nina fished in her satchel and pulled out one of her cards. "I'm going back to New York for a few days, but I'll come back whenever it's convenient. Call me, won't you? If you have a chance. I would really appreciate it. Oh damn, there's the bus."

Nina began to run. Hagen studied the card and then tucked it carefully into the inner pocket of his corduroy jacket.

17

"GODDAMMIT," Nina cried, as the bus driver, ignoring her frantic signals, sailed up the street toward the turnoff for the parkway. She had narrowly missed being at the bus stop in time. Would it have killed him to stop? she thought angrily. Nobody will give you a break in this world anymore. Shaking her head, she began trudging up the avenue cursing the fact that she would now have to rush to get to the shoot on time.

At that moment, a burgundy-colored Honda pulled up in the road beside her and stopped. The driver lowered the window and hailed her. Nina looked up and saw Gemma waving at her. Nina blushed, immediately thinking of her encounter with Patrick at Lindsay's store. Had Gemma found out somehow? Was she about to ask about Patrick and Lindsay? Nina felt her stomach churning at the prospect of lying for Patrick's sake. She could see that Gemma was calling to her, but the wind made it difficult to hear. Nina stepped off the curb and bent over so that her face was beside the open window.

"Nina, are you going into the city?" Gemma asked.

Nina nodded. "Eventually. I just missed the bus."

"Do you want a ride? We're on our way there. I can give you a lift."

"You could? Are you sure?"

"Sure. I'm going right into Manhattan," said Gemma.

"That would be great," said Nina, truly relieved.

The driver behind Gemma honked his horn.

"Hop in," said Gemma, pushing the button that unlocked the doors. Nina opened the back door and threw her bag in the well of the backseat. She bent down and smiled at the twins, who were buckled into their seats. "Hi, guys."

Simon, who had a mouthful of cookies, attempted to smile and say, "Hi, Aunt Nina." In the process he sprayed his brother with cookie crumbs. Cody whacked Simon with a plastic action figure and Simon shrieked indignantly and then began to cough.

"Cody, stop it," cried Gemma.

Before the fight could begin in earnest, Nina pointed out the window on the street side. "Look, you guys, look out there. A motorcycle." Both boys quickly swiveled their heads to look, as if the hog were an exotic bird.

Nina slammed the door, walked around to the passenger side, and slid into the front seat, brushing her tangled, windblown hair back off her face. "Gemma, you are a lifesaver," she said.

Gemma was looking in the rearview mirror, and gliding out into the traffic. "I'm glad we saw you. I thought you must be headed to the bus."

Nina nodded. "I have a commercial shoot today and I was going to catch the last bus, but I was waylaid at the police station. I thought I'd have to wait another hour."

"At the police station? What was that all about?" Gemma asked.

"Well, it was about my dad," said Nina. "Did Patrick tell you . . . ?"

"Tell me what?" Gemma asked.

She really doesn't know, Nina thought. Immediately, she regretted mentioning Patrick. How could he keep the information that Duncan had been murdered from his own wife? Didn't they communicate at all? "I was there to find out if there were any new developments," Nina said carefully. "They're now working on the assumption that my dad did *not* commit suicide. They think he was murdered."

"Murdered," Gemma exclaimed.

"Yes," said Nina. "They're sure now that it was murder."

"My God," said Gemma. "Do they know who . . . ?"

"No." Nina didn't want to tell the whole seamy story in front of the twins. But she felt as if Gemma was entitled to know. She was a part of the family. Nina tried to think how best to explain it.

Gemma interrupted her thoughts. "Does Patrick know this?"

Nina could hear the anxiety in her voice. The idea that her husband might not give her such a significant piece of information was beginning to dawn on her. Gemma clutched the wheel and stared straight ahead, but Nina could see that her bony wrists were trembling.

"Just the barest details," said Nina, trying to sound reassuring. "There's very little to know at this point." Nina was a little taken aback that Gemma would be more interested in her husband's mind-set than in learning about Duncan's murder. Of course, Duncan was a stranger to her. A man she barely knew. Patrick was the one she lived for. Nina thought of Patrick, caught in Lindsay's office, defying his sister to criticize his behavior. She felt as if she were watching a marriage heading toward the edge of a cliff. It's not your business, she reminded herself. They have to work out their own problems.

"I don't understand your brother no matter how hard I try," Gemma said.

Nina glanced over at Gemma's drawn, anxious-looking face and felt a stab of pity for her. "My brother," Nina said, with as much circumspection as she could muster, "can be very self-centered."

The twins, who had been fairly quiet, suddenly erupted into a battle. Gemma glanced in the rearview mirror. "Stop," she yelled. "Please."

Nina swiveled around in her seat and saw that Simon was hoarding several toys, impervious to his brother's shrieking. Nina rapped him on the knee. "Hey! Give your brother one of those," she said.

"This is mine," Simon started to protest.

"I don't want to hear about it," said Nina. "Just pick one and give it to him. Or *I'll* pick one." Nina turned back around in her seat. Before Gemma could say any more about Patrick, Nina changed the subject. "So, you guys having a day in the city?" she asked.

"No," said Gemma. "We're going to pick up the new house-keeper."

"The new housekeeper," said Nina, surprised. "What happened to Elena?"

"She had to rush back to Panama. Her sister was in an accident."

"Oh, that's too bad," said Nina, remembering the Mass card, the compassion in Elena's eyes.

"The new person is named Cora," Gemma said.

NINA slammed the car door with effusive thanks and rushed into her building and up to her apartment to get dressed for her appointment at the studio in SoHo. She didn't bother with any makeup. The photographer would have his own makeup artist at the studio. Her nerves were jangled by the time she caught a cab and got back downtown, but she arrived on time, and allowed herself to be moved about numbly, like a prop, while technicians adjusted lighting and tried different makeup and outfits on her and the photographer shot endless Polaroids, which he and the director then mulled over. Nina learned her few lines and then was leafing through a magazine when she thought she heard her cell phone ring in her satchel on the floor. She could hardly tell if it was hers, given the general hubbub in the studio. As she reached into her bag she saw two set carpenters and a makeup artist reach for their phones at the same time. Nina pulled out her ringing phone as if it were a grab bag prize, while the others tucked theirs back away in disappointment.

"Nina?"

Her heart leaped. "Andre? How are you? Where are you?"

"I'm in Sante Fe. I just got here. Listen . . ."

"How was the trip?" she asked.

"All right," he said, deflecting her question and abruptly getting down to business. "I just wanted to tell you—I did what I said I'd do. I checked around with my . . . contacts among the prison population. No luck there. Nobody had given anything to Duncan to deliver. A lot of the guys were quite broken up about your dad's death, by the way."

"Thanks. Thanks for trying. I found out from Detective Hagen—he's the detective who worked on my mother's case— that my dad *was* trying to track down information about my mother's . . . murder. He told Detective Hagen that he had some new imformation."

Andre was silent for a moment. "Did he say what it was?"

"He didn't know," said Nina.

"Do you think that might be related to his murder?" he asked.

Nina hesitated, then finally admitted it to herself, and said, "I think it's possible. Don't you?" She felt a sudden, overwhelming closeness to Andre, the only other person who seemed to really care about what had happened to Duncan Avery.

"Well, it might be. If it is, you have to be very careful, Nina."

"I suppose," she said.

"It worries me," he went on. "Because if Duncan was killed for stirring this whole thing up . . ."

She smiled, happy in spite of herself to think that he might be worried about her. "I know, I know. Don't worry. I'm not even in Hoffman. I'm in New York on a job right now . . ."

"Nina, can you join us?" the director called out with an edge in his voice.

"Andre, they need me. I have to go. Can I call you back?"

"I didn't mean to interrupt," she heard him say as he ended the call.

The day drew to a close without a single foot of actual film having been shot, and the director announced that they would have to postpone shooting for three days. When Nina got back to the apartment, it was growing dark, and gloom seemed to have settled over her spirits as well. She sat down in an armchair in the living room and stared out at the city lights, which were winking on all over the skyline as evening fell. It was good to be back in the city, she reminded herself. She felt at home here. I should call someone, she thought. Go out to dinner. The thought of getting ready was exhausting, but her friend Francine lived just around the corner on Amsterdam. Francine worked for a newsmagazine and always had lots of great stories, not to mention romantic troubles. They could go to a neighborhood place, where all she needed to do to get ready was to comb her hair. They could drink some wine and catch up over Thai food or a burger. She dialed Francine's number and waited while it rang. When the machine came on, Nina hesitated, and then hung up.

She could try her friend Sara, who lived in Tribeca, but it seemed too much like work to go all the way downtown. Maybe she was better off staying in, anyway. She needed her beauty sleep. Once she and her friends got talking they could stay out late, and she could end up drinking more wine than she intended. If she stayed in, she could have one glass, an omelette, and go to bed early. There was an open call she wanted to go to tomorrow. Nina sat back down in the living room. She found her mind wandering to Andre. She closed her eyes and felt a little weak at the thought of him. Then she shook her head and opened her eyes. Animal attraction to a stranger, she thought. An *engaged* stranger. Even though she thought he might feel it, too, it didn't mean anything. He was already taken.

Just then the phone rang, and she jumped. Andre, she thought, her heart lifting. She rushed to pick it up. "Hello?"

"Nina? This is Frank Hagen."

"Lieutenant Hagen?" She felt curious and alarmed all at once.

"Yeah. Look, after what we talked about this morning, I decided to ask a few questions of my own. I thought you might want to know. It seems they already found that woman they were looking for. The hooker."

"They did?" Nina cried. "Was she . . . did she tell them what my dad wanted? Why he was with her?"

"No," he said with a sigh. "And she's not gonna be telling them anything. They found her in the morgue."

"She's dead?" Nina's heart skipped a beat.

"Yup," said Frank. "It turns out she's been in the hospital for the last week. She was admitted with pneumonia. Nobody knew where she was because she kept quiet about having AIDS. I guess she figured it was bad for business. Anyway, from what I heard, she wasn't too good about taking care of herself. She was more interested in scoring some crack than in taking her AIDS cocktail, so when the pneumonia hit she couldn't fight it off and she checked out."

"Checked out, like . . .?"

"Like died," said Frank bluntly.

"Shit. Pardon my language," said Nina.

"Yeah, Chief Perry's put 'case closed' to it," said Frank sarcastically.

"But he can't. My dad didn't. . ."

"I tried to tell him they were barking up the wrong tree, but he wasn't interested," said Hagen. "He reminded me that I was retired and that the force could get along just fine without my help."

Nina could easily picture it. She had heard the chief express disdain for the retired detective with too little to do. "So that's it?" she protested.

"Well, not exactly. It wasn't a total loss. You see, the hooker's name was Perdita Maxwell. It's one of those names you don't forget," said Frank Hagen with a chuckle. "I recognized it the minute I heard it."

"What about it?" Nina asked, frowning.

"I recognized it because she was one of the many people we interviewed when your mother was murdered," said Hagen. "Perdita Maxwell, that was the name she used for customers. Her real name was Penny. Penelope Mears. Does that ring a bell? She was the mother of that druggie friend of your brother's. The one who thought he was a rock-and-roll star. Calvin Mears."

Nina's heart started to pound. She sat up straight, clutching the phone. "Calvin Mears? Jimmy's friend."

"That's the one," said Frank Hagen. "I looked it up in the file to be sure, but I knew the minute I heard the name."

"My father was looking for Calvin's mother?" she said.

"My guess is, he was trying to locate Calvin," said Hagen.

"Right. Of course," she breathed.

"But," Frank cautioned, "Calvin Mears is long gone. He had to leave town years ago. He was involved with some girl who died of an overdose."

"Yes. I remember Jimmy saying something about that," said Nina. "Did he give her the overdose?"

"Well, he was definitely on the scene when it happened. It was one of those things where everybody knew but nobody was saying anything," said Frank, in a tone of reminiscence. "We picked Mears up for it but we had to let him go. We couldn't really make anything stick. Not long after that, Mears disappeared."

"But his mother probably knew where he was," Nina said, thinking out loud.

"Probably," Frank Hagen agreed.

They were both silent for a moment.

"You know . . ." said Nina.

"What's that?" Hagen asked.

"Well, I'm just thinking. If Mears finds out that his mother died, he might come back. You know, just to pay his respects. Don't you think?"

"I doubt it," said Hagen. "That girl that died? Keefer was her name. Her father wanted revenge. Keefer let everybody know that he was going to kill Mears if he got a hold of him. Mears knows better than to come back."

"Dammit. What did my father want with Calvin Mears?" she mused aloud.

"I don't know. Ask your brother."

Immediately, Nina remembered Jimmy telling her on the

way to the funeral that he had paid Duncan a visit. He had insisted that they didn't discuss anything important. He certainly hadn't mentioned the name of Calvin Mears. "I believe I will," she said.

"If you want, I can go talk to him," Frank said.

Nina pictured Jimmy hyperventilating in the church when she told him that Duncan had been murdered. "No," she said. "I'll talk to him." The thought of Jimmy pretending not to know anything filled her with fury. Was he protecting Calvin Mears at the expense of his family? Could he have stooped that low?

"It might be a good idea to have someone else there," said Frank.

Nina felt as if her heart had turned to stone. "Thank you, Lieutenant," she said. "I appreciate your help. But I'll deal with my brother."

18

By ten o'clock the next morning, Nina arrived at her aunt's house. She went inside only long enough to drop her bag on the piano bench and pick up the car keys. She looked around, knowing there was housekeeping she should do, but not now. Now she had to find Jimmy. She started out to the Volvo. The day's newspaper, still in its sleeve, was lodged in a tangle of bushes near the driveway. She tucked it under her arm, unlocked the car door, and tossed the paper on the seat beside her. In fifteen minutes, including a stop for gas, she was climbing the wooden steps and ringing the bell of the Connellys' neat bungalow.

George Connelly came to the door. "Nina," he exclaimed. "I don't see you for years and now it's getting to be an everyday thing."

"Hi, Mr. . . . George. Is my brother here?"

George frowned. "No, he's not here. I don't know where he is."

"Isn't this his day off?" said Nina.

"Yeah," said George. "We take the same day off. Planned it that way so we could spend some time together. But I got up today and he was gone. Rose probably knows where he is, but she left me a note that she'd gone to the store. Do you want to come in and wait? She should be back . . . Oh, wait a minute— here she comes now." He waved as Rose's car pulled into the driveway. "Let me help her," he said. "She's got groceries."

Before Nina could reply, he was off the porch and down the steps, meeting his wife by the trunk of her car. Nina watched as he lifted the bags out of Rose's arms and insisted that she precede him into the house. They walked up the path chatting amiably about someone Rose had seen at the grocery store.

"Nina, could you hold that door open?" George asked.

Rose's smile faded as she looked up at Nina in the doorway. "Well, Nina."

"Hello, Mrs. Connelly."

"She's looking for Jim, honey," said George. "Do you know where he went?"

Rose stopped just inside the porch door, holding a paper sack as if it were a baby in her arms. "No, I don't."

I don't believe you, Nina thought.

"Can I give him a message when he comes back?" Rose asked.

"This is . . . something personal," said Nina stiffly.

"I hope this isn't more about your father. I only say that because after what happened in church the other day, Jimmy was quite upset," said Rose. "And he doesn't need that. He has his own struggles and he's done a magnificent job. He doesn't need to be constantly reminded about unpleasant things."

"Unpleasant things?" Nina cried. "Both of our parents have been murdered. You can't very well just forget that."

"Yes, we read that in the paper. Now they think your father was murdered," said George. "Terrible. That poor man."

"I don't expect Jimmy to forget it," said Rose sternly. "But Jimmy has come a long way, and I don't want anything to drag him down again."

"You mean, like me," Nina said bitterly. Her face flamed. She wanted to start shouting at Rose Connelly that it was none of her business what Nina said to her own brother, but years of being cautioned to respect her elders inhibited her, and she kept silent.

"Don't take that the wrong way, Nina," said George soothingly, giving his wife a reproving glance. "We may be a little overbearing when it comes to Jim. It's been such a struggle for him. And he's like a son to us. You know that. We're very aware that he doesn't cope well with turmoil in his life."

"I do know that," said Nina, a note of sharpness in her tone.

Rose looked at Nina sympathetically. "I didn't mean to offend you, Nina," she said. "I could never forget all you children have suffered. And please believe me, I'm only thinking of your welfare. The both of you. It's not healthy for you either, Nina. I think you might need to talk to a counselor or someone about this anger of yours. Before you let it ruin your life."

"My life is fine," said Nina.

"Well, I'm not going to tell you what to do. You're a grown woman," Rose said. "But I'd prefer if you didn't get Jimmy involved."

Involved? Nina thought. Isn't Jimmy an adult? she wanted to demand. But she already knew the answer. It was as if Jimmy had become a child again, in the family he really wanted to belong to.

"So you won't tell me where he is," said Nina.

Rose looked at her with a tranquil gaze. "I told you. I don't know where he is, Nina. He doesn't tell me everything he does."

"You could try the gym. He's often there," said George, trying to be helpful. "Or the church. He helps out there. He might be at a meeting. Usually he goes to the meetings at the Fellowship Hall of the Presbyterian Church. At any rate, we'll let him know you were here," George said, more gently, "when he comes home."

"Thanks," said Nina. Thanks for nothing, she thought.

"We'll pray for you," Rose said.

AN hour of driving from one of the places George had mentioned to another yielded no clues to Jimmy's whereabouts. When she stopped at a light opposite the Claremont Diner Nina's stomach rumbled and she suddenly realized that she was hungry. She'd been in such a hurry to get the bus at Port Authority that she hadn't even had a chance to pick up something for breakfast. Part of her was tempted to keep on looking, but physically she was running out of gas. She pulled into the lot and parked. For a moment, she recalled the night of her father's funeral, when she had come here with Andre. She wondered when he would get back, and then she reminded herself that his life was no business of hers.

As she started to get out of the car she saw the newspaper on the seat beside her and decided to bring it in with her. It would be something to do while she waited for her order. Maybe she would find an article in it about the police investigation of her father's death.

Inside the diner, she took a two-person table by the window and waved away the giant menu, asking the waitress for a roll and coffee. She pulled the plastic sleeve off the local paper and unfolded it, paging through it. There was a brief article about Duncan headlined, "Woman sought in Avery murder inquiry dies in hospital." Nina pounced on the article and read it, but it left her feeling more frustrated than ever. All it said was that Perdita Maxwell, a.k.a. Penelope Mears, whom police believed may have been involved in the death of

Duncan Avery, had died in the hospital from pneumonia, complicated by AIDS. Nothing more was said about the investigation except that it was ongoing. Instead, the newspaper devoted several column inches to rehashing the murder of Marsha Avery and Duncan's conviction. Nina flipped the page impatiently.

The waitress brought her order, and Nina ate, her eyes glazing over as she scanned the Kiwanis Club photos and editorials about property taxes. But when she came to the obituary page, she stopped short.

"Mears, Penelope, 47," read a small headline over a paragraph, without a photo, near the bottom of the page. The obit offered only the briefest, most sanitized summary of a life Nina now knew to be rather sordid. Penelope's occupation was listed as massage therapist, and her only surviving family was a married sister named Sally Jenkins living in Seaside Park, N.J., and one son, Calvin, of Los Angeles. Nina tried to put a face to the name of Calvin's mother, but she couldn't remember ever meeting her. When she was a kid, she remembered the adults talking about Mrs. Mears as a mother who didn't care what kind of trouble her son got into. Nina had always somehow understood that about her, but she'd never realized what it was that Mrs. Mears had done for a living. It must have been a well-kept secret at the time. She wondered if her own parents had known the truth about Calvin's mother. Nina read over the funeral arrangements, and then, with a start, she looked again at the date and time listed. She glanced up at the clock over the diner counter. This was an opportunity. Maybe. She hesitated, remembering what Frank Hagen had said—that Calvin wouldn't dare show his face in Hoffman because of that vengeful father. But it was surely worth a try.

• • •

BY the time she got to the funeral home, there were only two cars in the parking lot. A ponytailed attendant in a shiny suit, standing under the portico outside the doors, told her that the Mears mourners had already left for the cemetery.

"You can catch them if you hurry," he said.

Nina got back in the Volvo and drove as fast as she dared to the stone pillars that marked the entrance to Shadywood Cemetery. She drove slowly, looking right and left for signs of life among the quiet markers. She passed a black Dodge pickup truck with tinted windows parked by the side of the road. Nina glanced over and saw that someone was sitting in the car. She looked away, not wanting to intrude on their grief, and continued on along the winding road through the cemetery.

The small party of mourners was not hard to spot. They were on a hillside that sloped up from the road. Nina parked the Volvo and got out, walking up to where the knot of people were standing. The blustery gray November wind rattled the few leaves left on the trees around them, and a shower of flakes, looking more like cinders than snow, whirled around the tiny group. The priest was intoning a blessing while a sad-eyed middle-aged woman in a navy blue dress and a gray coat chewed the inside of her mouth. Beisde her, a man in a checked sport coat and a fedora stood with his feet apart, his hands folded in front of him, in a straight-backed stance.

There were two other women, both dressed in black, one a bleached blond, the other a redhead. The blond's tight black dress had sequins across the yoke. The redhead wore a short skirt and tight sweater. There was a huge run in her dark stockings. Both of the women were red-eyed from weeping, and if appearances were any indication, Nina thought, they might have been Perdita's colleagues.

Between these disparate pairs stood a lean man with filthy hair and classic features. He wore an open-collared black shirt and a gray pinstriped suit over unbuckled black boots. He swayed slightly, and his large, glittering gray eyes stared blankly down at the coffin.

Calvin Mears, she thought, her heart skipping an anxious beat. He still had the tired, lost look she remembered from their teenage years, which made him appear both unhealthy and strangely compelling. There were large bags under his gray eyes and a faint pinkish tinge to his nose, which indicated that Calvin had shed tears over the death of his mother, Penelope, a.k.a. Perdita Maxell.

A large, hulking man, his hands clasped in front of him, his head bowed, loomed behind Calvin protectively. Nina realized, with a start, that it was Jimmy. His eyes widened as he looked up and saw her approaching.

He frowned at her as she came closer. Don't worry, Nina thought. I'll mind my manners. She bowed her head and said a brief prayer along with the priest. She didn't intend to disrupt the funeral. Her questions could wait a few minutes more.

The last prayers were said, and then Calvin stepped forward and took a white carnation from one of the two small arrangements that had been set beside the grave. He placed it on the top of the plain coffin, sniffed, and wiped at his eyes. The woman in the gray coat turned and gave him a perfunctory hug as the priest signaled that the service had ended. Her husband stood by, his gaze darting around the deserted graveyard.

Nina walked over to her brother and pulled him aside.

"What are you doing here?" Jimmy asked.

"I came looking for Calvin," said Nina. "Don't play dumb, Jimmy. You have to know his mother was the"—she lowered her voice and turned her back on the mourners—"the hooker that the cops were looking for. About Dad's death."

"What?" Jimmy asked.

"What?" Nina mimicked him impatiently. "Come on,

Jimmy. Why was Dad looking for your friend, Calvin Mears? You know, don't you?"

Jimmy lowered his eyes, and a flush crept up his neck.

"Jimmy?" she asked. "What's going on?"

"Nothing," he said. "I can't talk about it here."

Calvin was being embraced by first one and then the other of his mother's friends, the blonde and the redhead.

"I thought you didn't associate with Calvin anymore," said Nina.

Jimmy looked around anxiously. "Look, I hadn't talked to him in years. Yesterday Calvin called me. He told me about his mother and he . . . asked me to meet him here." Jimmy shrugged. "I figured I should come. The cops are saying that his mother killed Dad. I wanted Calvin to know that I don't believe it."

Nina crossed her arms over her chest. "Why not? What do you know?" she said.

Calvin shook hands with the priest and then came over to where Nina and Jimmy were standing. He fumbled for a pack of cigarettes in his breast pocket, shook out a cigarette, and lit it, offering them one before he put the pack away. Nina declined, but to her surprise Jimmy took a cigarette and accepted a light from Calvin. He inhaled deeply. The priest and the two hookers made their way down the hill toward their separate cars while the middle-aged couple stood resolutely behind Calvin.

"Calvin, are you ready to go?" asked the woman in the gray coat.

"My aunt and uncle," Calvin said apologetically to Jimmy and Nina. He turned back to the older woman. "Just a minute. My friends are here." He exhaled a cloud of smoke and closed his eyes in relief. "God, I'm glad that's over," he said. He took another deep drag and clapped Jimmy on the back with his free hand. "Thanks for being here, Jim."

Jimmy blushed, and indicated Nina, who was standing quietly, looking around the cemetery. "You remember my sister, Nina," Jimmy said to Calvin.

"Yeah, thanks for coming, Nina," said Calvin.

The cemetery was peaceful and apparently empty now except for the black pickup truck that had been parked on the shoulder when Nina came in. She saw it rolling slowly toward them down the winding road. Calvin turned and looked at his mother's coffin for a moment, a thoughtful look in his gray eyes. "This bites," he said. Then he turned to Jimmy. "Look, man, we gotta talk. I mean, she had a shit life, but still, it's not fair for them to go saying she killed your old man. 'Cause she did not do it. She had a cup of coffee with him and she gave him my phone number. That's it." Calvin's restless gaze traveled over the nearby headstones, as if seeking something. "That's all it was."

"Did he call you?" Nina asked abruptly.

"Yeah," said Calvin. "He called me." Calvin looked at Jimmy accusingly. "He said you told him everything."

"Mears!"

They all turned around. The black pickup truck had come to a halt at the foot of the sloping hillside and a heavyset man with graying hair had emerged from the car. He was wearing work boots and a bulky hooded sweatshirt, and he was holding a baseball bat in his meaty hand.

"Oh shit," said Calvin, his gray eyes widening. "It's Keefer." Calvin turned to his uncle. "It's him," he said. The stocky man in the checked jacket nodded and slid silently into place beside his nephew.

"Don't say anything to him," the older man advised. "Let me do the talking."

"I told you I'd catch up to you, Mears," the man in the sweatshirt announced in a threatening voice as he started up the incline. "You thought you could just slip in and out of town without me knowing. Sorry, buddy. There's a lot of people around here with long memories."

"Hey, man, this is my mother's funeral. Have a little respect," Calvin called out indignantly, but his voice had a quaver.

Calvin's uncle nudged him. "I told you to shut up." He turned around and spoke in a low voice to his wife. "Sally, go get in the car."

The woman in the gray coat let out a little cry, but her husband scowled at her. "Now," he said, and this time the woman obeyed, looking anxiously back at them as she descended the little hill to their sedan.

Keefer continued advancing on them, swinging the bat like a pendulum.

"Oh, Christ," said Jimmy. "This could get ugly." He dropped his cigarette, ground it with his boot, and started toward Calvin. Nina grabbed her brother by the hand and tried to jerk him back.

Calvin's uncle unbuttoned his jacket to reveal a shoulder holster. "Look, Mr. Keefer," he called out to the man in the sweatshirt. "My name is Joe Jenkins, and I'm a police officer, so before you start anything, you should know that. I know all about your beef. My nephew here don't want no trouble. We just buried his mother, and we want to leave this place in peace, understood?"

Keefer stopped where he was and glared at the man's gun in the holster.

The two cemetery workers who had been watching this encounter crouched down behind a headstone.

"You gonna shoot me?" Keefer demanded.

"If I have to," said Jenkins.

"That bastard killed my little girl," Keefer cried.

The veteran policeman spoke calmly. "It was a drug situation, sir. I'm not defending him, believe me. But your daughter died because she did too many drugs."

Keefer raised the bat and shook it at Calvin. "He gave them

to her. He knew what would happen. She was pregnant with his baby and he didn't want to support a kid."

Calvin's uncle shook his head sadly. "Mr. Keefer," he said, "Calvin didn't have to kill your daughter because she was pregnant. All he hadda do was walk away. Which is just what he would have done. Wouldn't ya, Cal?" he said, cuffing Calvin on the head.

Keefer stood staring at them, the bat raised, his shoulders hunched.

Jenkins walked slowly toward the enraged father and spoke quietly. "I'm guessing you've got a wife, and other kids, and maybe even grandchildren. They all need you. You probably got a job and a house. You crack his skull and you lose everything."

"But he killed my baby," Keefer protested, and his voice cracked. "He's the one who gave her the dope."

Jenkins shook his head. "You go on home now, Mr. Keefer, and don't get yourself in any trouble. Because this guy's not worth it."

Keefer glared at Calvin, who stood stock-still, watching the exchange. Calvin's uncle turned and grabbed his nephew by the upper arm. "Come on," he said. He pointed a finger at Keefer. "Stay right where you are, sir," he advised, as he dragged Calvin along with him. Calvin kept looking back at Keefer, but Keefer's shoulders had slumped. He watched them depart and then walked heavily over to a cast cement bench under a nearby tree and sank down on it, dropping the bat to the ground.

"We better get out of here, too," said Jimmy.

Nina did not budge. "What did he mean, you told him everything? What did you tell Dad?"

Jimmy was stone-faced.

"I swear to God, Jimmy. If you don't answer me . . ."

"Okay, okay," he said with a sigh. "But not here. Follow me in your car."

19

SNOW flurries swirled around the Volvo as Nina followed Jimmy's car. She hunched forward in the driver's seat, her neck muscles tense as she kept the Saturn in view through the mist of flakes.

Where the hell is he going? she thought angrily. She hadn't thought to ask him where he was heading, and she hated driving like this, not knowing where he intended to lead her. For one terrible moment she realized that he might be trying to shake her. They had left the Hoffman city limits and entered Port Regent, a run-down, working-class town. Nina didn't recognize the neighborhood where he had led her, a deserted area where rows of warehouses stored freight for trucking lines. Nina started to mutter at Jimmy under her breath when suddenly she saw his blinker indicating that he was pulling over. Through the dingy white veil of flurries in the sky she saw a blinking neon sign over a low corner building that read THE END

ZONE. The window of the old building also had a neon sign, partially lit, which read BAR AND GRILL.

Jimmy parked and turned off his lights. Nina followed suit and got out of the car. A few scattered cars were parked near the corner. In this neighborhood of featureless warehouses the bar was the only place in sight that did not look utterly lifeless.

Sliding a little on the leather soles of her boots, Nina shuffled along holding on to a chain-link fence to where her brother stood waiting.

"What are we doing here?" she said.

"Let's go in," he said.

"It's a bar, Jimmy."

"I know it's a bar, Nina," he said irritably. "Our carpet warehouse is just across the street. So when I have time to kill I come in and relax a little bit. Okay?"

"Okay, okay," she said. She followed him down some steps to a heavy double door, which he opened. Inside, she saw darkness and smelled cigarette smoke and stale beer.

Jimmy took his coat off and hung it up on a hook just inside the door. When he reached out a hand for Nina's, she shook her head.

"No, thanks, I'll keep it," she said.

Jimmy shrugged. "All right," he said. "Follow me."

It was easier said than done, at first, but in a few moments her eyes adjusted to the gloom. It was a long narrow place with an old mahogany bar, obviously the pride and joy of the owner, because despite its many scars, it did have a rich patina. The floor of the bar was tiled in tiny white octagons, many of which were missing, with grout gone to dirt in the empty spots. The ceiling was tin and the tables were round and battered, with glass ashtrays liberally distributed on the tabletops and utilitarian wooden chairs surrounding them. In the back were a pool table and an ancient jukebox. It was the kind of bar that would get a gentle refurbishment in midtown Manhattan, Nina thought, and quickly become a fashionable hangout. Here in the suburbs, people's idea of a bar was Applebee's or T.G.I. Fridays. This bar was in a neighborhood few people from Hoffman would want to frequent.

This gloomy afternoon The End Zone was about half full of men in down vests and heavy work boots. Guffaws and smoke rings hung in the air. At the end of the bar, ESPN was playing on the suspended television, the sound too low to be heard as anything other than more noise. Aside from the two waitresses, Nina was the only woman in the place.

Jimmy took a table and sat down, pointing out a chair for his sister. Nina sat and looked around her, studying the crowd and the atmosphere.

"You don't need to look so superior," said Jimmy.

Nina turned and looked at her brother. "I'm just looking around. Do you mind?"

"Take your coat off," said Jim.

Nina removed her coat and laid it on a chair beside her.

A blond-haired girl with coarse-looking skin came up to their table holding a tray under her arm. She was wearing jeans and a tight black T-shirt that said BABY LOVE on it. "Hey, Jimmy," she said.

"Hey, Rita," Jimmy said sheepishly, avoiding Nina's questioning gaze.

"Who's your friend?"

"My sister, Nina. This is Rita."

Nina smiled thinly and then looked at Jimmy. Clearly, he was no stranger here. "What'll you have?" asked the waitress.

Jimmy tapped his fingertips lightly on the edge of the table. "I'll have a . . . Guinness," he said.

"No Coke for you?" Rita asked, clearly surprised.

"I'm not working today," he said. "It's my day off."

Nina looked at him in consternation. She didn't want to make a scene in front of the waitress. "Just club soda," she said.

"And bring us some chips," said Jimmy, still not looking at Nina.

The waitress left and Jimmy sat with his back against the wall, pretending to be absorbed by the game of pool that was going on at the table beyond where they were sitting.

"Jimmy," said Nina.

Jimmy turned and she saw the baleful look in his eye. "What?" he demanded.

"What about . . . I thought you didn't drink," said Nina.

"One isn't going to kill me," he said.

"I thought that was against the rules," said Nina.

"What rules?" he demanded. "I'm a grown man, Nina. I make the rules."

"You know what I mean," said Nina. "Your program."

"I know what you mean. You don't think I can handle it," he said defensively.

"I'm not judging you," she said.

"Right," said Jimmy.

Nina hesitated. "What about the Connellys . . . ?"

"What?" he cried. "You going to call my family and tattle on me?"

Nina was silent. His family. It still stung to know that he regarded other people as his family. Then again, there wasn't much left to the family he had started with. Maybe she just envied him that luxury. People who really cared, who would really be upset if they knew that he was going to have a beer. "No. I'm just worried about you."

Rita returned and set down their drinks. Jimmy stared at the dark beer but did not pick up the glass. "Don't. Please. Don't worry about me."

Nina saw the expression of dread in his eyes. He looked like a man facing his own execution, and she knew it was their conversation that he was dreading. Maybe she shouldn't force him. Maybe if she dropped the whole thing, he would pour out his beer and they could leave. But at the same time, she knew that intentionally or not, this was exactly what he wanted her to do. He wanted her to feel guilty and stop hounding him for answers. No, she thought. I won't. I can't. She took a deep breath. "Why did Dad call Calvin Mears?"

"I'm not sure," Jimmy said evasively.

Nina peered at him and when she spoke there was an edge in her voice. "I don't believe that for one minute. You told me yourself that you talked to Dad while I was in New York. What did you two talk about? What did it have to do with Calvin?"

Jimmy sighed and stared at his glass. But he didn't pick it up. For a minute, Nina thought he was going to refuse to answer her. Then, at last, he spoke. "I went to see him," said Jimmy. "I told you that."

"Yes," said Nina. "While I was out of town. You mentioned that. Why? It wasn't just to talk about old times, was it?"

Jimmy shook his head and sighed. "One of the steps in AA—you're supposed to apologize to the people you wronged. You know, make your peace with them. Admit that what you did while you were drinking may have hurt them. You know?"

"Yeah. I remember when you did that with me. That was years ago. And I remember telling you that you hadn't ever really wronged me. I said that the only one you hurt was yourself," she said.

"Well," he said, staring at the drink sitting in front of him. "That wasn't exactly true. There was something that I didn't tell anyone. Not you, not anyone. I never really finished with that step because . . . I never actually . . . apologized to Dad."

"Apologized for what?" Nina asked. Then she looked at him through narrowed eyes. "Jimmy, are you trying to avoid my question? What has this twelve-step business got to do with Calvin Mears?"

"I'm not avoiding anything," he said. "I'm trying to explain . . ."

"All right. Sorry," she said. "Go on."

He reached out to his glass and put his hand around it, studying the drink in his hand as if it were a jewel with a curse on it. "I never wanted you to know any of this. You're going to hate me."

Nina's stomach turned over and she suddenly felt sick. The smoke in the air seemed suffocating. "What are you talking about, Jimmy? Why should I hate you?"

Jimmy picked up the glass.

"Jimmy, don't," she said.

For a minute he hesitated, obviously torn. Then he set down the glass and pulled his hand back.

"What?" she prodded him.

Jimmy looked around the bar anxiously, as if worried that he might be overheard. Then he leaned slightly closer to Nina. "No matter what Dad did—you know, no matter how bad a thing he did. Well, I did something too. The night Mom died."

Nina's eyes widened, and her heart beat a tattoo.

Jimmy hesitated, and then continued. "The night Mom died, Calvin and I . . . we went over to our house. The place looked dead. I thought no one was home . . ."

Nina was staring at him. He glanced up at her, and then looked away.

"Calvin stayed outside. He was my lookout. He was supposed to let me know if anybody was coming. I . . . went into the house by the back door to . . . steal the money from Mom's purse."

"What?" Nina yelped.

"We were high and we wanted to score some more drugs.

We didn't have any money. You know I was very messed up in those days . . ."

"Jimmy!" Nina cried.

"So, I remembered Mom went to the bank on Fridays. I figured . . ." Jimmy sighed. "I knew where she kept her purse. I sneaked into the house and went to their room and found it. I stole the money and I ran out."

"Wait a minute. Wait a minute," said Nina. "You were the thief?" She was having a hard time absorbing this information. She had always believed that the thief was also the murderer. "Where was Mom when you were in the house? Are you saying that she was there in the house and she didn't hear you come in? That's impossible."

"No, I'm saying that it had already . . . that she'd already been attacked. Stabbed. I just didn't know it."

"And you didn't see her in there? Our mother, lying there like that, in a pool of blood on the living room floor?" Nina cried. "You didn't notice the blood all over the kitchen, on the walls?"

"I didn't go in the living room. It was dark in there!" Jimmy cried. "And in the kitchen. That was pretty dark, too. Just that little light over the stove . . ."

Nina remembered. Jimmy was describing the house as she'd found it, that long-ago night. But what he was saying— she didn't want to admit to herself that it could be true. "Oh, give me a break. You expect me to believe that you went in and took the money and left and you never saw her?"

Jimmy nodded miserably. "I didn't want to see her. I . . . was being quiet. I wanted to avoid her. But . . . I guess it didn't matter because she was . . ." Jimmy fell silent. He tipped his head back against the wall and did not look at Nina.

"Because she was already dead," said Nina grimly.

Jimmy shook his head. "No. She wasn't dead. That's what makes it even worse. It turns out she was still alive."

20

NINA felt like the room was spinning. "Still alive?" she cried. "How could you possibly know that? You just said you didn't see her."

Jimmy looked at her sorrowfully, but there was no compassion in her eyes. He hesitated, and then continued. "When we talked the other night, Dad told me that she was still alive. He said she was still alive when *he* came in and found her. He found her lying there in the living room in all the blood . . . She was barely alive, but she was able to speak—whisper, I guess."

"She could speak?" Nina said, going over that night as she remembered it in her mind. "He never said that. He told me she was dead."

Jimmy nodded sadly. "I guess she was by the time you came home. But when Dad found her, she was just clinging on. When Dad lifted her up, she was looking him right in the eye and saying my name, and Dad thought she—you know—mistook him for me. He didn't realize, I guess . . . She must have known I was in the house. She must have heard me come in. Maybe she even saw me there. She was probably trying to call to me to come and help her. But I was too busy looking for the money. I was going through her purse, stealing from her, while she was lying there bleeding to death on the living room carpet, trying to call to me to help her."

"Oh my God, Jimmy," Nina said, filled with revulsion.

"I know. I was just too fucked up to even hear her. I might have been able to save her life. But all I cared about was getting the money."

His face wore an expression of sheer misery. Nina had a slight impulse to reach out for his hand, to comfort him, but she felt paralyzed. "Jimmy, why didn't you tell the police all this?"

Jimmy ran a hand over his bristly head. "Because Dad kept saying that whoever took the money must have killed her. I was afraid they would blame me. You know, they might think that I killed her."

Nina had a sudden terrible thought. "Jimmy, you didn't . . ."

Jimmy looked at her balefully. "I didn't hurt Mom. Come on, Nina. How could you even . . .? I would never have laid a hand on Mom."

"But you had information that might have helped the investigation. Maybe they would have found out who really killed her. Instead they blamed Dad," said Nina.

"They had other evidence," he reminded her.

She looked at him with narrowed eyes. "So you assumed that they were right. That Dad killed her."

"I didn't know," said Jimmy feebly. "Mom and Dad were always mad at each other. When the cops arrested him, I just figured . . . I mean, they're cops. They know about this stuff. I didn't know what else to think."

"I never believed it," she reminded him angrily.

"I didn't want to believe it. But during the trial, when it

came out about how he wanted to divorce her. And then that business about him sleeping with Mrs. Ross." He shrugged his broad shoulders. "I started to think . . . It sounded . . . possible."

"And what do you think now?" Nina said slowly.

Jimmy sighed. "I think they must have been wrong. When he told me that part about how he found her there and she was whispering my name, I knew. I knew he was telling the truth. She heard me in the house. I just didn't hear her. She was too weak to call to me. He didn't kill her. She wasn't even dead when he found her."

"I hope you told him that," said Nina bitterly. "I hope you told him that you realized he was innocent so that he heard it from your lips before he was killed."

Jimmy shook his head slightly. "I wanted to. But . . ."

"Oh, Jimmy!" Nina rolled her eyes in exasperation. Part of her wanted to just get up and leave him there in disgust, but there was more that she wanted to know. She took a deep breath and tried to compose her thoughts. "So when you told him you were the one who took the money, what did he say?"

"What do you think?" said Jimmy defensively. "He was mad at me."

"Do you blame him?"

"No," Jimmy retorted. "It's what I expected. That's why I didn't admit it for so many years."

Nina chewed her lip and stewed in silence for a moment. "Okay, what else?" she asked.

Jimmy spoke in a monotone. "He asked me all about it. I told him how Calvin was waiting outside, being the lookout, and Dad wanted to know if Calvin had seen anything or anyone. You know, someone leaving the house as I was going in. He said the killer must have just left when I was arriving because Mom couldn't have been lying there like that for long. Not as badly wounded as she was."

"So you gave him Calvin's number . . ."

"I didn't have Calvin's number. I told you, I hadn't talked to him in years. I told Dad to call Calvin's mother."

"Penelope Mears," said Nina, "a.k.a. Perdita Maxwell. And she told him how to get in touch with Calvin."

Jimmy shrugged. "I guess so."

"And what did Calvin tell him? Did he remember anything from that night? Anything or anyone he might have seen?"

"I don't know," said Jimmy.

The bar was noisy around them, but they were an island of silence. For a moment they each pondered the wreckage of their family and wondered if it could have been avoided.

Finally, Jimmy took a deep breath. "When the cops told us that he killed himself," he said, "I lost it. I felt so guilty."

Nina softened toward him a little at this admission. "But Dad didn't kill himself. Remember?"

Jimmy nodded. "I know."

She hated to see him looking so lost and hopeless. "Look, Jimmy, what's done is done. Right now we need to find out what Calvin told him."

Jimmy seemed too lost in his dejection to rise to the challenge.

"Right now we don't know where Calvin is or what he said," Nina said.

Jimmy shrugged. "He said he was going right back to California. Or maybe he'll stay with his aunt and uncle for a little while. I don't know. When he gets back to L.A. I can call him and find out what he told Dad. If anything . . ."

"I can't wait that long," said Nina. "I'll track him down myself."

The waitress ambled over to the table, holding an empty tray against her hip. "Can I get you folks another round?" she asked.

"No, just the check. We're leaving," said Nina.

The waitress nodded and departed.

"Do you hate me now?" said Jimmy.

She didn't want to look at him. "I don't hate you. But I'm not going to pretend that it doesn't matter."

The waitress returned with the tab and set it on the table. Nina reached into her satchel for her wallet.

Jimmy picked up the bill and set it down in front of him. He picked up the glass of Guinness and gazed at it. "On second thought," he said, "I'm gonna stay."

Nina stared at her brother. "What do you think you're doing?" she asked.

Jimmy looked at her defiantly. "Having a drink."

"Are you trying to make me feel guilty for making you tell me the truth?"

"No. I just need a drink, okay?"

Nina hesitated. Much as she wanted to deny it, she did feel guilty. She didn't want to see him fall back into the habits that might lead him to the gutter. What would her mother want her to do? she wondered. She knew the answer. She took a deep breath. "All right, look, Jimmy. It's bad. All this you told me. But it's not the end of the world. We can get past this. It'll all work out somehow." She was scraping the bottom of her emotional barrel for some platitude that would assuage him, although, admittedly, her supply of optimism was low. But she had to try.

"You don't mean that," Jimmy said.

Nina looked around helplessly. "Well, I'm saying that somehow it will all be okay, Jimmy. All right? Now just put your coat on and come with me. Don't undo all the good you've done. Dad was so proud that you'd straightened your life out. That was really important to him. To all of us. Please, Jimmy. Come back with me. Now."

Jimmy lifted the glass and gazed at it as if mesmerized. Then he raised the glass to his lips and took a sip. For a minute he closed his eyes and the tense muscles in his face relaxed, his expression some cross between ecstasy and despair. He sighed.

"Jimmy, stop!" Nina cried. She leaned across the table and grabbed his upper arm. "Let's get out of this place."

He glared at her and jerked his muscular arm out of her grasp. "Leave me alone, Nina," he said. "Mind your own business. I know what I'm doing. I've been needing a drink for the longest time."

21

IT was growing dark by the time Nina turned onto Aunt Mary's street, and the flurries, which had stopped for a while, had begun again, swirling and dancing in her headlights. She was still trying to come to grips with what her brother had told her and with her repeated, futile attempts to dislodge him from the bar. Her head ached from the effort. She pulled into the dark driveway at Aunt Mary's house, wishing she had put the porch lights on before she left. She got out of the car, slammed the door, and trudged up toward the front steps.

All of a sudden a dark figure rose up in front of her.

Nina screamed and stumbled. The man stepped forward and caught her.

"Nina, it's me."

Nina looked up at the man who was holding her by the arms and saw that it was Andre. For a minute her heart lifted, and then she suddenly became angry. "What are you doing? I didn't see you there. You scared me half to death."

"Sorry," he said. "I was sitting on the step. I've been waiting for you," he said.

"I didn't see your car," she said accusingly.

"I parked it on the street so you wouldn't have to move yours to let me out."

"Jesus, Andre, you really scared me." She knew she sounded irritable, but she couldn't help it. She didn't want him to know how glad she was to see him. He looked so handsome in the moonlight, with a dusting of snowflakes on his shiny black hair. He was wearing a tan shearling jacket over a dark turtleneck. The jacket was open at the neck and she could see its woolly sheepskin lining. For a moment, she wished fiercely that he would open his jacket and pull her in, so she could bury herself against the warmth of his broad chest. She banished the thought, reminding herself that it didn't mean anything that he had come here. He wasn't here to console her. On the contrary, he was a bystander, agape at the spectacle of her family's destruction.

"That was kind of a quick trip, wasn't it?" she said coldly. "How long were you gone? Overnight?" She brushed past him and mounted the stone steps, fumbling in her pocketbook for the house keys.

"It was long enough," he said. "Nina, I've been concerned about you."

Nina stuck her key in the lock. Concerned? she thought. He sounded like a high school guidance counselor. "Nothing to worry about. Do you want to come in?" she asked without enthusiasm.

Andre looked down at his clothes. "I'm kind of damp," he said with a grimace.

"Another time then," she said, not looking at him.

"We could sit outside," he said. "I noticed there's a patio around back. I've been on planes and in airports all day. I could use the air." He held up a paper sack. "I even brought drinks. I've got two coffees in here—decaf."

Nina hesitated. Her head ached and her clothes stank of cig-arette smoke from the bar. Her eyes met his shadowed gaze. Andre's expression was guileless. She suddenly recalled the night of her father's funeral, when she'd felt so alone, and he had shown up at the door, worried about Duncan's death. He had not created the quagmire that she found herself in. He was a friend, was making a welcome offer after the miseries of this day, and the idea of sitting outside in the darkness appealed to her. "All right," she said. "If you're not too cold."

"Me? Nah," he said, smiling broadly. Andre came down off the step and started around the house toward the patio in the backyard. Nina followed him, walking over the fallen leaves, now dark under the thin layer of snow. She noticed the smell of chimney smoke in the air, and felt a sudden longing for a hearth that she did not have. Behind the house, the cushioned patio chairs were circled around a glass table with a center hole for a nonexistent umbrella. Andre skimmed off the snow and set the two Styrofoam coffee cups down on the tabletop. He pulled out a chair for her, brushing snowflakes off the seat. Then he pulled out a chair for himself. The house loomed dark and unwelcom-ing behind them, but the backyard was silvery, the dancing flakes lit by a misty moon on the rise.

Andre reached into the paper bag and pulled out stirrers, creamers, and sugar packets. "Let me just doctor these up," he said. "How many sugars?"

"Two," she replied.

"Sorry they're not hotter," he said. "I've been outside here for a while."

Nina nodded, but once again an irrational hostility toward him reasserted itself. "I didn't ask you to wait," she said, in a voice that was meant to sound offhand but came out sounding mean, even to her own ears.

"I know," he said wearily.

Immediately she was sorry for her tone. Sorry for making

him feel weary. "How come you're back so soon?" she asked.

Andre frowned and tapped his fingers against the side of the cup. "Things didn't go exactly as planned," he said.

"With Susan?" she asked.

He nodded. "Yeah. She . . . kind of sent me packing," he said.

"Really?" Nina asked, her heart leaping. "Why?"

Andre sighed. "She said she wasn't . . . sure anymore. About us," he said.

"Oh. That's too bad," said Nina, although part of her was undeniably elated at this news. She tried to sound sympathetic. "Did she say why?"

Andre hesitated. "It's a lot of things. I think it's been coming for a while," he said vaguely.

"Does this mean you're not going to move out there?" she asked.

"I don't know," he said. "I'm still . . . sorting it out."

"Are you still engaged?" Nina asked.

"She still has the ring," he said.

Nina blushed and was grateful for the darkness. She imagined him begging Susan to keep his ring and promising that they would find a way to work it out. "Well, then, there's still hope," Nina said, forcing herself to sound cheery, although the mental image of him pleading with his faceless fiancée made her feel dead inside.

Andre was silent for a moment. "That's one way to look at it," he said. He set his cup down on the tabletop. "But right now I want to know what's going on with you. Did you find out anything more about Duncan's death?"

Nina shrugged and took a sip of the coffee. It was sugary and barely warm. "Oh yes. I found out a lot. Too much, you might say."

Andre frowned. "Like what?"

After another sip, Nina set down her cup and recounted her conversation with Jimmy as fully as she could.

When she finished, Andre blew out his breath with a soft whistle.

"Damn," said Andre, frowning. "Well, that explains Duncan's renewed hope about finding your mother's killer."

"I know," she said.

"So," said Andre. "What do you intend to do now?"

Nina took a deep breath. "I'd like to talk to Calvin Mears and find out what he told my father. But Jimmy thinks Calvin may have turned around and gone right back to L.A. Some guy came after him at the cemetery with a baseball bat."

"A baseball bat?" Andre cried. "Why?"

"To settle an old score," she said. "Luckily for Calvin, his uncle was there. Apparently he's a cop down in Seaside Park. At least, it said in the obituary that they come from Seaside Park. Anyway, the uncle was armed and headed the guy off."

"Wow," said Andre, shaking his head. "And you're certain your brother is telling the truth about all this."

Nina nodded. "I believed him. He was a mess. Jimmy's a reformed alcholic. When I left him he was diving into a beer."

"God, that's awful. Did you try to stop him?"

Nina felt insulted by the question. She thought of how she had begged Jimmy to leave the bar and come back with her. "Of course I did!" she cried.

He reached out across the cold glass top of the patio table and took her hand. "That was stupid of me," he said. "I know you did."

She met his gaze and felt a tightness in her chest and a lassitude in her limbs. The desire to touch his skin, to feel his lips, to fold herself against him was like a drug in her veins. A weakness, she reminded herself, that she could not afford. He was engaged. He belonged to someone else.

She drew herself back. "So?" she said, deliberately misunderstanding him. "You think I didn't handle it the right way with my brother? Maybe you think I should have physically dragged him out of there. Or called the cops."

"I didn't mean it like that," he said.

"I don't care how you meant it," she snapped. "I'm cold. I'm going in."

Andre turned his face away from her and looked at the ground. Instantly, she felt sorry for taking out all her frustration on him. He had done nothing but try to help her. He didn't deserve her bitterness.

"You're right. It's getting cold out here," he said. "I better be going."

Apologize, she thought. You are deliberately twisting his words. But no apology rose to her lips. Her heart seemed to be roiling with anger and disappointment. "That's a good idea," she said, standing up.

Andre nodded, as if he understood something unspoken, and then he got up from the patio chair. He dumped out the leftover coffee, gathered up the empty cups and packets, and put them in the bag. Then he jammed the bag into the pocket of his coat.

"Nina," he said, "I don't think you should go pursuing this guy . . . Mears, is it?"

"Calvin Mears. And I don't really need any more advice. Thank you, but I'm sure I'll be fine," she said coldly.

He turned away and she thought she heard him sigh. He started to walk around to the front of the house, and she followed the tracks of his boots in the gauzy snow. When they reached the walk they separated. He headed down toward his car, which was parked on the street. She thought to wave to him, but he did not look back at her.

• • •

"JIMMY?" Rita leaned over and searched her customer's face. "I'm going off my shift. Can I call somebody to come and get you?"

Jimmy looked up at the waitress's face through a fog. He knew what she was saying. She was saying that he was in no shape to drive. But he wasn't that far gone. He tried to say "No" but ended up making a grunting noise.

"How about one of the guys from work that you come in here with? Pete. I could call Pete for you," Rita suggested.

Jimmy's half-closed eyes widened in alarm. Not Pete, he thought. Not anybody from work. If they saw him like this, half in the bag and needing a ride home, he might not have that job for much longer. His dulled brain made a sloppy search through the possible names and faces. Not Nina. Not after this afternoon. And not Rose. Definitely not Rose. Or George. They would look at him so sadly, and what would he say? After all the pep talks and the prayers, how could he explain?

Jimmy's eyes closed, and then he started and looked up at Rita's kindly face. "Call Patrick," he said.

"Do you have a phone number for Patrick?" Rita asked.

Jimmy patted himself up and down, trying to remember. Patrick's phone number. He used to know it by heart.

"Is it in the book?" Rita asked.

Jimmy looked up at her gratefully and nodded. "Patrick Avery," he said. "In Hoffman."

"Okay," she said, putting a glass of water down in front of him. "Here's some water. I'll give Patrick a ring."

Jimmy grabbed her forearm as she tried to turn away. " 'Smy brother," he said.

Rita nodded, and pried his fingers off her arm. She disappeared behind the bar as Jimmy tried, with a trembling hand, to lift the water to his lips.

The water slopped onto his hand and onto the table. He set it down carefully and tried to think. He knew what they would ask him. Why did you do it? Why did you start again? All these years and now here you are. Over the edge in one precious day.

He knew when he was driving here, leading Nina here. He knew he wasn't going to make it through his confession without something. He'd tried praying in the car, but it didn't work. His mind kept drifting away from redemption. He knew what the look on Nina's face was going to be. The contempt in her eyes. Nina had no idea what it was like to live as he had lived. His heart, his mind, everything cried out for oblivion.

But it wasn't only that. If he were honest, he'd admit he had known what was gonna happen when he saw Calvin today. When he'd walked into that funeral home and looked at Calvin's face, he'd felt like an old man. A tired old man who had resigned himself to penance, and given up everything that had ever made him happy. Given it up and accepted being half alive. Never doing too much of anything. Never caring too much about anything or anybody. Never really laughing. When he saw Calvin he remembered what it was like to feel high. High and alive. He remembered. And he wanted it back.

Now Nina knew everything about that night. He was like a man turned inside out. All his secrets were on the outside now. Well, not all his secrets. He still had to tell Patrick. He knew that. He had to. He had to confess to Patrick before he could really be free. And once he was free, he planned to celebrate. That's right. Celebrate.

"Is that your Jag out there, mister?" he heard a man at the bar saying in a loud, taunting voice.

Jimmy looked up. Patrick had come in, still wearing his good suit and his Burberry raincoat. The men at the bar were looking at him with dislike. Dislike tinged with envy.

"Yes, it's mine," said Patrick in an impatient voice.

"Runs kind of ragged, don't it?" asked another man.

"I know," said Patrick. "It needs a tune-up."

"You think you'd take care of a piece of machinery like that," one of the men at the bar said to the other. "Not just drive it into the ground."

Patrick was looking around, searching the dark corners of the bar. Jimmy raised his hand weakly and Patrick's irritated frown turned to a glare. He strode up to the table where Jimmy still sat.

"What the hell happened to you?" he demanded in a low voice. "Jesus, Jimmy. You're going right down the fucking tubes."

Now that Patrick was here, Jimmy knew what he had to do. He had to tell Patrick. About the robbery and Calvin and everything. He had to tell him everything. Just like Nina. Jimmy reached up and hooked one of the buckles on Patrick's coat.

"Let go of that," Patrick said, pulling his coat free. "Come on. You can sleep at my house tonight. Is your car here?"

"My car?" Jimmy repeated, confused.

"I'll drive you by in the morning," said Patrick. "You can pick it up then. Come on. Did you pay yet?" Jimmy blinked at his brother. Patrick reached under Jimmy's arm and around his back and hoisted him to his feet. Jimmy swayed above him. "You fucking moron," said Patrick, throwing money down on the table.

Jimmy let himself be led outside. The cold air hit him like a bucket of water, and he felt suddenly much more lucid than before. He looked up at the night sky. There were still some snowflakes coming down but nothing much was sticking to the ground. Patrick hauled him to the Jaguar and opened the door.

Jimmy leaned on the open door. "Patrick. I have to tell you . . ."

"That's fine," said Patrick. "Get in the car, Jim."

"Issabout what happened. Issabout Mom . . . and Dad . . . and Calvin."

Patrick's jaw tightened and he shook his head. "Just get in the goddamned car."

"Lemme tell you, Patrick . . ." Jimmy pleaded. "I gotta tell you."

Patrick pushed him down roughly into the passenger seat. "Yeah. Yeah. Tell me when we get home," he said. "Now get your hand inside before I slam the door on it."

22

NINA'S cell phone rang in her coat pocket as she closed the front door. Answering it as she shrugged off her damp coat, she was surprised to hear her great-aunt's thready voice on the other end.

"Aunt Mary," she said. "What's the matter?"

"Nothing, dear," her aunt said. "I hate to bother you. But I talked to the doctor today and he said I can go home tomorrow."

"That's great," said Nina, trying to hide her dismay. Tomorrow she planned to track down Calvin and get the answers she needed about her father's last days. But she couldn't let down her aunt. All right. Tonight, she thought. I'll do it tonight. He's got to still be in Seaside Park with his relatives. There has to be a way to find him. And then she had another, dismal realization. Her aunt's bedroom was still torn apart. Only half the trim was painted. All the furniture was still in a covered heap in the middle of the room.

"I know how busy you are, Nina, and I hate to put you out," Aunt Mary said. "But do you think you could come out to Hoffman and pick me up and bring me home?"

Nina's headache, which had abated slightly while she was sitting on the back patio, came rushing back full force. She wasn't about to tell her aunt that she was already in Hoffman, or why. But she knew she had to quickly rearrange her priorities. "Of course," she said. "Of course I can. When shall I come for you?"

"How soon can you get here?"

There was only one right thing to do. "I'll be there in the morning," said Nina. She was so tired that all she wanted to do was lie down and close her eyes. But the room was not going to paint itself. She had to get it done tonight.

Nina put on her painting clothes, laid out the painting supplies, and set to work. The work went quickly once she got started. Luckily she and Duncan had already done most of it. She just had to finish the trim. And she had long ago washed the curtains, which had required several washings, but were now ready to be rehung. When the painting was finished, Nina looked around and felt a glimmer of satisfaction at the result. She had picked a light yellow, which she hoped was close to the original color. She uncovered the furniture and pushed the pieces back into place, being careful not to scuff the new paint. The pictures she would rehang in their original places in the morning, when she hung the curtains. She'd started to close up her paint can when she noticed the closet. Should she paint it? It would be such an effort to clear it out.

She looked at the closet critically. It really needed a coat of paint, and there was no way she was ever going to do this job once Aunt Mary was back in the house. All right, she thought with a sigh. It'll keep my mind off everything else. She reached into the closet and began to pull out the clothes, laying them across the bed still on their hangers. She put the shoes in a plastic bag and moved them out. She had emptied the closet of all the shoes, clothes, and accessories, and was about to begin to sweep it out, when she noticed a couple of cardboard boxes in the corner. She was tempted just to leave them there, but her sense of order was offended at the idea of painting around them.

Just pull them out, she thought. It's not that much. She had to get down on her knees to reach the boxes. She was grateful that her aunt was not a hoarder like lots of old ladies. I'd never get finished, she thought. Aunt Mary probably doesn't even remember these boxes are here. Nina dragged the dusty cartons onto the floor beside the closet. I should probably leave them out for her to go through and throw them away if she wants. But even as she thought this, she lifted the top off the first box and saw that it was filled with newspapers. The headline on the top paper struck her like a blow. "Doc's wife stabbed to death."

Nina sank down onto the rug and stared at the photos of her parents and the picture of their old house, which were splashed across the yellowed front page. With trembling hands she reached in for the next paper, neatly packed in the box. In this edition, Marsha's murder shared top billing with the discovery of a baby's body in the park. Again she saw the photo of their old house and, below the fold, a photo of the baby's shallow grave. She lifted off the next couple of papers. Each day, her mother's murder was the lead story. The next time the murder got the entire banner was a headline reading, "Doc arrested in wife's murder."

Oh my God, Nina thought. Aunt Mary saved every one of these. She took the lid off the other carton and saw that this box, too, was filled with papers. She couldn't remember ever having seen the newspapers or watched the news at the time of her mother's murder. But her aunt had saved every single paper dealing with her niece's death. Part of Nina wanted to throw them away, but the desire to read about these events that had changed her own life so completely was far too compelling. She reached for the first paper and began to skim the various reports.

In one edition, a crudely drawn crime scene sketch showed, with arrows and broken lines, how Marsha had crawled from the kitchen to the living room, leaving a trail of blood. Nina had always known that Marsha was killed in the kitchen with one of their knives from the block on the counter. But why did she crawl into another room, mortally wounded like that? Nina wondered. It must have been some instinctual urge to escape, or perhaps aberrant thinking brought on by the attack.

The mental image of her mother doing that, knowing she was about to die, made Nina start to shake. She pulled the afghan off Aunt Mary's bed and wrapped herself in it, waiting for the chills to subside before she went any farther. The wind outside the house had begun to howl and rattle the shutters. You shouldn't do this to yourself, she thought. But she felt like a smoker telling herself she should not light up, knowing that she would. Finally, she picked up the papers again.

The papers published during the trial had minute accounts of the crime, but she was unprepared for a picture published in a Sunday newsmagazine article about the case. It was a photo of her mother, dead on the living room floor. Nina closed her eyes against the gruesome image and steeled herself before she opened them again. She forced herself to look. There was her mother's body, splayed out on the rug, the newspaper bunched beneath her outflung arm. Nina was grateful that she could not see her mother's eyes in the photographs. Marsha's face was in shadow.

Oh, Mommy, she thought. How could anyone hurt you? Her mother looked so gentle and vulnerable, the roll around her midriff exposed where her turtleneck shirt had ridden up.

Her mother had always been embarrassed by that stubborn excess weight. She was always trying to diet or walk it off. On her feet, her white ankle socks were splattered with blood. Marsha often padded around the house in her socks. Nina could see that the socks, in addition to being bloody, were slightly grimy on the bottom. Who could be so cruel? Nina thought.

Nina could not stand any more. Enough of this, she thought. Enough. I can't look at this anymore, she thought. Forget painting the closet. No one will ever even notice. I'll put all this stuff away tomorrow. I have to get out of this room and away from all this.

She shrugged off the afghan and felt chilly again. Shivering, she dragged herself up to her old pink bedroom, and fell down on the bed in her clothes. She knew she should get up and take a shower, but she was too exhausted. I'll do it in a minute, she thought. Almost before she could finish the thought she was asleep.

Nina's dreams were a jumble of images. She dreamed, finally, of her mother. Marsha, alive and cheerful, was standing in the kitchen of their old house. At first Nina felt elation at the sight of her. She started toward her mother, wanting to embrace her. All at once she realized that Marsha was chopping something on the counter with a large carving knife. Nina was frozen, horrified by the sight. She knew she had to warn her mother about the knife, but the words stuck in her throat.

"Go upstairs and paint your room," her mother said. Nina was afraid to leave her mother there in the kitchen, but she could not speak. "Go on now," her mother said. "There's not much more to do. Finish it up."

The next thing Nina knew she was in the pink bedroom at Aunt Mary's house. She knew in the dream that this was somehow wrong, but she didn't know why. She went to the closet, but it was empty—no clothes on the hangers. All she saw was a box in the back of the closet. The sight of the box filled her with dread. Suddenly, her brother Jimmy appeared in the doorway to the room.

"Don't open that," Jimmy said. But when she looked up to answer him, he had disappeared. She turned back to the box and pulled it toward her. She lifted the lid, her hands trembling. When she moved it away and looked inside, she saw a baby, its eyes open, its skin cold and bluish.

Nina sat up in bed, her heart pounding. In the room she thought she could hear the echo of her own scream. "Oh my God," she whispered. She covered her face with her hands. Calm down, she thought. It was just a dream. As her racing heartbeat subsided to a normal rhythm, she reminded herself that it was obvious where the dream had come from. The newspaper stories had brought it all back to her. The baby they found in the park on the day her mother was murdered. It was all mixed up in her dream. I brought it on myself, she thought, by reading those newspapers. She shook her head and sighed.

Looking down, she saw that she was still in her painting clothes. Painting clothes, she thought. Just what her mother always wore. Nina knew she should change—put on a nightshirt or something—but she did not want to get out of the bed. She lay back down and pulled the pink blanket at the foot of the bed around her. But she didn't sleep. She thought of Jimmy, drinking beer, and wondered if he had got home safely. She thought of Andre, and how she had been cold and driven him away. She tried not to think of the dream. She lay there in the darkness, her eyes wide open, and listened to the wind whipping the trees and howling against the window.

23

ANDRE walked down a long corridor to the desk where, after a variety of security precautions, he and all prison employees were required to show their identity badges and sign in each morning. The guard at the desk, Joe Estevez, was sitting, reading a magazine. He looked up as Andre signed in. "Hey, Doc."

"Joe," said Andre. "I was wondering. Is Stan Mazurek coming in today?" The guard, injured in a prison melee, had started coming back to work part-time. He was assigned to a desk job in the warden's office until he was able to fully resume his duties.

"Yeah, he's here," said Joe. "You want to talk to him?"

"Yeah, send him down to the infirmary, will you?"

"Sure thing, Doc."

Andre waved, walked past the desk, and entered the bureaucratic maze of offices on the first floor that led, at last, to the infirmary. Andre's new assistant, Dwight Bird, was already set-

ting up the examining room. Bird, a young man with dread-
locks and wire-rimmed glasses, looked up at him. A highly intelligent college student, Bird was not an inmate, but had pleaded
nolo contendere to a charge of hacking into his university reg-
istar's computer and changing grades for a fee. He'd been given
a fine and a sentence of community service, and the judge had
recommended that he do his community service at the prison,
saying he wanted this bright young man to see where he would
end up if he continued to follow his hacker proclivities. Dwight
had shown an aptitude for his work in the infirmary and was
invaluable to Andre with his skill on the computer.

"Dwight," Andre said, as he put on his own lab coat. "How
you doin' today?"

"Doin' my time," Dwight said amiably as he unpacked test
kits from a box.

Andre leaned over and put his hands on his desk. "A question."

Dwight shrugged. "Shoot."

"Would it be possible to find out if a certain passenger is
leaving any of the area airports on flights to California today or
tomorrow?"

Dwight raised his eyebrows. "Sure it's possible."

"But is it legal?" said Andre. He knew that Dwight would
know better than he.

Dwight grimaced and waggled his hand. "You know. That
airline thing."

Andre nodded. "I was thinking that. Never mind."

"I could do it for you," Dwight said eagerly.

Andre shook his head. "Forget it. It was just a thought."

Dwight shrugged. "Whatever you say, Doc." He resumed
unpacking the test kits.

Andre frowned and tapped his pencil on the tabletop. He
wasn't the least bit surprised to hear that checking on an air-

line's passenger list was illegal. He was just grabbing at straws because, for Nina's sake, he had to find Calvin Mears. He had lain awake the night before thinking about their discussion. Nina had been angry, but Andre knew it stemmed as much from the brutal truth about her brother as it did from anything he had done. Well, he thought, it might have had something to with his trip to Santa Fe. Of course, that would presume that she was beginning to care about him the way he had come to care about her. At any rate, it was a badly timed trip, even though he hadn't planned it that way. And she must have been feeling betrayed everywhere she turned, he thought. Even though she was angry, she was also right—she didn't need more advice. She needed help. Once he'd made up his mind that he was going to help her, no matter what he had to do, he was able to get to sleep.

There was a knock at the door and Andre looked around. A uniformed guard with a pugnacious face was standing in the doorway. "Hey, Doc. Estevez said you were looking for me."

Andre smiled. "Hey, Stan. How's the reentry going?"

Stan Mazurek automatically reached for the spot in his chest where he had been stabbed and patted it. "I can't wait to get back on the bloc. I hate the desk job."

"Well, for a while it makes sense," said Andre.

"Yeah. And my wife's in no hurry for me to be in with the prisoners again."

"I can imagine," said Andre.

"So what'd you want, Doc?"

Andre walked up to the man and spoke quietly to him. "Stan, something's come up. I was . . . uh . . . visiting with Doc Avery's daughter last night."

Stan Mazurek shook his head. "That poor kid. Just gets her old man out of the joint and what happens? Did they catch the son of a bitch who killed him yet?"

"Not yet," said Andre. "The local police seem to be dragging their feet on this."

Stan nodded. " 'Cause he's an ex-con."

"I think you're probably right," said Andre. "But it might be helpful if you could find out for me where I could locate this guy." Andre reached into his pocket and pulled out a clipping of Penelope Mears's obituary. He underlined the name of Calvin's aunt. "The guy I'm looking for, Calvin Mears, may be staying with these people. I tried calling Directory Assistance, but they have an unlisted number."

Stan looked at the name, perplexed. "How would I know where to find them?" he asked.

"The guy's a cop in Seaside Park. I thought maybe through the police fraternal organization or something . . ."

"Oh sure, that's easy," said Stan. "My buddy's recording secretary of the FOP in the county."

"That's great. I need it yesterday," said Andre apologetically.

"No problem," said Stan.

"Think of it as a favor to Doc Avery," said Andre.

Stan tucked the clipping into his pocket and patted it. "Consider it done."

NINA went to the grocery store, stocked up on soup, frozen dinners, and a few of her aunt's favorite candy bars, and brought them back to put in the refrigerator. She looked at her watch. She needed to finish up in Aunt Mary's room before she went to pick her aunt up at the nursing home. She took a minute to try and get the phone number of Calvin's aunt and uncle in Seaside Park, the nearest shore town to Hoffman, but it was unlisted. She figured she would try Jimmy at work when she got back from the nursing home. Surely he would know. At least Rose and George hadn't called looking for Jimmy. That was a good sign that he had probably made it home all right yesterday. She checked her watch again and hurried down to Aunt Mary's refurbished bedroom.

In the daylight, it looked pretty good, she thought. She threaded the laundered curtains onto their rods and hung them up again. She stepped back to admire them, and bumped up against the boxes of newspapers she had looked through the night before. As she replaced them in the back of the closet, the memory of her nightmare came back to her. That image of the baby in the box made her shudder. Don't think about it, she told herself. It was just a dream. Get busy. You've still got a lot to do. She reached for the paintings, which she had stacked on the dresser when she'd taken them down.

Which one goes where? she wondered, as she began to rehang them. There were a couple of small flower paintings that hung on either side of the large mirrored bureau. Nina put them up, moving them around until she thought they looked right. Aunt Mary could always change it, she thought, if she had gotten the order wrong.

The largest painting was one of Nina's mother's watercolors, which Aunt Mary kept over the bed. It was her last painting, the one she'd been working on at the time she died. It was a spring scene that had been painted at the Madison Creek Nature Preserve. To Nina's untrained eye the painting looked finished, although her mother might have had more she wanted to do to it. The dominant colors were pastels—yellow, lavender, and spring green. The painting showed two boys fishing on the bank of the creek. Lilacs were in bloom all around them, the flowers reflected in the surface of the quiet water. It was a painting full of light and joy, and Nina's eyes filled with tears at the sight of it, knowing that it was the last her mother had ever done.

She rehung the picture, and then took a final, satisfied look at the room before she closed the door, gathered up her bag, and headed for the car. But as she drove toward the nursing home, her mind wandered back to the painting, and her mother.

Each day, Nina remembered, fair weather or foul, Marsha would carry her paints and easel down to the park and set up among the trees, out of sight and careful not to disturb the birds and the squirrels or the people who were strolling, or, as in the case of these two boys, fishing. Patrick used to tease their mother that her green sweatshirt was her camouflage outfit. Nina could picture her mother there, hidden among the leaves, those sweet, keen eyes focused on the scene in front of her.

Nina had actually recognized the very spot her mother had painted in the picture over Aunt Mary's bed. It was one of Marsha's favorite locations. It was right near the spot where . . . Nina's heart skipped a beat. She forced herself to watch the road, but her concentration was jolted. It was right near the spot where that baby had been found on the day of Marsha's murder. The baby who had disappeared. She tried to remember what had happened. The boyfriend—what was his name? Travis something. He told the police that someone had kidnapped the child. But everyone thought he had killed the child and gotten rid of it. He had, as it turned out, brought it to the park to bury it. To bury it right near where Marsha used to sit so quietly and paint. Was that it? Nina wondered. Had her mother seen that man, Travis, burying that poor dead baby? Did he find out somehow that she was a witness? Or did he notice her watching him and follow her home? Was that why she was killed?

Nina turned the car into the nursing home driveway, shaking her head. No. Impossible. If Marsha had seen someone doing that, she would have called the police right away. The police would have dug up the baby and arrested the man. And her mother never said a thing about it. Which was impossible. Marsha would have told all of them about it immediately. No, that wasn't what had happened. Thinking hard about it, Nina remembered. A dog had dug up a black plastic garbage bag. The dog probably tore the bag open and the dog's owner must have seen the baby inside and called the police. That's what had brought the police out. It had nothing to do with her mother. It was just a coincidence. It was her dream that made her think that. The dream had merged the headlines in the paper. She parked the car and took a deep breath. Stop imagining things, she scolded herself. Go get your aunt.

24

AUNT MARY was sitting up in the armchair of her room, fully dressed, when Nina arrived. "It's not like you're anxious to get home or anything," Nina said wryly.

"I admit it," said the elderly woman with a smile. "I'm ready to go. I hate to think I might end up in a place like this one day. Promise me you won't move me out of my house unless I'm a hopeless case."

"I promise," said Nina gravely.

An aide in a pink smock, with a name tag that read TAMALA, bustled in and began stripping the hospital bed. "Is she telling you how mean to her we are around here? Here, honey, take these last few pills."

Aunt Mary obediently swallowed the pills with a cup of water and then shook her head. "I told her you are all angels of mercy, but I can't wait to get home."

The aide gave a boisterous laugh. "I don't blame you, honey."

Nina picked up Aunt Mary's little suitcase. "How about these flowers?" Nina asked.

"I told Tamala to put them in the common rooms," said Mary.

"I guess you're ready," said Nina, glancing up at the clock. She wondered if she would be able to get her aunt home and situated and still be able to hunt down Calvin Mears. She had to talk to him. It was the only way she was ever going to find out the truth. "I'll take this suitcase out and bring the car around," said Nina.

Nina's aunt noticed her looking at the clock. "I'm such a bother," she said.

Nina immediately felt guilty. "Don't talk like that," she said.

ANDRE palpated the abdomen of the middle-aged black man lying on the examining table and made some notes on a clip-board that lay on the rolling stainless steel tray beside the table. "Okay, " he said to the patient. "You can sit up now and pull down your shirt."

The inmate grunted as he swung his sturdy legs over the edge of the table. His dark skin had an ashen tone to it, and there were large dark circles under his eyes. "So, what's the matter with me, Doc?" he said, as he stretched his T-shirt over his belly and adjusted the orange tunic top over it.

"I need a little more information before I know the answer to that," Andre said. "I'm gonna send you out for X-rays. After I get them back we'll talk more."

"All I got left on my sentence is two years," the man said. "I don't want to die before I see the other side of that wall."

"We'll try to make sure that doesn't happen," Andre said. He walked over to the barred window of his examining room and called out to the armed man sitting beside the door. "Eddie. You can take Mr. Bishop back now."

"Thanks, Doc," murmured Bishop wearily.

Andre clapped the inmate gently on the back as he opened the door and delivered the man to the guard in the hallway. Then he sat down at his desk to record his notes.

Dwight Bird, his hands encased in disposable plastic gloves, entered the examining room from the infirmary, cleared the paper off the table, balled it up, and put it in the trash. Then he replaced it with another long sheet.

Andre looked up from the desk.

Dwight glanced around before he spoke to be sure they were not overheard. "Your boy's not flying," said Dwight.

"What?" asked Andre.

"You heard me," said Dwight with a sly smile.

"How did you . . . ?"

"I was eavesdropping when you were talking to Mazurek."

"Dwight . . ." Andre protested. "You want to get in more trouble?"

"Don't worry," said Dwight. "I am never ending up here. I promise you that. Besides, if anybody gets in trouble for this, it's gonna be you."

Andre nodded ruefully. "I suppose you're right."

"You're welcome," said Dwight, ambling back to the intake area.

Andre sat and thought for a minute. So Calvin Mears was still in the area. Stan had already delivered the Seaside Park address along with the phone number. But Andre knew better than to call and inquire. If Calvin was staying with his aunt and uncle, a call like that would send him running. Andre knew what he had to do. He got up, walked to the door, and looked out. The guard who had accompanied Bishop, relaying him to another colleague, was returning to his post. "Eddie," Andre called to the young man as he resumed his position outside the infirmary door. "This is an emergency. I'm gonna have to leave."

ONCE they arrived back at the house, Nina came around to the passenger side of the car and unfolded her aunt's walker. Aunt Mary inched her way up the path to the front steps and into the house while Nina hovered beside her.

"It takes me a while," said her aunt.

"You're doing fine," Nina assured her, although she felt her own anxiety rising as they hobbled along slowly.

As they crossed the threshold, Aunt Mary sighed. "Oh, it's good to be home."

"Why don't we get you settled in your room?" Nina asked.

Her aunt nodded. "It would feel good to get in my own bed for a little bit."

They inched across the living room and down the hall. "When we get to the door here, I want you to close your eyes," Nina said.

"Close my eyes?"

"Come on. Just do it."

Obediently, Aunt Mary closed her eyes. Nina switched on the bedside lamp and the one on the bureau, and then told her aunt she could look.

Mary's eyes widened. "Oh my goodness. Nina. What did you do?"

"This room seemed a little gloomy. I decided to brighten it up," Nina said proudly. As she spoke, she helped her aunt to seat herself atop the newly washed bedspread.

"It's wonderful," said Aunt Mary. "It's absolutely beautiful. And you're right. It had gotten so dingy. Ever since Uncle John died I've been meaning to have it painted but I never got around to it. Oh, Nina, you are an angel. I just can't get over it," said Aunt Mary. She pulled her afghan up over her legs and sat up against her pillows, gazing around in amazement.

"When did you have time to do this, Nina? With all that's happened . . ."

"Well," said Nina, placing the suitcase on the bed and unpacking it, "my father helped me." She felt tears rising and pressed her lips together. Then she took a deep breath. "We got a good start on it together, but I have to admit, it was only half done when you called to say you were coming home. I stayed up most of last night finishing."

"Oh, you shouldn't have. You need your rest," said Aunt Mary.

Nina went to the closet and took out a hanger to hang up her aunt's bathrobe. "I didn't get it all done. I didn't do the closet. I started to empty it out, but then . . ." Nina stopped, not wanting to mention the old newspapers she had found in the boxes. "I didn't have time to finish," she said, her voice trailing away.

Aunt Mary grimaced. "Did you find the newspapers?"

Nina turned around and met her aunt's gaze. "Yeah. I found them."

Aunt Mary gazed at her sympathetically. "I hope it didn't upset you too much. I would have warned you if I thought you were going to be in there."

Nina shook her head. "I was a little . . . surprised at first."

"I kept them away from you at the time it happened," said Mary. "There was so much going on. It was all so terrible. I felt like I had to shield you from it as best I could. I never turned on the news when you were around. I hid the papers. But I knew . . . I had a feeling that someday you might want to see them."

Nina sat down on the edge of the bed. "In a way I didn't want to read about it, and in another way I couldn't stop myself."

"Of course," said the old woman.

"It brought that day back to me so vividly. You never know until it's too late that it's a day that will change your life forever.

That afternoon I was thinking it would be the best day of my life."

"You were? How come?" her aunt asked.

"Well, I had a crush on the boy next door and he asked me to the movies. Oh, I was on cloud nine. And I remember it was a great day for Patrick, too. He found out that day that he was accepted at Rutgers. We were both so excited. We had no inkling of what was about to happen." Nina shook her head at her own innocence. "I had no idea that was the last time I would ever see my mother. I can still picture her . . . wearing that old green sweatshirt of hers. She'd gone down to the Preserve to paint that afternoon, but she had to come home 'cause all the police and reporters were in the park. That was the day they found that missing baby, remember? The one that was killed by his mother's boyfriend, or whatever?"

Aunt Mary frowned. "You mean the Kilgore baby?"

"That was it. The Kilgore baby."

Aunt Mary shook her head. "That wasn't the Kilgore baby they found."

"It wasn't?"

Aunt Mary shook her head. "They never did find April Kilgore's baby. Although no one doubts that that boyfriend of hers killed the baby. He ended up in jail for hitting April Kilgore so hard that she lost the hearing in one of her ears."

"That wasn't the Kilgore baby?" said Nina. "Whose baby was it?"

"I don't know. I don't remember if they ever found out. It was a newborn. The mother had smothered it and put it in a trash bag and buried it in the park."

"A newborn?" Nina said, shaking her head.

"They figured out that it had only been there for a day or two. I guess you missed that when you were reading the papers."

"I was only reading about Mom," said Nina.

"Naturally," said her aunt.

Nina frowned and continued to unpack her aunt's suitcase. The phone rang on the bedside table and Mary picked it up.

"Yes, I'm home," Mary said cheerfully. "Just got here a few minutes ago. Thank you. Nina's taking good care of me."

Nina glanced at her aunt, who was smiling warmly at her as she spoke. Nina smiled back.

Aunt Mary put her hand over the receiver. "It's for you, dear," she said. "It's Rose Connelly."

Oh no, Nina thought. She took the phone from her aunt. "Hello?" she said in a guarded tone.

"Nina, it's Rose. I wonder if you could come over. I need to talk to you."

Nina was fairly certain that Rose wanted to talk about Jimmy, and Nina didn't have time for that discussion today. "I'm really . . . kind of busy here."

Nina's aunt was shaking her head. "You go ahead," she said. "I'll be fine."

"Nina, it's urgent," said Rose.

"Okay," Nina sighed. She turned back to the phone. "All right. I'll be over in a little while."

"Please hurry," said Rose, and the catch in Rose's voice gave Nina a feeling of dread in the pit of her stomach.

THE drive to Seaside Park didn't take long, although it involved crossing several bridges built to span the swamps of the wet-lands. Once past the welcome sign, the atmosphere changed. The shore town was completely different from Hoffman. For some reason, the hordes of New York City commuters who clamored to live in the suburbs eschewed this sprawling bungalow-filled town. It was an extra half hour away from the city, and there was a distinct lack of shopping centers in the vicinity. And, of course, the suburban ideal of having the best schools and cultural life for students was clearly not the highest priority here. Instead, the town offered ocean, peace and quiet, a lot of seafood restaurants, and sunsets over the wetlands year-round. Not a bad trade-off, Andre thought.

Because it was midweek and off-season the town was fairly deserted. Andre had no trouble finding the street and the neat gray frame house where Lieutenant Jenkins and his wife, Sally, lived. Andre parked at the curb beyond the driveway and climbed the steps to the aluminum storm door with an elaborate metal J at waist level. He rang the bell and waited.

After a few minutes the inside door was opened by a midde-aged woman with bleached hair in a perm that had lost most of its curl. She was wearing blue pants and a Fralinger's Salt Water Taffy T-shirt with a colorful Victorian design on the front. She frowned at the sight of the exotic-looking man on her doorstep.

"Yes?" she asked, keeping the storm door securely locked.

"Mrs. Jenkins?" he asked.

"Yeah," she said.

Andre thought about the story he had prepared, given what little he knew about Calvin Mears. "My name is Andre Quinteros. I'm a physician."

Andre could see her shoulders relax a little bit when she heard that he was a doctor, but she still regarded him suspiciously.

"I treated your, uh . . . sister for several years on and off," Andre lied.

"I don't remember seeing you at the hospital," Sally said.

"Well, unfortunately, I was away when she contracted her final illness. And then, her death was so sudden. I feel terrible about it. She was still a young woman."

Sally reached down and unlocked the storm door. She pushed it open just enough to rest against it. "She went quick," agreed Sally.

"Tragic," said Andre. "I'm so sorry for your loss."

Sally Jenkins cocked her head to one side. "Thank you. You came all the way down here to offer your condolences?"

"Well, actually." Andre held up an envelope. "I have something I have to deliver. She knew she had a terminal condition, and she asked me to do her a favor. She wanted to be sure that . . . um . . . this went to her son."

"She didn't have no money," Sally said.

"It's true that she was virtually indigent, but that was why she left this with me. So that she wouldn't be tempted to spend it when she got desperate. She asked me to put it in Calvin's hands, and she said that in the event of her death, you people would probably be taking care of him. You know. Being his aunt and uncle."

"How come she didn't go to a lawyer?" said Sally.

"She couldn't afford a lawyer," said Andre.

Sally nodded at this, as if confirming it was true.

"I volunteer at a clinic. She used to come and see me there," Andre said. "I guess she figured she could trust me."

Sally snorted. "That figures. You're good-looking."

Andre smiled thinly. "In any case, I wanted to deliver this to her son." Andre tapped on the envelope in his hand.

"He's not here," said Sally. "You can leave it with me."

"I'm afraid I can't do that," said Andre. "I promised your sister I would bring this to him and put it into his hands."

Sally peered at the envelope. "How much is it?"

Andre gave her a reproachful look. "It's not a great deal of money. But it was her wish for her son to have it."

Sally gazed at him thoughtfully. "This isn't some scheme you cooked up with that Keefer guy to get to Calvin, is it?"

"Excuse me?" Andre asked politely.

Sally looked out at Andre's car at the curb. The M.D. plates were clearly visible. She looked back at Andre and then sighed. "This sounds like something Penny would do. Oh well. All right. He's not staying with us. We crowd him, he says. He's staying over at the Ocean Breeze Motel. Unit 408. You know where that is? It's a few blocks in from the boardwalk."

"I imagine I can find it," he said.

"I'm gonna call Calvin and tell him you're coming," she said. "If he don't want to let you in, that's his business. You can slide it under the door."

"That's fine," said Andre. Despite her lackluster appearance, this woman was nobody's fool, he thought. He wondered if he could get to the Ocean Breeze Motel before Calvin decided to bolt. Of course, Calvin would be curious about the envelope with the money. That might be enough to make him stick around. Andre had to hope so. "You have a nice day," he said.

Andre walked back to his car and was leisurely about getting into the driver's seat, for the benefit of the cop's wife still watching him from the doorway. He adjusted his mirrors and checked all his locks before pulling slowly away from the curb. Once out of her sight, however, he navigated through town screeching around corners, past blinking red lights, and accelerated to the speed limit on the deserted road that ran past the wetlands toward the boardwalk.

The Ocean Breeze Motel was not difficult to find, and luckily he had the room number already. There was a large parking lot in front of the fifties-style motel, but room 408 was in back. Andre drove around and parked his car. There were a few other cars scattered in the parking spaces, and beyond the parking lot, an empty swimming pool with a single round table and a few overturned plastic chairs beside it. Outside of a room down the walkway was a chambermaid's rolling cart, piled high with towels and cleaning supplies, but no signs of the chambermaid.

Andre got out of his car and, noting the sequence of numbers on the doors, walked in the opposite direction from the cart until he spotted room 408. He could see a sliver of light inside the room, like a glaring crease along the seam of the blackout drapes. He lifted his fist to knock on the door, but before his hand made contact with it, the door was pulled open from within.

A lean young man with dishwater-blond hair and startlingly handsome features opened the door. He was pale and sweaty, and his fine gray eyes were wide with fear.

"Are you the doctor my aunt called about?" he demanded.

Andre frowned and took a step back. "Yes," he said slowly.

"Thank God." He looked anxiously up and down the deserted walkway and grabbed Andre's sleeve. "You gotta help me. He's dying."

25

THE inviting smell of cinnamon and yeast emanated from the Connellys' house when Rose opened the door. But the look on Rose's face was anything but welcoming. She did not smile at Nina as she asked her to come in, and every crease and sag on her middle-aged face seemed more pronounced than usual.

"It smells good in here," said Nina, trying to be pleasant.

"I made bread. It was something to do with my hands," said Rose abruptly. "Sit down, Nina."

Nina sat on the taupe love seat. Rose sat at a right angle to her on the couch. Over Rose's shoulder, Nina could see a framed photograph of Jimmy and young Anthony, arms around each other's shoulders, smiling for the camera. "What's the matter?" said Nina. "You sounded upset on the phone."

"I'll get right to the point," said Rose. "I want to know what happened yesterday. With Jimmy. You left here looking for him. Did you find him?"

"Well, yeah. Actually, I found him at . . . Didn't he tell you?" Nina asked.

"He was out all night," said Rose. "He said he slept at Patrick's. He was surly this morning when I tried to talk to him."

At least he came home, Nina thought. Maybe Rose didn't know he'd been drinking. "Maybe he was tired," Nina suggested.

Rose looked at Nina with a disappointed expression on her face. "Please, Nina. Don't try to fog me. I'm not the sharpest tack in the box, but I'm not a fool either."

Nina reddened and looked away from the older woman.

"I think . . . Jimmy was drinking."

Nina tried to look surprised.

"Jimmy thinks I don't know," said Rose calmly. "He forgets the years we went through with him when he was trying to kick the drugs and the alcohol. This morning it was obvious. I could still smell it. I could see it in his behavior. He's like a different person when he's high. Where was he when you found him yesterday? Was he drunk?"

Rose was obviously not inclined to hysterics or to mincing words, Nina thought. She was not going to be put off with excuses. "He was at a funeral," Nina said.

"Whose funeral?" Rose asked, surprised.

"Penelope Mears. She was the mother of . . ."

"Oh, God," said Rose. "Oh no. It's Calvin Mears, isn't it? Calvin Mears is back in his life." She shook her head. "Lord help us."

"Well, actually, I don't know about that. Calvin was in town for his mother's funeral. I think Jimmy was just trying to be . . . . supportive, you know."

Rose shook her head. "That's who called him this morning. I could see the difference in Jim right away. That's where he is," she said grimly.

"What do you mean?"

Rose looked at her balefully. "This morning he told me he was going to change his clothes and go to work. But his boss called from Hoffman Flooring. Jimmy never showed up. He just . . . disappeared."

Nina tried to think of something reassuring to say, but the words stuck in her throat.

"He's with him," said Rose. "With Calvin. I'll bet you any money." Rose shook her head and then looked up at Nina. "Was he drinking when he was with you yesterday?"

Nina didn't want to be a snitch. But apparently her face gave her away.

"I see," said Rose grimly. She shook her head. "I'm afraid for your brother."

Nina chewed her lip and thought it over. Then she spoke quietly. "So am I."

For a minute, they sat in silence. Then Rose sighed. "No one can make him stay straight if he doesn't want to be. No one can do that for him," she said. "But I'm afraid if he goes into another tailspin, he won't be able to pull himself out of it."

Nina thought about her brother and Calvin Mears. "You said Calvin Mears called," said Nina. "Do you have Caller ID on your phone?"

Rose frowned. "Yes. I think maybe we do. I never use it. Anthony wanted it."

"Can I see?" said Nina. "It's worth a try."

Rose led her to the phone and Nina picked it up and scrolled the Caller ID messages. "Ocean Breeze Motel," she said. "Do you know anybody there?"

Rose shook her head.

Nina showed her the time on the identification window. "Is this about the time when Mears called?" she asked.

"Yes," said Rose.

Nina dialed the number and asked the woman who answered for the motel's location. Then she put the phone back in its vertical cradle. "It's a motel in Seaside Park. I'm going down there," she said.

Rose shook her head. "Nina, it's up to Jimmy. You can't make him give up his addictions. He has to do that himself."

Jimmy is with Calvin Mears, Nina thought. "I just want to find him," she said.

WHILE she gassed up the car at the local service station, Nina called Gemma's house. The machine picked up. She tried Gemma's cell phone and this time Gemma answered.

"I hear Jimmy spent the night at your house," said Nina. "Where are you? You sound like you're in the car."

"I was at the university library," said Gemma. "Yeah. You're right about Jimmy. Patrick had to go pick him up at a bar."

"I think he's in trouble," said Nina. "He told the Connellys he was going to work this morning, but he never made it there. I think he went to meet up with Calvin Mears. You probably don't remember him . . ."

"Yes, I do," said Gemma flatly. "He used to call me Bones."

Nina winced. She knew that Gemma had endured a lot of teasing about her scrawny appearance in school. "Well, he's a jerk. He always was. Anyway, I'm going to try to find Jimmy. Calvin and Jimmy are a bad combination. Listen, Gemma, I need a favor. Can you pick up my aunt's prescriptions at the Village Pharmacy and bring them to her? The pharmacist said she can't have all of them ready for at least an hour, and I want to get on my way."

"Sure," said Gemma. "No problem."

Nina thanked her sister-in-law, paid for the gas, and headed toward Seaside Park.

Dark clouds were gathering over the deserted beach town by the time Nina arrrived. She stopped at another service station for directions and made her way slowly to the street, two blocks from the beach where the Ocean Breeze Motel was located. As soon as she turned the corner and saw the neon sign for the Ocean Breeze, she also saw that there was some sort of commotion going on around it. There were police cars and an ambulance in the parking lot, and people were clustered outside the motel office talking and pointing. A yellow police line had been set up, blocking access to the motel rooms. A few angry customers were demanding that they needed to get in. Nina's heart was in her throat as she parked at the curb and walked up to where a knot of police officers were standing.

Before she could even open her mouth to ask a question, one of the officers said, "All right, move along here."

"What happened?" she said.

The officer did not look at her. "Everybody move along. We need everybody to get out of the way."

A heavyset girl in a barn jacket and blue jeans was making notes on a pad. "They had a shooting," she volunteered.

Nina's heart skipped a beat. "Who got shot?" Nina demanded.

"I don't know. I'm trying to get some answers myself. I work for the weekly paper. Somebody who was staying in the motel."

"My brother was . . . visiting here," said Nina anxiously. "Do you have any names?"

The girl looked at her pad. But before she could find the name, Nina saw a car door open and two people she recognized got out. The stocky, balding man was wearing fishing gear and waders, and the woman was wearing stretch pants and a T-shirt with some sort of Victorian design on it. It took Nina a moment to recognize them as one of the officers, apparently in charge, went up to them and shook hands with the balding man. Calvin's aunt and uncle, from the cemetery, she thought. The uniformed officer leaned in and spoke earnestly to the two of them. The woman let out a startled cry and sagged against her husband.

"Calvin . . . Mears," said Nina.

"That's right," said the female reporter. "He was killed. The ambulance took the other two away. Hey . . ."

Nina rushed past her and up to the police line, behind which the plainclothes officer who had been speaking to Calvin's aunt and uncle was talking with a woman wearing plastic gloves. "Excuse me," she said. "Excuse me. Please, I need help."

The officer turned to Nina with a frown. "Get back from there, please," he said.

"My brother was with the man who got killed. I need to know . . ."

"What's your brother's name?" asked the detective.

"Avery . . . James Avery."

The officer looked at his notebook and his frown deepened, but his impatient look disappeared. "I'm sorry, miss. What's your name?"

"Nina . . . Avery." Her mouth was so dry she could hardly get her name out, and her heart was hammering.

"Your brother, James . . . uh . . . he's been taken to Shore Medical Center. If you want, I can have one of my men drive you over there to see him."

"Oh my God," said Nina. "Oh my God. Who shot him?"

"Your brother . . . no, he wasn't shot. The other two men were shot. Your brother . . . he apparently was the victim of a drug overdose. He's . . . uh . . . he's critical right now. He's in a coma. Here, you want to sit down? Can somebody bring this lady a chair?"

One of the uniformed officers ducked into a nearby room.

"What was your brother doing here with Mr. Mears? Do you know?" asked the detective.

"I don't know," said Nina. "They were old friends."

An officer appeared from inside one of the rooms carrying an armchair. He put it on the walkway, and Nina sank down into it, her legs feeling like rubber.

"Are you all right?" the young officer asked solicitously.

Nina nodded.

"Sepulveda, go get her a drink from that machine in the office," said the detective. "When she's ready, drive her over to Shore. Her brother's the one who OD'd."

OD'd, Nina thought. Oh God. "But . . . who, what happened?" Nina whispered.

"Detective Milgram," said another uniformed officer, who was approaching with a woman wearing a cotton shirt, with mirrors sewn around the neck, a long skirt, and sandals. She had walnut-colored skin and shiny dark hair pulled back in a messy knot at the back of her head. "Here's the chambermaid. She just got back. You said you wanted to ask her . . ."

"Yeah," growled the detective. "Miss . . . Patel, is it? I want you to tell me everything you saw . . ."

"I'm not a chambermaid," the woman protested. "My uncle owns this place."

Nina, still in the chair, looked down the walkway at Calvin Mears's aunt and uncle, who were talking to another detective. Calvin's aunt was sniffling into a tissue and shaking her head miserably. The uncle was speaking angrily, making a gesture as if he were wielding a club, and suddenly Nina heard him say, "He had a bat with him." Nina realized that Jenkins was telling the police about that guy, Keefer, at the cemetery. The guy with the baseball bat.

"What about the other guy?" his wife cried. "The Puerto Rican guy. The one that came to the house."

The detective, whose back was to Nina, murmured something, and they both nodded.

Officer Sepulveda, a serious-looking young man with a long

narrow face, returned from the soda machine and handed Nina a can of Sprite. Gratefully, Nina took a drink.

"You ready to go over to the Medical Center now, miss?" he asked.

"It's all right. I'll be all right. I can drive there," Nina said faintly.

"It's no problem," said Sepulveda. "If you're too shook up to drive."

"I just need to sit a minute," she said. She closed her eyes and sipped at the soda. The chambermaid was droning on about the mess she had found in 408 and how in India her parents had servants who cleaned up after her.

"So, did you see anything at all . . . anything unusual?" the detective asked. "Anything that might help us find out who did this."

"No, not really," said the woman apologetically in a singsong accent. "Well, maybe one thing," she said.

"And what was that?" the detective asked.

"Well. I saw a Jaguar parked out in back there. You know. The British sports car. Silvery blue color. Brand-new. Really a beautiful car. You don't see many of those in a place like this; I can tell you that. It was only there a short time."

"Did you notice the plate?" the detective asked.

The woman shook her head. "Jersey plates, I think. I didn't pay attention."

Officer Sepulveda put a hand on the back of the chair and leaned over to speak to Nina. "How you doing?" he asked. "Are you ready to go?"

Nina did not reply. She was staring straight ahead, thinking about what the chambermaid had said. A late-model silvery blue Jaguar, Nina thought. Parked right outside the room where Calvin Mears was gunned down. The room where Jimmy was dying of a drug overdose. A silvery blue Jaguar. No, she thought. It couldn't be.

26

"OKAY, miss," said the nurse kindly. "We've got him stabilized and he's in an ICU cubicle now. You can go up, but only for a few minutes."

Nina had been sitting in the Emergency Room waiting area of the Shore Medical Center for nearly two hours, waiting to see her brother. She understood that the doctors and nurses were busy trying to save him, and she was patient. Occasionally a nurse would come out and give her an update on his condition. Now, at this latest bulletin, Nina stood up. "How is he?"

"He's still critical," said the nurse apologetically. "He's not conscious, but . . . maybe he'll know you're there anyway. Sometimes they do."

Nina thanked her, and made her way through the maze of the unfamiliar hospital, following the signs to the ICU. Directed by a receptionist, she entered the curtained cubicle timidly and saw her brother lying in a hospital bed, lit by a fluorescent halo from the harsh light over the bed. Nina tiptoed up to Jimmy and put a hand on his clammy forehead, which was about the only visible part of him that was not crisscrossed with wires and tubes. His eyelids were a grayish color, closed over his sunken eyes. There was no sound in the cubicle except for the whoosh of the ventilator. The tube, taped to his face, snaked out of his mouth between his parched-looking pale lips. What happened to you in that motel room? she wondered.

"Jimmy." She leaned over and spoke into his ear. "It's me. Nina. You've got to come back to us. Come on. Open your eyes. You can do it."

There was no response from the man on the bed. Nina straightened up and looked down at him. All the way over here, all the time she had been keeping a vigil for Jimmy, she kept thinking about the silver-blue Jaguar in the motel parking lot. Last night, Patrick had picked Jimmy up at the bar. Jimmy had probably told him about how he and Calvin had conspired to rob their mother on that long-ago day. Maybe it made Patrick angry enough to want to confront Mears himself. Maybe Patrick walked in on them and found Jimmy overdosed like this and went crazy. Jimmy, what happened in there? She asked the question in her mind. But now, with Jimmy comatose and Mears dead, she wondered if she would ever know the answers.

A nurse poked her head between the curtains and spoke quietly to Nina. "Keep it short, hon," she said.

Nina nodded and then bent over to kiss her brother's forehead. "I'll be back," she said. She thanked the nurse on her way past the central command desk in the ICU, and the nurse smiled at her sympathetically.

She held her breath as she passed through the busy unit. She opened the door and stepped gratefully out into the relative quiet of the waiting area.

"Nina!" Nina looked up and saw Rose and George Connelly,

who had just arrived. They hurried toward her, their eyes full of pain. Nina had dreaded this encounter ever since she called Rose from the hospital. They had tried so hard for Jimmy, and now they would have to endure even more suffering on his behalf.

"How is he doing?" George cried.

"Not too good," said Nina, and for the first time since she had entered the hospital, tears welled in her eyes.

"The Lord will protect him, Nina," said George, putting an arm around her. "Have faith." Is that your secret? Nina wondered. Is that how you can stand the blows?

Rose shook her head. "Ever since you told me that Calvin Mears was back, I was afraid something like this would happen."

"I'm sorry, Rose," said Nina.

"Oh, Nina," said Rose. "Don't apologize. It's not your doing. You have nothing to be sorry about." Rose reached out for her and enveloped her in a motherly hug that felt like forgiveness, and Nina allowed herself, for a few moments, to let down her guard and have a good cry.

HUNGER and exhaustion overwhelmed Nina as soon as she left the hospital, and at the first rest stop she pulled in and closed her eyes for a minute. Nearly an hour later, the chill in the car woke her from a deep sleep. She went into the restaurant and got herself a quick bite. Then she drove the rest of the way back to Hoffman.

Nina was surprised when she pulled into the driveway to see the little wine-colored Honda Civic parked there. She trudged up to her aunt's front door and reached for the knob. The door opened and Nina was greeted by her sister-in-law.

"How is Jimmy?" said Gemma, as Nina brushed past her coming into the house.

"Not good," said Nina.

"Will he live?" Gemma asked.

Nina shook her head. "I don't know."

"What about the other man?"

"Calvin Mears?" Nina asked. "He's dead."

"No, there was a Hispanic man. They said on TV he was still alive but he was critical."

Nina shook her head. "Oh, I don't know. I don't know anything about that. I've been with Jimmy. I'm numb." Nina took her jacket off and sat down in a chair, rubbing her eyes. "The Connellys are with Jimmy now. Have you heard from Patrick?"

Gemma shook her head. "Not yet. He's still at work, I suppose. I want to get down there to the hospital, but I need to wait for Patrick."

Nina stared at her. "He hasn't called you back?"

Gemma shrugged. "That's not unusual. He hates for me to bother him at work. And he's often late."

Nina couldn't meet Gemma's inquiring gaze. She had been thinking dark thoughts about Patrick for the last few hours. "Where are the boys?"

"With the new housekeeper," Gemma said.

"How's my aunt?"

"Sleeping. She took her medication," said Gemma.

Nina exhaled a little sigh of relief. "Thanks for doing that. And for staying with her."

"No problem. Well, now that you're back," said Gemma, "I'll be going."

"Gemma, can I talk to you for a minute first?"

Gemma looked surprised. "Certainly, Nina." Gemma sat down on the sofa, her wiry frame barely making a dent in the cushions. Her fingers moved restlessly in her lap, twisting her rings. Her large brown eyes studied her sister-in-law. "What is it?"

Nina glanced behind her at the hallway leading to her aunt's bedroom. "We have to talk quietly. I don't want my aunt to wake up and hear any of this."

"Any of what?" Gemma asked.

"I've been thinking about this the whole way home in the car. Trying to think why . . . I don't know where to begin." Nina took a deep breath. "I have to ask you something. It's about Patrick."

Gemma frowned. "What about Patrick?"

Nina clasped her hands and rubbed them together. "All right, I know this is going to sound . . . Look, I've been very worried ever since I heard that . . . well, someone saw a silver-blue Jaguar at the motel where they found Jimmy."

Gemma stared at her. Nina could see her pulse beating in her throat.

"It may not mean anything because there are lots of blue Jaguars . . ." Nina backpedaled.

The expression in Gemma's eyes turned stony. "You are . . . sick," said Gemma. "You think your brother did this?"

Nina drew back in the face of Gemma's anger. "I don't know what to think. I'm sorry, Gemma—I couldn't help thinking about it. I mean, Jimmy spent the night at your house. I'll bet he told Patrick all about what he and Calvin Mears did on the night my mother was killed—about the robbery."

Two spots of color appeared in Gemma's normally pale cheeks. "Jimmy was carrying on about that. Yes," she said. "He maundered on till all hours. I don't think that Patrick believed him though. Jimmy was dead drunk."

Nina leaned forward in her chair. "I know, but maybe today it was bothering Patrick. Maybe he decided to go down to the motel where Calvin was staying and confront them both—find out for sure. And maybe he walked in and found Jimmy like that, and—you know—went crazy. If I'm not mistaken, he does have a gun. I think he told me that once."

"Patrick is at work," said Gemma. "In New York City."

Nina thought of the other times when Patrick had said he was at work. Times when he was with Lindsay Farrell. "How do you know?" Nina asked. "He could have left work and driven down to Seaside Park."

Gemma studied her through narrowed eyes. "Did you tell all this to the police?"

"No," Nina admitted. "They questioned me, but when they mentioned the blue Jaguar I never said anything. No matter what you might think of me, I wasn't about to rat out my brother. I'm just . . . worrying out loud."

"Well, stop it," said Gemma. "Why would you want to think the worst of Patrick? Are you trying to ruin us? He's my husband. He's the father of my children. Do you want him to go to prison?"

"I just want to know the truth," Nina said stubbornly.

"Give me the phone," said Gemma, holding out her hand. "I'll call him again. I'll prove it to you."

Nina reached in her satchel and gave the cell phone to her sister-in-law. Gemma punched in a number.

"Yes," she said. "I want to talk to Patrick Avery. Tell him it's his wife, and this time it's an emergency. No matter what he's doing, tell him I need to speak to him."

Gemma waggled her foot impatiently as she waited for Patrick to get on the line.

Nina watched her cautiously.

"Yes, I'm still here," said Gemma. Suddenly, all the fire went out of her eyes. "He's not? Since when? When did he leave? I see." Gemma punched the phone off and sat holding it for a moment. Then she stood up and handed the phone to Nina. "I have to go," she said.

"Where is he?" said Nina.

"I don't know," Gemma said.

Nina shook her head. "Gemma, I don't want this to be true. Look, I'm not going to tell the police anything about this. But you have to prepare yourself. If the Puerto Rican guy lives, he may be able to identify the shooter. If it was Patrick . . ."

Gemma hesitated and then turned toward the door. "Go to hell," Gemma said, grabbing her coat. She slammed the door as she left.

Nina grimaced. She didn't blame Gemma for being angry. She felt guilty for even thinking these thoughts about her own brother. But she had to find out for sure. She knew that there was one other place that Patrick could be. Somewhere that Gemma didn't know about.

27

ANDRE awoke, shivering, in a room filled with bright lights. He looked around and saw railings on his bed and a thin white cotton blanket covering him. There was an IV needle inserted in his hand, a splotch of blood dark against the transparent tape. He tried to shift his weight in the bed and felt the pain radiate throughout his upper body. What am I doing here? he thought groggily. And then he remembered.

"Hey, somebody's awake," said a nurse, as she approached his bed and rested her thick forearms on the bed rail. She was middle-aged, with a short, graying haircut and a broad, pleasant face. She cocked her head and looked down at him kindly. "How you feeling now? You're a mighty lucky fellow," she said. "They took three bullets out of you."

Andre tried to speak, but his mouth was dry and he couldn't form the words.

"Here, let me help you," said the nurse. She produced a tiny sponge on a stick and wiped his parched lips with it. "There, is that any better?"

Andre nodded slightly. "Time?" he murmured.

The nurse checked her watch. "It's about five o'clock. You were on the table for several hours. You're still in the recovery room. We're going to keep you here until everything's stable and then we'll move you upstairs. But you know the drill, Doc."

Andre smiled faintly and nodded. As his awareness returned, he was overcome with a feeling of intense anxiety.

"At first they didn't realize who you were," the nurse continued cheerfully. "The police thought you were into drugs like the guys they found you with. Then somebody went through your things and figured it out."

Andre tried to lick his parched lips with a sticky tongue and the nurse swabbed his mouth again, a concerned look on her face.

"Water?" he managed to ask.

"Not just yet," she said, "but I can get you some cracked ice if you want."

"Please," Andre muttered, his coated tongue barely functioning.

The nurse bustled off and Andre closed his eyes. He tried to remember what had happened. There were blanks in his memory. He struggled to piece the events together in his mind. He'd been worried about Nina. Worried she would never rest until she found Calvin Mears. He knew they would never get together until this was resolved. It was all she could think about. So he had decided to just go ahead and do it, without even telling her. He had tapped into the Corrections Department grapevine, gotten the address . . . Faces floated into his mind. Stan Mazurek and Dwight Bird. The woman in Seaside Park, Calvin's aunt . . . He closed his eyes and tried to focus his mind. Like a weary man seeking repose, he let his mind rest on Nina.

Nina. Nina wanted to know . . . What was it? He remembered taking the address that Stan gave him and driving to that house in Seaside Park. He had his story all prepared.

"Here we go," said the nurse. She reappeared at his bedside and lifted a small piece of ice from a cup with a little plastic spoon and placed it on his tongue. Andre felt the coldness fill his mouth and trickle down his throat. All of a sudden, a wave of nausea came over him, and his mouth began to water. He tried to take a deep breath.

· "What is it, Dr. Quinteros? Are you feeling sick?" the nurse asked.

Sweat popped out on his forehead. Andre tried to quell the nausea with his will.

"I can give you some Compazine if you need it."

"No," said Andre. Compazine would knock him out again. "Phone," he said. He swallowed hard. "I need the phone."

The nurse wagged a finger at him. "No phone for you. You know better than that, Doctor. You're still in recovery. You have to stay quiet. Now you just lie back there and stop worrying. There will be time for the phone when you get into a regular room. Whatever it is will just have to wait."

She started to walk away from the bed.

"Nurse," he croaked in a hoarse voice.

She came back and looked him over, frowning. "You're sweating something terrible. Let me get the thermometer."

She walked away again and Andre fell back against the pillow. He had to get word to Nina. Tell her what happened. The skinny young man with dirty hair and desperate eyes had opened the door a few inches and stared at him.

"Are you the doctor my aunt called about?" he had asked. Then: "Thank God. You gotta help me. He's dying."

Andre had gone into the room. It was dark and in disarray. The whole room smelled of vomit. There was a large man on the bed with a rubber tube tied around his upper arm and vomit all over his shirt. He was barely breathing.

"What happened?" Andre had asked Mears.

Calvin Mears had stared at the man on the bed. "I don't know. He just collapsed."

Andre had rushed to the man's side, examining his eyes. His pupils were pinpoints, his pulse feeble. His skin was pallid, cold to the touch. His breathing slow and shallow. "What drug did he take?"

"Drug? I don't know," said Mears.

"You're a liar," Andre had cried, groping around until he found the syringe on the floor. "What was it?" he demanded.

"Heroin," Mears had said. "It was heroin."

"Shit," Andre had said. "We need Narcan. Call nine-one-one." And then he had heard the knock at the door. Mears had gone to answer it.

The nurse returned with the thermometer, poked it into Andre's ear, and pressed a button. She took it out of his ear and peered at it.

"What is it?" Andre breathed.

"It's climbing on us a little bit. That's normal though. Right after surgery. We'll keep an eye on it."

Andre reached out and grabbed her hand. "Please, nurse. A phone call. Can you do it for me? It's urgent."

"Now, listen," said the nurse. "You may be a doctor, but I'm in charge here and I say no phone calls, no questions from the police, nothing, until we get you into a little better shape."

"Police?" he whispered.

"They're out in the hallway," she said. "They've been asking to come in here for the last hour. They want to talk to you about what happened. But they're not getting in until I say so."

"I want to tell them . . ." he said.

"Oh no. I don't want them in here disturbing everything.

There's plenty of time for that," said the nurse. "Now lie back." Shaking her head, she took the thermometer and his chart and went back to the nurses' station. She recorded the patient's temperature, filed the chart in the appropriate slot, and then went to check on an elderly man who had had his gallbladder removed by laparoscopy. The old man seemed to be faring pretty well. He would be heading up to his room in no time. She moved on to a woman who'd had several ovarian tumors removed that afternoon. Everything was benign, but she'd had a rough couple of hours. A bad reaction to the anesthetic. The nurse started to walk around the side of the bed to take the woman's pulse when the woman called out in a weak but alarmed voice. "Nurse, that man, look!"

The nurse turned and saw the doctor with the gunshot wounds. He had managed to slide off the bed. He was on his feet, but wobbling, holding the bandages on his stomach with one hand and the wall with the other as he tried to make his way to the door. The back of his johnny was flapping open but he did not seem to care.

"Dr. Quinteros," she cried. "Stop that!"

He ignored her, continuing to shuffle toward the door holding on to the wall.

"You stop right there," she cried, as she rounded the bed and headed toward him. "You'll start bleeding."

Just as he got to the door she reached him and tried to grab him. He turned toward her, his coppery skin now gray. Blood was seeping across the front of the johnny where he held his hand. Before she could catch him his eyes rolled back and he collapsed against the wall and slid down to the cold tile floor.

28

NINA had called Farrell's Antiques and the salesman, Arne, answered. He told her that Lindsay was out. When Nina persisted and said she would come to the store and wait for her, Arne had finally admitted that she was out appraising the contents of an estate for a young banker named Cowley, whose parents had recently passed away. She would probably be working there late into the night. Reluctantly, he gave her the address, warning her that she was not welcome to barge in on Lindsay while she was working. Nina was beyond caring about being unwelcome.

The Cowley estate sat at the end of a winding driveway that passed through an apple orchard and over a bridge above a man-made pond surrounded by weeping willows. In the moonlight, the fronds of the willow trees were silver, and the onyx surface of the pond was split by a corrugated trail of light. Nina drove slowly toward the enormous Norman-style house at the foot of the driveway. The place was probably breathtaking when it was all lit up, Nina thought, but tonight it was dark except for several glowing windows on the first floor. Nina parked the Volvo beside the lone car in the driveway, a black BMW, and stepped out onto the cobblestones. There was no sign of the Jaguar. This one time, Nina wished that she had found it here. Maybe he came and went, she told herself. Go and find out.

She walked up to the front door of the Cowley house, which was standing ajar, and pushed it open. She stuck her head in the door and called out in a loud voice, "Lindsay? Are you in here?"

Nina heard a distant voice say something, and she stepped into the grand, open foyer with a winding staircase that faced the front door. She looked down through the corridor of rooms on either side of the foyer. One of the corridors was dark, but through the other she could see the tasteful muted tints and wallpapers of the succeeding rooms. "Lindsay. It's Nina Avery," she called out in the direction of the lighted rooms. She listened for a reply and heard one voice, and then a second voice.

Frowning, Nina began to walk in the direction of the lighted rooms and the voices. As she got closer she could distinguish the timbre of the two voices—it was a man and a woman speaking. Lindsay and, if she wasn't mistaken, Patrick. Patrick. Nina fumed as she passed through ornately decorated rooms that already had colored tags attached to the vases, paintings, and furniture. She arrived at the doorway of a book-lined room and steeled herself for what she might see when she looked in. She knew she should announce herself, but she decided it was time they were caught in the act. She stepped through the doorway and looked. At the opposite end of the room, in front of a bank of mullioned windows, Lindsay and Patrick were huddled together. As she looked closer she saw that they were examining the underside of an upended settee.

"Look at that webbing," said Lindsay, shaking her head.

"Reupholstered," said Patrick. "So that takes it out of the five-figure range."

"Exactly," said Lindsay.

"Excuse me," said Nina.

Lindsay shrieked and Patrick looked up, glaring. "Nina," he said. "For Christ's sake. You scared us. What are you doing here? Why did you sneak up on us like that?"

Nina stared at the two of them, dressed in sneakers and filthy clothes. Lindsay had her hair knotted up in a scarf. "I'm sorry," Nina mumbled. "I didn't . . ."

"Let's lower this," said Patrick. Lindsay nodded, and the two of them replaced the settee on the jewel-toned oriental rug.

"I'm going to get started in the dining room," Lindsay said to Patrick. "I want you to get to work on those Japanese porcelains. We'll go over it when you're done."

"Okay," he said.

Lindsay edged by Nina and exited through the library doorway. "Always nice to see you, Nina."

Patrick indicated a tapestry-covered chair. Nina took the seat. Patrick sat down on the edge of the leather sofa.

"Patrick, what's going on here?"

He folded his hands together and sighed. "I could lie," he said, "but I guess I may as well tell you. My mind is pretty well made up. Although I'm going to catch hell about it from all directions . . ."

"Patrick . . ." Nina said sharply.

Patrick frowned. "All right. Here's the short version. I'm quitting my job, and I'm going to buy Lindsay's business."

"This is about the business?" Nina said.

Patrick nodded. "That's what I was doing the other night in the office when you came by. Going over the books. She's got a lot of stock and overhead, but there are people with money around here who are ready to buy. Lindsay and Arne are getting married and they're going to move back to Europe."

Nina felt stunned at how completely she had misread the situation. "Arne? The salesman in the store?"

Patrick nodded. "Yeah. I think he's a little . . . flaky, but hey, who am I to talk? Anyway, it seemed like a perfect opportunity. I just . . . I don't get any satisfaction anymore out of what I'm doing. I mean, we have money, and everything money can buy, but the only time I'm really happy is when I'm doing this—digging around old estates, going to auctions, hunting through old books to find obscure paintings. I thought I would be satisfied when I finished my house, but I found myself hating work and wishing I could start all over again. And, I don't know, maybe it's because both our parents are dead at such an early age, but I keep thinking that life is too short. You have to do the thing you love, even if it means you don't have all the luxuries another kind of work can bring. Well, you know. You do what you love to do . . ."

Nina shook her head. "Patrick, I'm . . . I don't know what to say. Does Gemma know about this?"

Patrick made a sour face. "No. And she's not going to like it. We're not going to have the kind of money she's used to . . ."

"Oh, come on, Patrick. Gemma's not exactly materialistic," Nina reminded him.

"No, but things are gonna be tight for a while. She may have to find herself a job where she can make some money," he said.

"I guess she can always go back to the university," said Nina.

Patrick looked at Nina with an incredulous expression on his face. "Uh, no, I don't think so."

"Sure. They'll take her back. She can work on her mother's book on weekends or evenings."

"She didn't tell you, did she?" Patrick asked. He shook his head. "She asked me not to. She said she was going to. I should have known."

"Tell me what?" Nina asked.

Patrick shook his head. "Nina, she didn't resign to work on any book. She was fired. She was fired for falsifying results in the research lab for a paper she prepared for publication."

Nina stared at him. "Gemma?"

Patrick sighed. "Don't feel bad. She didn't tell *me* about it for six months. She pretended she was going to work."

"You're kidding," said Nina.

"I wish I were. Don't look so surprised. This is vintage Gemma. I've gotten used to it over the years. Anyway, I'm not all that concerned with what she thinks about my job change. She'll have to live with it. And Lindsay's been helping me with the things I don't know too much about. That's why I'm here. She thought it would be a good opportunity for me to price some things I wasn't too familiar with—chinoiserie, American antiques—all that. So, now that you know, what do you think?"

Nina felt like her head was spinning. "I think . . . if that's what you want to do, you should go for it."

Patrick smiled broadly, and Nina realized it had been a long time since she saw her brother smile that way. "Thanks," he said. "That means a lot to me. I doubt my wife will agree." He shrugged. "But I don't care anymore. It's my life." Then he looked at Nina curiously. "By the way, how did you find me?"

Nina shook her head. "I . . . I . . . just took a lucky guess. I wanted to tell you about Jimmy."

Patrick rolled his eyes. "Is he drunk? He was drunk last night, you know. I had to go pick him up at a bar. And before you ask, yes, he told me all about him and Calvin robbing the house the night Mom died. I thought about punching his lights out but he was too drunk to even feel it."

"Patrick," Nina interrupted him. "Jimmy's in the hospital. A drug overdose. He's in a coma."

"Oh my God," said Patrick.

"Gemma's been trying to call you."

Patrick grimaced. "Shit. I was ignoring the messages. I knew I'd be late with all this. Shit. We have to get to the hospital. Where is he?"

"Shore Medical. I'm on my way down there again. He was with Calvin when it happened."

"Surprise, surprise," said Patrick disgustedly. "Nina, will you take me with you? I don't have my car. Some guy at the bar was hocking me about how ragged it was running. So I took it to the garage after I dropped Jimmy off this morning, and I grabbed the bus into the city."

Nina's heart suddenly felt positively light. He didn't even have the Jaguar. Her suspicions of Patrick were completely off base. "So it wasn't your car there," she said.

"Where?" he asked.

"Never mind. Come on. We better go."

"All right. Let me clean up. My business clothes are in the powder room under the stairs. I'll tell Lindsay what's going on and meet you outside."

Nina nodded and watched him go, calling out to Lindsay that he had to leave. Nina could not remember the last time she had felt so relieved. Hoisting her leather satchel on her shoulder, she walked out of the library toward the entrance of the house. As she passed through the dining room, Lindsay set down a silver candlestick she was examining and looked over at Nina. "Will he be coming back?"

"Not tonight," said Nina. "Our brother—well, you know Jimmy—he's in the hospital. He's in a coma."

"That's awful." said Lindsay. "What happened?"

Nina felt an irrational desire to protect Jimmy, even from the consequences of his own stupidity. "It was an accident," she said.

"Nina, where are you?" Patrick demanded from the hallway. "Let's go."

29

ᴸWHILE Nina drove, Patrick adjusted the knot in his tie and tried to reach his wife on the telephone. There was no answer at the house or on the cell phone. "Where is she?" he said irritably.

"She may have gone down to see Jimmy. She was very worried about him," said Nina loyally. She was admittedly surprised at the news about Gemma's being fired from her job, but everybody knew that the academic world was a high-pressure, results-oriented environment. Nina was willing to give her sister-in-law the benefit of the doubt, even if her husband wasn't.

"She was worried. Right," Patrick scoffed.

"Come on, Patrick. Gemma's been under a lot of stress lately. In addition to everything else, I think she's been a little anxious about your relationship with Lindsay. I mean, I know I was suspicious. I thought you might be . . . messing around with her. It was a natural assumption, given your history with Lindsay."

Patrick shrugged. "Well, I'd be a liar if I said it didn't cross my mind. Lindsay's a beautiful woman. But she's taken."

"And so are you," Nina reminded him.

"Right," Patrick said glumly. He peered out the car window at the darkened street. "Hey, Nina, if you don't mind, can you swing by the garage?" said Patrick. "If my car's done I can pick it up. It'll be closed by the time we get back, and with all that's going on, I may need it tomorrow."

"Where is it?" she asked distractedly. "Whitey's?"

Patrick nodded and Nina made a left turn in the direction of the garage they had used for service for as long as she could remember.

"Make it quick," said Nina. "We have to get to Jimmy."

"That fucking Calvin Mears," said Patrick. "When I get my hands on him . . ."

"Oh, I guess I didn't tell you. Somebody beat you to it," said Nina. "He's dead. Someone shot them in the motel room where they were partying . . ."

"Shot them? Why? Jimmy, too?"

"I don't know why. But no. Not Jimmy. He'd already over-dosed. They shot Mears and some other guy who was there. A Puerto Rican guy."

"Jesus Christ. Jimmy can pick 'em, can't he? Here, turn here. We can go around Whitey's the back way."

Nina followed his instructions and pulled up by the lighted pumps in front of the garage. The garage doors were closed and dark. "Even if it's ready," she said, "you may not be able to get it."

"Don't worry," said Patrick. "I know the kid at the pumps. He'll give it to me. I'll be right back. Wait for me."

Nina nodded as Patrick jumped out of the car. She watched her brother go up and start talking to the young guy in the lighted booth between the gas pumps. Patrick and the attendant had a brief conversation and then Patrick headed back to the Volvo. The kid picked up the magazine he had been perusing and resumed reading. The kid won't give him the car, Nina thought. He'll probably have to come back in the morning.

Patrick opened the door of the Volvo and slid into the passenger seat.

"What happened? It's not ready or he can't give it to you?" Nina asked.

"Neither," said Patrick. "They fixed it first thing this morning. Brought it back to the house. Look, it's getting late. Why don't I just ride with you? You don't mind, do you?"

Nina was staring blankly through the windshield.

"Nina?" he said.

Nina shook her head. "No. No, of course not."

The drive to the hospital only took half an hour, and Nina drove there without any wrong turns or mishaps, but when she pulled into the well-lit parking lot and turned off the engine, she could not remember having made the trip. Her mind had spun, turning over and over the events of the day. When she told Gemma about the Jag being seen at the motel where the shooting occurred, Gemma acted indignant. How dare Nina accuse Patrick? But Gemma knew all along that Patrick didn't have the Jag. That it was home. In their garage.

"Nina," said Patrick. "Are you in there?"

Nina started, and looked at him. "What? Yes."

"You didn't say a word the whole way down here."

Nina turned and looked at him. "Patrick, does Gemma ever drive the Jag?"

"Sure," he said. "Though I don't give her a lot of opportunities. Why?" He opened the car door and started to get out.

Nina got out of the car, closing the door behind her and locking it. "She never told me that you didn't have the Jag today. That it was at your house."

"Why would she tell you that?" he asked.

"Maybe the garage guys just left it and she didn't know," Nina mused aloud.

"Nobody just leaves a Jag," Patrick scoffed. "That's a lawsuit waiting to happen. Somebody has to sign for it. Do you know Jimmy's room number?"

Nina shook her head. "Um . . . He was in ICU. Let's check there first."

"Fine," said Patrick. He took the lead, opening the hospital doors for her and checking with Patient Information. They still had Jimmy listed in ICU, and the woman at the desk gave Patrick directions through the hospital to the Intensive Care Unit. Nina trailed after her brother, grateful that he was taking charge.

Patrick was already talking to a nurse at the ICU nurses' station. Nina thought about Jimmy, who had been in the motel room but hadn't been shot. Patrick came up to her and shook her by the upper arm.

"Hey, I think this is good news. They moved him to a private room."

Nina blinked at him. "They did?"

"Yeah. Here's the number. We have to walk back around to the elevators."

"Okay," said Nina. "You lead the way."

Patrick did so, impatiently pushing the elevator button a half dozen times before they heard the ping that meant it was arriving on their floor. They stepped in and rode up to Jimmy's new floor, then walked down the hallway, checking over the doors for his room number.

"This is it," said Patrick.

While Nina would have peered inside first, Patrick strode in. Nina followed him and saw Rose and George Connelly, sitting, talking quietly at the foot of Jimmy's bed. They both looked up and then rose to greet Nina and her brother. Brief hugs were exchanged, and then Nina and Patrick looked toward the bed. Nina felt a sudden letdown to see that Jimmy looked exactly as he had when she'd left him earlier in the afternoon.

Patrick grimaced at the sight of his brother. "Oh my God," he said. "James."

Rose got up and joined them, looking at the young man in the bed. "The doctor was just in and we talked to him. He said there's three possibilities. If Jimmy comes out of the coma, he may recover. Or he could just slip away from us."

"What's the third possibility?" Nina asked.

Rose reached out and touched Jimmy's hand, avoiding the part that was black and blue where the IV needle was taped. "He could stay like this. Possibly for a very long time."

Patrick shook his head. "Oh my God," he said. "Jimmy, you idiot." But when Nina glanced at him she saw tears in his eyes.

Nina turned to George and Rose. "Why don't you two go home and get some rest. You've been here for hours. Patrick and I will stay with him for a while."

"Oh no," said Rose, sitting back down next to her husband. "We're fine. We just took a break a while ago. Your wife was here, Patrick, and she stayed with Jimmy while we went down to the cafeteria."

"Gemma was here?" he said.

"She just left a few minutes ago," said Rose. "Anyway, we need to stay because we're expecting Anthony. He's flying in from Boston to be with his brother."

Patrick reached out and rubbed his hand over Jimmy's burr haircut. "That's good of Anthony," he said.

George got up and said, "Here, let me get you two a chair." Before they could protest, he was out in the hallway questioning a passing nurse.

Nina's stomach growled and she felt the headache returning. She wanted to be alone to think. "Rose, what time does the cafeteria close, do you know?"

Rose looked up at the clock. "You'd better hurry," she said. "You can just make it."

"Patrick, I think I'm going to go down there and get something to eat. Can I get you anything?"

Patrick shook his head. "I ate with Lindsay," he said.

"I'll be back soon," said Nina. She left the room, making note of the number and the location, found an elevator, and rode to the basement, where the hospital cafeteria was located. It was painted a muted aquamarine and had all the warmth of a fish tank. There were only a few tables occupied, and the cafeteria workers were beginning to wipe off the empty tables and put up the chairs. Nina grabbed a yogurt and a bottle of juice, paid the cashier, and sat down not far from a couple who were sitting silently, eating off trays.

Nina started to eat the yogurt, and it felt good going down, but she also was glad to be away from Jimmy's room in a spot where she could sit and think. Her hands shook as she lifted the spoon to her mouth and tried to remember everything she'd heard about the shooting today. It was some kind of madness to suspect Gemma just because she'd had access to the Jag and lied about it. What reason would Gemma ever have had to shoot Calvin Mears and the other guy? None. There was no reason. It was not as if Calvin Mears had seen *Gemma* leaving their house that long-ago April night. Gemma had no reason in the world to kill Marsha. Thinking back on that afternoon, she remembered Marsha urging Patrick to take Gemma out to celebrate. Nina's mother had always been more than kind to Gemma. She'd always felt sorry for the girl who was forced to live with a father and a stepmother who didn't really want her around. No, there was no reason. Everything that day had been perfectly normal. Nina and her mother had talked about what a great student Gemma was, and what a help to Patrick. And then a thought struck Nina. A thought that made her feel faint. The newspaper her mother had pulled off the coffee table in the living room when she fell, dying of her wounds. Gemma's picture had been on the front page that day, for receiving the Delman Prize.

The couple at the other table stood up. The woman had her back to Nina. Nina could see that she had frizzy brown hair cut into a shag. The man had blond hair and a bulldog face. Nina took a last bite of her yogurt and stared at the pair. She was sure she knew them from somewhere. The man picked up the trays to bus the table. The woman, whose coat was hanging over the back of her chair, picked up the coat and put it on. On the front of the coat was a large laminated button with a photo of two girls in Christmas party dresses.

Omigod, thought Nina. Of course. She stood up, still holding her yogurt, and approached their table shyly. "Mr. . . . Mazurek?" she said.

The bulldog-faced man scowled at her suspiciously.

"My name is Nina Avery," she said. "You testified at my father's parole hearing. Duncan Avery."

The man's furrowed face broke into a broad smile. "Oh yeah. Hey there. Hey, honey. This is Doc Avery's girl, remember? Did you meet my wife, Carla?"

Mrs. Mazurek looked at Nina with narrowed eyes, as if she couldn't really remember her, but she smiled all the same and extended a hand. Nina put the spoon in the yogurt in her left hand and shook hands with both of them.

"So," Mazurek said, nodding. "Are you here to see the doc? We just come from his room, but we didn't see you up there."

"I'm sorry?" said Nina, shaking her head slowly.

"Dr. Quinteros," said Mazurek, looking at her curiously. "You didn't know he was here?"

30

NINA grabbed the sleeve of his coat. "I didn't know anything about this. What happened? Is Andre all right?"

Stan shrugged. "He was pretty groggy when we were up there. Well, he's been through a hell of a lot today. He was in surgery this afternoon. Then they had him out in the recovery room and he hurt himself trying to get up, so they had to go back in and sew him up again. I figured you knew about it."

Nina's stomach was churning. She had to force herself to remain calm. "I didn't understand what you said. What did this have to do with me?"

"Just this morning," said Stan. "He asked me to find out the address of this cop named Jenkins in Seaside Park. Something to do with your father's murder. So I called around and got it for him. The next thing I know the doc left work. A couple hours later we get a call at the prison that Dr. Q is in surgery. Apparently, he went looking for this cop's nephew in some sleazy motel in Seaside Park. Some guy came in and shot at them. The nephew's dead. The other one's here in the hospital, too."

Oh my God. *Andre!* she thought. He did it for her. He tried to find Calvin Mears for her. A Puerto Rican guy got shot, Mrs. Jenkins had said. A Hispanic man, someone else had said. *Gemma.* She had asked about the condition of the Hispanic man. And Nina had never even put it together that it might be a doctor of Mexican descent.

"Are you all right, honey?" asked Carla Mazurek. "You look a little green around the gills. Do you want to sit down? Stan, let her sit."

But Nina waved away their concern. "Where's his room?" she asked.

Stan peered at his wife. "What was it, hon? Three . . ."

"Three ten," said Carla promptly. "But they wouldn't even let me go in. They let Stan go, but I had to wait in the lounge."

"Thank you," said Nina. "Thank you both."

"You can't just go up there," Stan warned her. "You have to have . . ."

Nina was not listening. She tossed her yogurt into a trash bin near the door and began to run.

THE elevator door opened on three, and Nina quickly looked at the room number guide and rushed off to the right. Down the hall she saw an armed cop in full uniform standing outside the door of one of the rooms, his hands clasped over a clipboard in front of him. Without even looking at the number, she knew. That was Andre's room. They were protecting him. He was a witness to the shooting and he was still alive. She exhaled a deep sigh. He was still alive.

She walked up and spoke politely to the officer. "Excuse me," she said. "Is this Dr. Quinteros's room?"

The officer studied her with an unsmiling stare. "The patient in this room is not allowed to have visitors," he said. "Not unless they've got clearance."

"I really need to see him," said Nina. "He's . . . he's my fiancé," she said.

The cop picked up the clipboard and studied it.

"Name?" he said.

"Susan . . ." she blurted out.

"Susan what?" he asked.

Nina blushed, realizing she had been caught out in her lie. She didn't even know what Susan's last name was. "Look, I'm sorry," she said. "That was stupid of me. I'm not really his fiancée. I'm a friend. A good friend. In fact, he's in there because he tried to . . . do me a favor."

"Name," the cop repeated stubbornly.

"My name is Nina Avery . . ."

The cop ran a pen down the list of names on his clipboard. "I'm sorry, ma'am," he said. "You're not on this list."

"But . . . if you would just stick your head in there and ask him, I'm sure he'd tell you that he wants to see me. Please, could you just ask him?" Nina knew she could be seductive when she wanted to be. She summoned all her powers of persuasion and tried to win him over. "Please."

The cop glared at her. "You are not on the list," he said. "And if you don't move along now, I'm going to have to get somebody up here to escort you out of the building. Is that clear?"

Nina closed her eyes for a second and pictured Andre's face. His fierce, intelligent eyes, which seemed to be able to look into her heart. She thought she had driven him away the other night. But it turned out that he had simply decided to take on her problems and tell her about it afterward. You did this for me, she thought, and you don't even know I'm here. But I'm not going to leave until I see you and let you know . . . She took a deep breath and nodded. "Okay," she said. "I get it. Okay. I'm leaving."

The cop watched her go suspiciously. She started back down the hall in the direction of the elevators, trying to think of some way she could get in. When she reached the nurses' station, she stopped. The nurse behind the desk was fairly young and had long shiny curls.

"Hi," said Nina.

"Hi," the nurse said pleasantly.

"I love your hair," said Nina. "It's really beautiful."

The nurse smiled and patted her healthy curls. "You wouldn't want to have to wash it every day," she said.

Nina forced a smile. "No, I'm sure. Listen, can you tell me how Dr. Quinteros is doing? I'm a friend of his, and they won't let me in to see him."

"I'm sorry," said the nurse. "We're not permitted . . ."

"Well, how can I get my name on that list of visitors? I mean, we're really close and I know he would want to see me."

"I'm sorry," said the nurse. "We have nothing to do with that. That's a police matter."

Nina wanted to pound the desk in frustration, but she controlled herself. "Look, if one of you is going in there, could I give you a note to take to him, just to let him know I'm here?"

"I'm sorry," the nurse said, a slight chill in her tone. She swiveled around in her chair, reaching for some charts on the wall beside her desk.

All right, Nina thought. Plan B. Not that she had a plan B. She stepped away from the desk and looked down the hall toward Andre's room. The cop was still standing there, barring the door, staring straight ahead. Halfway down the hallway was an exit sign over a stairwell, and beside that was a lounge across the hall and one door down from Andre's room. Nina thought about it for a minute. She knew very little about Andre's life, but there were bound to be other people whose names were on that clipboard list who might come to visit him. If I wait in the lounge, she thought, and keep an eye on his room, maybe I can waylay one of the "approved" visitors as they are going in and explain it to them. Somebody who looks sympathetic. It was worth a try. She went and got a drink from the fountain and then slipped into the lounge.

It was a small room with a sofa and two chairs. There was a magazine rack with some dog-eared issues of *Newsweek* and *Ladies' Home Journal,* and a bunch of LEGOs scattered on the wall-to-wall carpeting. A TV was on in the corner, the laugh track blaring. There was no one else there at the moment. She was glad of that. She didn't feel like making small talk. Besides, it was immediately clear that she could not watch the door to Andre's room without the aid of a mirror, and she knew how strange that was going to look. She rummaged in her satchel and pulled out a compact. She opened it and moved her chair so that she could see the room in the mirror with her back to the door. It could prove to be a tedious wait, but it was worth doing. She only wished that Stan Mazurek hadn't already been and gone. She realized now that he'd been trying to warn her about this situation when they were talking in the cafeteria.

Nina held up the compact and looked into it as discreetly as possible. She couldn't really do anything else but sit there, and she was wondering what in the world she was going to do to pass the time. She couldn't read, or call anyone on the phone. She glanced at the TV in the corner occasionally, but only for a second. Then she resumed her vigil.

All at once, she saw the stiff cop moving and realized that someone was coming toward the door. This could be her opportunity. She sat up and stared hard into the mirror. But then her shoulders slumped as she realized it was only a nurse. She could see the side of the nurse's smock, and her painfully thin arm and bony wrist supporting a small tray.

The nurse moved the tray to her other hand as she reached for the doorknob with flashing, beringed fingers. Nina sighed, and then suddenly, a shock went through her like a lightning bolt. For one moment, the nurse was reflected in the tiny round mirror as she opened the door to Andre's room. It was only a glimpse, but in that glimpse Nina recognized the pale, narrow face. And in that second, all the doubts that had been nagging at her, swirling in her mind, coalesced.

Nina jumped up from her chair with a cry and bolted out the door. The cop's head swiveled at the sudden movement and he glared at her as she crossed the hall. "That woman that just went in there," Nina cried. "You have to stop her. That's not a nurse. I know her. I know who she is."

The cop put his hand on his holster. "I told you before that you can't go in there. What are you doing still hanging around?"

"Did you hear me?" Nina cried. "That is not a nurse who just went in there. She's . . ." Nina hesitated to say it. But it was too late for hesitation. "She's the one. The one you want."

"Get away from this door," growled the cop.

"Are you going in there?" Nina demanded.

"I'm warning you, lady . . ."

"Then I am," said Nina. He reached out to grab her, but she spun away from him and lunged for the door. She found the doorknob and turned it, pushing the door in.

The cop drew his gun. "Stop right there."

"Not a chance," said Nina, and she burst into the room.

31

GEMS flashed as the hypodermic needle, poised in one bony, beringed hand, punctured the IV tube that snaked down from the hanging bag and emptied through a needle into Andre's hand. Andre lay in the bed, his head tilted to one side, his eyes closed.

"Gemma, don't!" Nina cried.

Gemma, dressed in a blue nurse's smock and pants that ballooned around her skinny frame, looked up and met Nina's pleading gaze with an implacable stare. For a moment she flinched. Then she looked at the officer brandishing a gun who had just overtaken Nina.

"Officer," she said calmly. "What is this woman doing here?"

"I'm sorry, ma'am. I'm getting her out of here." He grabbed Nina roughly and twisted her forearm behind her back. Jamming his gun back in the holster, he reached for the handcuffs on his belt.

"That's all right," said Gemma pushing down the plunger on the syringe. "No harm done. Just finishing up here."

"Andre," Nina screamed.

The man on the bed started, and his eyes opened slightly. "Nina," he whispered.

. "Could you get her out of here?" Gemma asked, frowning.

"Right away," said the cop. He jerked Nina back by her shackled arms, but she strained forward with all her might, the cords on her neck standing out. "Don't you get it? She's trying to kill him. Andre . . ."

Andre was gazing at Nina from the bed with a puzzled, far-away look. "What?" he asked.

Nina was overcome with horror as she saw Gemma pull the syringe out of the tube.

"There we go," Gemma said. "Just something to help you sleep."

Andre lifted his right hand from the blanket as if to reach out to Nina.

Nina held his gaze and screamed at him over the curses of the officer as he attempted to drag her away. "Andre, pull the IV out of your hand!" Nina cried. "Do it. *Pull it out! Now!*"

"Are you crazy?" the cop said.

For a moment, Andre looked confused, and then, in one fumbling movement, he reached over to his left hand, ripped off the tape, and tore the IV needle from the back of his hand. Blood spurted up and showered down on the thin white blanket.

"Jesus!" cried the cop. "He did it."

Nina sagged in relief against the officer who was restraining her.

Gemma's face drained of all color. She looked at Nina with hatred in her eyes. Then she picked up the needle and tried to find a way to jam it back into Andre, who was turning away, shielding himself from her jabs with panic in his eyes.

"Wait a minute," said the cop. "Wait a minute. You. Nurse. Let me see that ID badge again." He let go of Nina and started toward the bed. Gemma stood frozen, staring at his approach. "All right," he said. "Hand over the ID."

Gemma hesitated for a second, grabbed the IV needle, and jabbed it into his outstretched palm.

Shocked, the officer cried out and yanked the needle from the fleshy part of his palm. Gemma fled the room while Nina, handcuffed, was helpless to stop her. "Get her," Nina shrieked at the cop.

The cop looked up from his assaulted hand, the whites showing around his eyes. "I can't. I can't leave him alone . . . I'll call," the cop said.

The officer picked up his two-way radio and began to yell into the static that there was an assault on the witness and the suspect was loose in the hospital. As he began to describe Gemma into the radio, Nina, still handcuffed, lurched toward the bed and gazed helplessly at Andre. "Are you all right?"

He reached out for her and grabbed the edge of her jacket in a feeble grasp. "That was the one," he said. "The one at the motel. Calvin opened the door and said, 'It's Bones.' I thought it was some sick joke. Then she came in with a gun and started shooting."

"I know," said Nina.

"You know her," Andre said.

Nina nodded miserably.

"She would have killed me just then," he whispered.

"Doc, is this going to kill me?" the cop demanded, holding out his palm for Andre to see.

Andre shook his head. "No. But you better have it looked at."

The officer heaved a sigh of relief. "All right," he said angrily, coming up behind Nina and unlocking her fettered wrists. "You have to get out of here right now."

"But . . ." Nina looked helplessly at Andre. The door to the room opened and three more uniformed officers entered, their guns drawn.

"Here," the cop yelled. "Clear the room. Everybody out but the witness. Get this woman out of here. Now."

A NURSE'S locker in the hospital basement was found broken open and rifled through. An orderly admitted that he let a woman matching Gemma's description into the nurses' locker room when she told him that she had forgotten her key. The hospital was searched, floor by floor and room by room, but Gemma had escaped.

Nina and Patrick were escorted to the police station, where they met with detectives. In response to their questions, Nina revealed all that she had discovered about her father's search for Calvin Mears. As Nina recounted what she had learned from Lieutenant Hagen and her brother Jimmy, Patrick stared at her.

"Wait a minute," he interrupted her. "Are you trying to imply that Gemma killed Calvin because she was the one he saw leaving the house the night Mom was killed?"

The senior detective looked at Nina with interest. "Well?" he said.

"What else can I think?" Nina asked faintly.

"Aren't you forgetting something?" cried Patrick. "Duncan killed Mom. He was just looking for someone else to blame."

Nina turned on her brother angrily. "Patrick, when are you going to wake up? How can you still insist on Dad's guilt with what we now know about Gemma? Are you so determined to hate him that you can't admit you were wrong?"

"I don't accept that," Patrick insisted. "What reason would Gemma have to do that? To kill Mom?"

"I don't know," Nina admitted.

"It can't be," Patrick said stubbornly. "I'll grant you she's a liar. God help me, I've known that for a long time. I've lived with her for twelve years. But, a killer . . ."

"Mr. Avery," the senior detective interrupted him, "that's not even a question. We know that your wife is a killer."

For two more hours, Nina and Patrick were grilled, until the police were satisfied that they knew nothing about Gemma's murderous activities. Patrick was informed that the police had a warrant and were on their way to search his house. Patrick, who was sitting with his head in his hands, looked up and said dully, "Make sure you send somebody who speaks Spanish. The housekeeper doesn't speak any English. She'll be freaked out."

The detective thanked him politely and went out to make sure they had a Spanish speaker on the search crew.

"Just like Elena," said Nina. "Why didn't she get someone who speaks English?"

Patrick stared blankly ahead. "So they couldn't keep track of her lies."

"Dad told me she was lying," Nina said. "He understood what she was saying in Spanish to Elena, and he told me Gemma lied about it."

Patrick shook his head. "I wondered why she let Elena go."

"Let her go? I thought . . . She told me Elena's sister was in an accident in Panama and she had to go back," said Nina.

Patrick turned and looked grimly at his sister. "Do you get it now? It's everything. It's a compulsion. It took me years to even realize . . ."

Nina returned his stare. "Do you think that's why she killed Dad?"

Patrick's gaze was anguished. "That's what they think, isn't it? That Gemma killed him. And Mom."

"Of course it is," said Nina flatly.

The detective reentered the interview room. "All right, you can go. Two of our officers will accompany you. The Hoffman police are cooperating with us and they will be watching both of your houses tonight because there is a possibility Mrs. Avery will try to return home, seeking refuge. If she should show up, don't try to reason with her. She is most likely armed, she is desperate, and she should be considered extremely dangerous."

Patrick's shoulders began to shake and he seemed almost too weak to stand up. Nina tried to comfort him and helped him to his feet, wondering all the while what he was feeling for his wife, now that he knew she was a killer. Was there still love there? Had there ever been? "Come on, Patrick," she said gently. "We have to go. The boys need you now."

NINA thanked Officer Kepler, who had accompanied her to her aunt's house. "I'm just going to have a look around the outside," he said.

"Please do," said Nina, ushering him in and taking off her coat. "Can I get you something? A cup of tea?"

"No thanks," he said, but he smiled at her appreciatively. He switched on his flashlight and started around the side of the house.

I'm going to have one, Nina thought. She went into the kitchen and put the kettle on. She could see the beam of his flashlight through the windows, roving across the backyard and around the garage in a jerky motion. Nina was glad to have him out there. She doubted she would sleep tonight. Not until she knew that Gemma had been apprehended. Patrick had promised to call the moment there was any news of Gemma's arrest.

While she waited for the kettle to boil, Nina went down the hall, opened the door to her great-aunt's room, and looked in. Aunt Mary was propped up on her pillows, dozing, the bedside light still on. She didn't want her aunt to wake up, but she noticed that her window was open a few inches, and Nina wanted to be sure that the house was locked up tight. She tiptoed over to the window and began to slide it shut as quietly as possible.

"Nina?"

Nina jumped and put a hand on her chest. She turned and looked at her aunt. "God, you scared me," she said. "I thought you were asleep."

"I was dozing," said Aunt Mary. "What are you doing?"

"Just closing the window," said Nina. "I thought it seemed a little chilly in here." Nina did not want to tell her the real reason she was concerned about an open window.

"I like the fresh air," Aunt Mary said in a groggy voice. "They keep that nursing home sealed up so tight."

"I know, I know," said Nina, "but you don't want to get a chill. You just got home. I don't want you going back to that place." Nina lowered the window and reached for the lock, which resisted her efforts to turn it. "Damn. I must have gotten this thing stuck when I painted."

"Oh, that lock is always stubborn," said Aunt Mary. "Where have you been all day, dear?"

Nina felt the lock give, and she turned it and then jiggled it. She decided a half-truth was her best option. "I went to see Jim," she said. "In the hospital."

"Gemma's in the hospital?" said her aunt. "But she was just here earlier."

Rubbing her hands together, Nina turned back to her aunt. "Not Gem. Jim."

"Oh, it sounded exactly like you said Gem," said Aunt Mary. "What's wrong with Jimmy?"

Nina's arms prickled with gooseflesh.

"Nina? What's wrong with Jimmy?"

"He had an accident," said Nina, distracted.

"Will he be all right?" her aunt asked.

"I hope so," said Nina.

"Nina," Aunt Mary exclaimed. "Is that a light out there in the backyard?"

Nina turned and looked. It was Officer Kepler's flashlight, still searching. "Oh, probably just somebody looking for their cat. I'll go take a look," she said. "Can I get you anything?"

"No," said her aunt. "I'm fine. I'm gonna read my book."

Gemma. It sounds exactly like Jimmy. Nina went down the hall to the kitchen, thinking about what Jimmy had told her. That their father had heard their mother whispering his name when Duncan found her on the living room floor, dying. *Gem,* Nina thought. It would sound just like *Jim* on the lips of a dying woman.

She opened the kitchen door and peered out into the darkness. "Officer Kepler?" she called out softly. "Is everything all right?"

The officer emerged from the darkness of the backyard onto the patio and switched off his flashlight. "All clear," he said. "Let me have a quick look inside."

"Everything seems fine, but be my guest," said Nina. "Let me just tell my aunt you're here."

The officer went through the living room and climbed the stairs. Nina heard him opening closet doors and sliding back the shower door in the bathroom. Nina went down the hall to her aunt's room. She opened the door and stuck her head in. "There's a policeman here. He's just having a look around because there's been a prowler reported in the neighborhood."

Aunt Mary lowered her book and looked up over the top of her reading glasses. "Oh my goodness," she said.

"Don't worry," said Nina, forcing herself to smile. "Everything's okay."

Nina pulled the door shut and went back down the hall, entering the kitchen just as Officer Kepler was emerging from the basement.

"Everything seems to be fine," he said. "I'm going to go now, but the Hoffman police will be watching the house. You sleep well, now."

"Thanks," said Nina. "I appreciate it." She walked him to the front door and waved to him as he got into his squad car. Then she closed the door behind him and locked it. The teakettle whistled, and she turned off the burner and poured herself a cup. As she started to carry it into the living room, she noticed that Officer Kepler had left the light on in the stairwell leading to the basement. She walked over to switch it off. As she pulled open the doorway, she heard a thud. It sounded as if it came from the basement.

Nina's heart began to hammer and she stood, undecided, at the top of the stairs. You're being paranoid, she told herself. The cop just looked down there. There's nobody here. But it was difficult not to be paranoid after what she had seen and learned tonight.

Just turn off the light and shut the door, she thought. It's nothing. Part of her wanted to go downstairs and look. Part of her knew she would not be able to forget the noise, even though rationally she knew it was probably her imagination working overtime. But it was foolish to go down those stairs. There wasn't even a light down there that worked. Nina stood at the top of the stairs, hesitating, and then she had an idea. In one decisive movement, she switched off the light in the stairwell, closed the door, and locked it. Then she dragged a chair from the kitchen table to the staircase door and wedged it under the doorknob.

"All right," Nina said defiantly. "If you're down there, stay down there."

She turned back to the stove to pick up her teacup.

Gemma was standing in front of her, her eyes wild, a gun in her hand. "I'm not down there," she said. "I'm right here."

32

THE shock buckled Nina's knees. "Jesus, Gemma!" she cried.

Gemma smiled slightly. "Sorry," she said. "I was in your aunt's closet. She was sleeping when I came in the house so I slipped in there. Now she's asleep again."

The thud. She'd heard a thud. But not a gunshot. "Is my aunt alive?" Nina cried. "What did you do to her?"

Gemma's smile faded. "I hit her with this," said Gemma, indicating the gun butt. "I had to knock her out. I just tapped her. Her head's like a little egg."

Nina's lip trembled, thinking of her frail, gentle aunt. "I want to see her. Let me see her."

"Not right now. Right now you have to help me," said Gemma.

"Help you? Why would I help you?" Nina cried. "You . . . you . . ."

Gemma shook her head. "Don't say anything nasty, Nina. I

can't take that from you. Now look. If you help me, I'll leave. And you won't be killed."

For a moment, Nina felt a reckless indifference to her own fate. All she could feel was hatred. "You are crazy," she said. "That's it. That has to be it. You have to be insane. Nobody could do the things you did . . ."

"Stop that, Nina!" Gemma cried, and shook the gun at her. "Do you think I won't shoot you? Do you think I'm bluffing?"

Nina shook her head slowly and struggled to calm herself down. "No," she said. "I don't think that. I know better."

"All right," said Gemma, her voice quavering. "All right. So. I know that I need to get away from here and I can't do that unless you help me."

"Why did you shoot Calvin Mears, Gemma? And Andre? Was it because Calvin saw you that night? You killed my mother, didn't you? Did my father figure it out? Did you kill him, too?"

Gemma pursed her lips and looked away. "This is not a conversation, Nina. I don't want to discuss anything with you. Just do what I say. I have no quarrel with you, Nina. I don't want to have to kill you."

"You had no quarrel with my mother. My mother was always kind to you," Nina cried. "She worried about you. She used to say how she felt sorry for you, because your father was always away and Didi was obsessed with wedding frippery. My mother cared for you . . ."

Gemma shook her head. "That wasn't real. As it turned out. Look, I haven't got time for this, Nina. Neither do you. Now listen. First I need money. Whatever you've got in the house. Your old aunt probably keeps some under the mattress. And then I need a car. I know the cops are out there. You may have to drive some distance with me, until we're out of their sight."

Nina felt a stillness come over her. She made a decision.

"I'm not going to do a thing for you until you tell me. I understand certain things. I understand that Calvin saw you that night. But he probably never thought much about it until my father questioned him. I imagine you killed my dad when he confronted you. But why did you kill my mother? I found her body that night, you know. I slipped in a puddle of her blood. I have had more nightmares than you could count. You have to tell me the truth. I won't budge unless you do."

Gemma looked at her indignantly. "You have nightmares?" She shook her head. "You? You don't know anything about nightmares."

Nina stared at her, trying to conceal her loathing. "Tell me," she said.

Gemma hesitated and then shook her head. "No. No. I'm not getting into this with you. Let me just say this. Your mother only pretended to care for me. When it came right down to it, she turned on me."

"How did she turn on you?" Nina asked quietly.

"Oh no," said Gemma. "Don't think you're conning me into telling you some secret. Because I am too smart for you."

Nina spoke in a calm voice, a voice trained by years in the theater. "Gemma, haven't I been your friend all these years?"

Gemma shook her head. "I have no friends. Every friend I ever thought I had, every person that I ever tried to care about . . ."

Tears rose to Nina's eyes. "I treated you like a sister. Even when other people were cruel, wasn't I your friend? Gemma, I have to know what happened . . ."

Gemma stared at Nina with her expressionless eyes, the gun wavering in her hand. "Fine. You want to know? Fine. You should know the truth about your mother. She was not the sweet, loving Marsha everybody remembers. She showed me her true self. I'll tell you. Although I'm sure you'll still take her side. Your mother called me," said Gemma matter-of-factly, "and asked me to come over. Said she wanted to talk to me about Patrick. But that was a lie. When I got there, she started asking me questions. She started out all kind and solicitous. And then she pounced. She said she saw me in the Preserve the day before, burying something in a plastic garbage bag. And then she heard that a dog had found the bag, and when the police opened it, there was a baby in it."

"A baby?" said Nina. "The baby in the Preserve? But where did you get a baby? You weren't . . . I don't . . . How did you . . . ?"

Gemma droned on, drowning her out. "It was a terrible experience. I was in school when the water broke. I felt it coming. So I went home. Nobody was there," Gemma said.

"You were pregnant?" said Nina, still trying to absorb this information.

"Nobody knew I was pregnant," said Gemma. "I only ate a little bit. I didn't gain much weight."

Nina remembered now. The baggy overalls and flannel shirts Gemma used to wear like a uniform, concealing the unwanted pregnancy. And no one noticed. Not her father or her stepmother. Or any of the Averys. "Did you tell the baby's father?" asked Nina.

"Patrick?" Gemma asked. "No. He never knew. He'd never even take my shirt off when he screwed me."

"Patrick?" Nina gasped. "Patrick was the father?"

"Yes, Patrick," said Gemma bitterly. "Is it so unbelievable?"

"But he and Lindsay . . . I mean, you were his tutor."

"I was crazy about Patrick. I did anything he wanted," said Gemma bluntly.

"And he wanted . . ."

"Sex," said Gemma. "Lindsay was holding out on him. She didn't love him the way I did. I never denied him."

"Why didn't you tell him about the baby?" Nina cried.

Gemma flinched ever so slightly. "He didn't want to know," she said.

Nina recognized the truth in her words and for one brief moment, she pitied Gemma, who had hoped for love and found herself used instead. Gemma's loyalty to Patrick was a kind of madness in itself.

Gemma shook her head. "Your mother reacted exactly the same way. As if I were the only one to blame. Not her precious Patrick. I thought if I told her the truth she would understand. Take my side. But all she could think about was the baby . . ."

Nina winced, and tried not to think about the helpless newborn, buried in a trash bag by his mother.

"She kept saying it couldn't be true and asking me why I did it," Gemma said. "And then, do you know what she said? 'That was my grandchild,' she said. 'You killed my grandchild.' As if the baby was all that mattered. As if the baby was everything and I was dirt. That's when I got pissed off."

Nina could not meet Gemma's indignant gaze.

"She kept talking about the innocent little baby and its precious little life. That's when I picked up the knife and killed her."

Nina was trembling all over. She didn't say a word.

"Now," said Gemma. "I've told you. Let's get going."

"Miss Avery!" There was a thunderous knock on the front door.

Gemma looked up, startled, and then jabbed the gun into Nina's belly.

Nina stared at her. "They know I'm in here. They're going to want to come in."

"Shit," said Gemma. She looked around the kitchen frantically. Then she spotted the chair wedged against the cellar door. "Move that thing," she commanded. "Quietly."

"It's no use, Gemma," said Nina, but she did as she was told. She freed the chair from under the doorknob and replaced it by the table.

"Open the door," Gemma commanded.

Nina pulled the cellar door open and went to turn on the light in the stairwell. Gemma jabbed her again. "Don't touch it. Move," she said.

Nina grabbed for the wall and began to descend the stairs slowly. Gemma pulled the door shut behind them.

"Miss Avery," the voices shouted. "We're coming in."

Nina began to shake her head. "It's no use doing this," she said.

Gemma grabbed Nina's long black hair and yanked it back. Nina stumbled on the dark staircase and managed to regain her balance. "You keep your mouth shut," Gemma growled, "or I swear to God, I'll kill you."

At the foot of the stairs, Gemma shoved Nina over to the wall beside the staircase, up against the cardboard boxes and paper shopping bags damp with mildew. Overhead, they heard the banging on the front door, and then the sound of the door bursting open. "Put your hands up," Gemma commanded. Nina raised her hands. Gemma stayed behind Nina, holding on to her hair and keeping the barrel of the gun pressed into her side.

Nina heard the police thundering through the house. One of them yelled to another. "In here. The old lady . . ."

"Is she dead?" she heard a voice demand.

There was a silence. Nina closed her eyes and prayed into the silence.

"She's breathing. Get an ambulance," said the voice.

"There's nobody upstairs," called another voice.

"The back door's open. Maybe they went out the back."

Nina stood with her face pressed against the wall of bags and boxes, her arms heavy from keeping her hands raised, hovering by her ears. The gun barrel pressed into her back. Gingerly, hoping for relief, she rested her palms lightly against the pile of boxes against the wall. Her right palm grazed scratchy canvas. It took her a moment to realize what it was and then, when she did, her heart leaped. People were shouting now and there were heavy footsteps from every direction in the house.

All of a sudden the door at the top of the steps burst open, and the voices were twice as loud. "Miss Avery. Nina," they called.

"Turn on the light," said one voice.

Light flooded the stairwell and two officers began to descend, guns drawn, flashlights scanning the basement. "There," one of them cried.

Gemma had dragged Nina by the hair away from the boxes, the gun barrel still pressed in her back, hiding behind her, using Nina as a human shield.

"Don't come any closer," Gemma yelled. "I have a gun. Now get back up those stairs and get out of my way or I'll kill her."

The cops exchanged a glance. "Let her go," said one. "You can't get away."

"Oh yes I can," said Gemma.

Nina, who had slipped her raised hand into that scratchy canvas bag in the dark while Gemma was occupied with the police, drew in a breath and said a silent prayer. She jerked herself away from Gemma, feeling a clump of hair tear away from her scalp. She turned, wielding her father's automatic pistol, the gun she had put in the basement, not knowing how to dispose of it. At her worst moment, she had suddenly realized that the canvas bag that held the gun was under her hand. Now she pointed it at Gemma. "No, you can't," she said.

For one moment, Gemma gaped at the gun in Nina's hand. Then she let out a cry of rage and lunged for it. Nina fired.

33

NINA, who was sitting in a chair beside Andre's bed holding his chilly fingers in her own warm hand, looked up as a nurse came into the room. "Don't tell me," she said. "I know. Visiting hours are over." Aside from a visit with her aunt and with Jimmy, who had awakened at last, she had spent most of the day by Andre's side. It was the best way she could think of to recover from her ordeal.

"Way over," the nurse said with a smile. "But your brother is outside and he wanted to know if he can come in."

"Patrick?" Nina said. She looked at Andre. "Is it all right?"

Andre nodded.

The nurse went out into the hall and in a moment the door opened again and Patrick came in. He was unshaven. His clothes were rumpled, and there were bags under his eyes. He approached the bed and looked at Andre sheepishly. "How ya doin'?" he asked. "I'm really sorry."

"It's not your fault. I'm all right," said Andre. "How about you?"

Patrick stuffed his hands in his pockets and shrugged. "My brother's recovering. That's one good thing. But my house is overrun with cops. My kids are freaking out. Lindsay took them to her parents' house just to get them out of there."

"It has to be tough," said Andre sympathetically.

Nina looked at her brother worriedly. "How are you holding up?" she asked.

"I'm coping. As long as I don't try to sleep," he said.

"Oh, Patrick, it must be so difficult to keep going."

Patrick shook his head. "I just keep thinking, how could I have lived with her and not suspected . . . ?"

Nina thought of all the things that Patrick had not suspected. Gemma's pregnancy all those years ago. The birth and death of his baby, which had begun a chain of disaster. Was it his own, willful ignorance that had brought his life crashing down around his head? Part of her blamed him, but still, he was her brother, he was suffering, and he did not need to be reminded of his own culpability. "No one suspected," said Nina. "You said it yourself. She was an expert liar."

Patrick sighed. "I spoke to Gemma's attorney. He's advised her that her best bet is to plead guilty and avoid the death penalty. She's considering it. I told him to beg her to do it for the boys' sake. I remember what it was like going through that trial."

Nina looked away from him. "Yes. That would be best."

"Too bad you weren't a better shot," said Patrick bitterly.

"Patrick," Nina cried.

"I'm sorry," he said. "I'm trying not to hate her. So far, it's a struggle."

Nina got up and walked over to her brother. She held him in a brief embrace. "We'll get through this, too, Patrick," she whispered. "I'll help you. I promise."

Patrick sighed. "You get back to your friend," he said. He

raised a hand in farewell just as the nurse bustled in. The nurse looked at Nina sternly. "Time to go. This guy needs to get some rest." She picked up Andre's chart, wrote something on it, and then headed for the door. "Five minutes. I'm gonna be counting." Patrick held the door open for her.

"Patrick," Nina called after her departing brother. "Wait out in the hall for me. I'll go home with you. Just give me a minute."

"Sure," said Patrick, and though he didn't smile, he looked relieved.

Nina sat back down and gazed at Andre. "I hate to leave you," she said. As she said it, she realized how profoundly she meant it. She had no desire to play it cool. "I wish I never had to leave you," she said.

"Will you come back?" he asked.

"Of course. I'm sure your family will be here tomorrow."

"My parents are on their way. You'll get to meet them."

"And your fiancée?"

Andre shook his head on the pillow. "No. Not Susan. That's over. I told her when I was out there."

Nina frowned. "But I thought. You said that she . . ."

"I was trying to be chivalrous, okay?"

Nina blushed, knowing her relief must be showing on her face.

"It had been coming for a long time," said Andre. "She never liked the fact that I wanted to work at the prison. We have different ideas about . . . a lot of things. The situation has been rocky between us for a long time. We probably should have broken up ages ago. It wasn't just about you."

Nina cocked her head and squinted at him. "Are you saying it was partly about me, Dr. Quinteros?"

Andre smiled. "Yeah."

"But she still has the ring . . ." Nina protested.

"Well, it's impolite to ask for it back," he said wryly. "We'll get another one."

Seeing his smile, realizing what he meant, she was filled with happiness for the first time in what seemed like ages. The recent horror seemed to vanish in its glow. All those she loved were still laboring under a load of grief, a dark cloud. Aunt Mary would need weeks, maybe months, to recover from her skull fracture. Jimmy would be facing another battle with his addictive demons. And Patrick—his agony would go on for a long, long time. She almost felt guilty to be so blessed. But blessed is what she felt.

"How can you say that?" Nina exclaimed. "How can you be so . . . sure? It's not like we were . . . dating. We never even— you know. Not even a kiss."

Andre looked down at their intertwined fingers. "No. But it's destiny. Your father used to tell me about you. 'Andre,' he'd say. 'She's the one for you.' "

"He did?" she said, smiling shyly.

Andre nodded. "When you came to visit, he always wanted me to meet you. It never happened. But he dreamed it. All he wanted was for you to be happy."

"I know he did," she said. And can I be happy now, Dad? she wondered. In spite of everything? She knew what his answer would have been. The same answer he always gave her when she doubted herself. You can do it, Nina. She remembered her father's eyes, the approval and the love she always saw there when he gazed at her. And though she would never see those eyes again, she realized, looking at Andre, that she would not have to live her life without the solace of a loving gaze. Her father had seen to it before he left her.